THEIR VIRGIN
CAPTIVE

THEIR VIRGIN CAPTIVE
Masters of Ménage, Book 1
Shayla Black and Lexi Blake

Published by Shayla Black and Lexi Blake
Copyright 2011 Black Oak Books
Edited by Chloe Vale and Shayla Black
Print ISBN: 978-1936596-06-5

THEIR VIRGIN CAPTIVE

Masters of Ménage
Book 1

Shayla Black and Lexi Blake

Enjoy exclusive excerpts at the conclusion of this book.

Chapter One

Gavin James put down his coffee and looked out over the Dallas skyline. From the top floor of the Black Oak Oil building, he could practically see all the way to Fort Worth. He knew the view well. The same buildings and trees, the same smog hanging over the same traffic jam this time of morning. Even the coffee was the same, just like every other morning. He rose long before the sun, nightmares chasing away any semblance of peaceful sleep. He always gave up and, after a punishing run, came in to the office. His employees thought he was dedicated, but the truth was he had nothing better to do.

His only reason for smiling anymore was the one person he must stay far, far away from. Hannah Craig.

Yeah, you did such a great job staying way far away from her, you idiot. You hired her as your admin. Way to keep the girl safe. She's a whole twenty feet away from you eight plus hours a day. Good going, James.

The phone ringing on his desk interrupted his nasty inner monologue.

"Hey, bro, I'm going to be a little bit late." Gavin's brother Slade yawned as he spoke.

"What a surprise. Another late night at the club?"

Maybe Hannah wasn't the only one who made Gavin smile. He couldn't help the way his lips quirked up, thinking about how his brother spent his nights. Spanking women was rapidly becoming a second job for Slade—and he was good at it. Often, Gavin wondered why he didn't go out with his brothers. Maybe not to the BDSM club they frequented, but dinner would be nice. He'd become so solitary in the last ten years since—

Nope. He refused to think about that.

Gavin forced a cheery tone to his voice. "Did Dex keep you out all night?"

"I did not keep him out," Dex said as he strolled into the office, proving once again that he was always on time. Of course, he also was the illegitimate child who felt the need to prove he belonged. "Slade managed that all on his own. He found a pretty blonde. Surprise, surprise. When I left the club they were getting mighty cozy."

Gavin's brief foray into a decent mood took a nosedive. Slade would have picked a pretty blonde for one reason and one reason only—to pretend she was Hannah. Of all of Gavin's many reasons for staying the hell away from his admin, the fact that both of his brothers were crazy about her sat at the top of his list.

Who are you fooling? That's not why you stay away. If you don't, you know what will happen. You know what you'd do to that girl. You already lost one. Do you really think you deserve a second chance?

Gavin took a deep breath and forced a smile. Dex already believed that he was indifferent. He didn't want to push his half brother even further away.

Punching the button on the phone, Gavin put Slade on speaker. "Tell me you're going to make the board meeting."

Dex snorted and tossed his big body into one of the chairs in front of Gavin's desk. He crossed one leg over the other, his beat-up cowboy boots poking from his tailored suit. That was Dex. Gavin could force him into a designer suit, but he was never going to lose the cowboy.

"Of course I'm going to make the meeting," Slade said with a long-suffering sigh. "I'm not late because I partied too hard. I just talked to the blonde. Mostly. Candy? Sandy? I don't remember. She was nice, but she wasn't…"

Hannah. Gavin watched Dex's mouth turn down. He was obviously thinking the same thing.

Slade continued. "It doesn't matter. Listen, I got a call about the Alaska site. We've had a little trouble there. Something's gone wrong with the infrastructure. I'm going to have to head up there for a few days. I spent the morning calling around to make sure the house is ready for me after the board disperses."

Gavin arched a brow at Dex, who waved him off. "It's an engineering problem, not security. I already talked to Mike in River Run. He said it's been really quiet there. The worst they've had is some kids deciding the base office needs new graffiti on the side. They have computer problems, too, but the IT guy is on it. The situation Slade is talking about just needs a little follow-up and supervision."

Well, at least security was one thing he didn't worry about. Since Dex had taken it over for Black Oak Oil, that function had been running smoothly.

Gavin grabbed the stack of mail he'd taken from Hannah's desk, waiting for her arrival in thirty-four minutes. God, he was an idiot. He knew the exact time she would walk in the door, and he waited on her like a dog waiting for a promised treat. Anxiously, he sorted through the mail. It was too early to expect anyone else to be in for meetings, and he had nothing else to do. She was far too efficient. He'd hired her straight off the bus from some no-name West Texas town, never imagining how quickly she would become essential. Sometimes, Gavin even found himself twiddling his damn thumbs because Hannah ran his workload so efficiently.

There was a slight pause on Slade's end of the line, and then his brother sounded almost reluctant. "Gavin, Dex and I want to talk to you about something. Do you think we could schedule lunch after the meeting?"

The mail was all crap. He could throw most of it away. He came to a large envelope that looked more interesting. Maybe it contained something other than an offer to halve his budget for bulk paper. Gavin sliced his letter opener neatly through the material as suspicion about this luncheon crept into his mind. "About what? Business?"

Dex shifted in his chair. "Not exactly."

Fuck. He didn't want to do this with them. "Is this about Hannah?"

Why had he even asked? He knew. His brothers had been sniffing around her since the day Gavin had reluctantly hired her almost a year ago. Somehow, they'd zeroed in on the fact that he wanted her, as well.

"What we want isn't going to change, Gavin," Dex

8

said, his mouth a stubborn, flat line. "No matter how much you want it to."

"She's an adult." Slade's voice was cajoling where Dex went straight to the fight. "She's smart and capable of making her own decisions. She'll be fine."

"She's what? Twenty-two or something." Practically a child. At least he kept telling himself that.

Dex leaned forward as if ready to fight if need be. "Gavin, you were running this company at twenty-two, don't forget. Besides, Hannah is twenty-five."

A chill raced across Gavin's skin, and suddenly the room seemed way too small. Hannah was twenty-five. They had just celebrated her birthday not a month before. He'd brought in a cake, and Dex and Slade had thrown her a party. Gavin remembered the jealousy he'd felt as his brothers had led her out of the office. He'd wanted to be there beside her, too, celebrating with Hannah. Holding her.

"If you're being at all honest with yourself, Gavin, you want what we want. Hannah is not Nikki, and you're not the same person you were then. You have to let it go and live again," Slade said. "I'll be there in ten minutes. We'll talk more then."

"Regardless of her actual age, she's naïve. She's not ready to take on multiple men or play your games." Gavin was pleased with how stable his voice sounded when all he could see in his mind's eye was Nikki's body laid out on the impersonal slab at the morgue.

Lately in his dreams, Nikki's body turned into Hannah's. The image seared itself in his head. He managed to breathe, barely. He had to focus or he would lose it. And he needed to find another job for Hannah. If he kept her this close… No, he just couldn't.

"Damn it, Gavin," Slade growled. "When it comes to Hannah, these aren't games, and we're not playing."

Gavin's heart stuttered. "Give the girl time to grow up."

He upended the large envelope in his hand and let the contents drift to his desk, hoping Dex didn't notice his shaking hands.

"Don't act like it's all just Slade and me. You're not fooling anyone," Dex said. For once, the big cowboy almost looked reluctant to speak. "I see how you look at her. You want her. You care. That's nothing to be ashamed of. Hell, if there's one thing both Slade and I understand, it's how a man can be crazy about Hannah."

Slade's voice came over the speaker. "Dex and I have given this a lot of thought. We think it's time, and all of us need to be on board."

"Exactly." Dex leaned forward. "We have a plan."

"What the fuck?" Anything else they were about to say got lost as Gavin saw what spilled out of the envelope. Photographs of Hannah. He frowned. Ten pictures, all of them of her gorgeous body wearing lovely, lacy creations in soft colors that showcased her plump breasts and gorgeous ass. In one, a shot of her backside, she wore nothing at all. Gavin's breath fled, and his cock stiffened at the sight.

Dex stood, peering down at the pictures on the desk. "What's that?"

Gavin had a sudden desire to hide the provocative images. Instead, he glared. At times, Dex had been known to think way outside the box when he solved a problem. Dex had said he a plan. Was taking these pictures a part of it? Or Dex's immature way of reeling him into their twisted little arrangement?

"Do you want to explain this?" He shoved the least seductive image in Dex's face.

"That's Hannah. What the hell?" Dex grabbed the picture.

"What's going on?" Slade asked, his voice rising in alarm over the phone. "What do you mean by 'that's Hannah?'"

Dex stared at Gavin, his face taking on that same blank expression he'd had for the first two years after Gavin and Slade had found him in a foster home. Dex had been the child their father hadn't planned on or wanted. It had been pure chance that Gavin and Slade even discovered that Dex existed. "You think I would do this?"

His half brother's indignant tone registered in Gavin's head, but rage rode him hard. "Do you know what Hannah could do to you if she found out about this? She could call in the cops, and I would let her. And your sick ploy won't work. You might be able to pull Slade into your perversions, but don't think you can do the same with me."

"Goddamn it, Gavin. Why would you say that?" Slade slammed a door, and Gavin knew that his brother was on his way.

Dex practically radiated fury. He was a huge bull of a man, and Gavin thought they were about to have the throw down he'd always suspected was coming. Dex loomed over Gavin, his fists clenched and ready, but then he shut down. Dex's shoulders relaxed, and his face became a mask of bland politeness. "Listen up, Gavin. The only reason I am not walking out the door right this second is that I want Hannah safe. After I figure out who's stalking her and make sure he can't do it again, I'm leaving. You won't have to deal with this perverse bastard ever again. But next time your rich-boy conscience takes over, don't you dare come looking for me."

Gavin looked at the pictures again and realized he'd made several terrible errors. He'd been so concerned about the photos that he hadn't taken time to really look at the envelope. It hadn't been addressed to him, but to Hannah herself. There was no stamp on the front. Some bastard had walked right into her office, stood at her desk, and made sure she would receive his "gift".

Dex flipped over one of the photographs and slapped it on Gavin's desk with a resounding thud.

You're mine.

The menacing words had been written in blood-red marker, the color a stark contrast to the white of the photo paper.

"This is not some prank I cooked up to trick you into joining us. You're really accusing me of becoming a stalker and trying to terrify the woman I love? And yes, I love Hannah. I won't not say it because you're too much of a pussy to handle it. I'm going to figure out what's going on, and when I leave, I intend to take her with me. And you, big brother, can go to hell for all I care." Dex turned on his boots and strode out the door.

Gavin tried to stop the queasy feeling in his stomach as everything Dex had said sank in.

"What the hell did you do, Gavin?" Slade asked, his voice barely audible over the sounds of traffic.

Gavin bit back the urge to put his head in his hands. He'd utterly mishandled everything. But that was the story of his whole fucking life. "Get your ass up here now, Slade."

He hung up the phone and couldn't help but stare at the pictures in front of him. Hannah was in her bedroom, and the pictures were obviously taken from a distance. They had a grainy quality. In most, Hannah was reading or watching television in her tiny bedroom. She wore a nightgown in two of the pictures, but the majority featured her in a lacy bra and barely-there panties. So fucking gorgeous. She hid that body under nearly shapeless clothes and always kept her hair in a ponytail. In the pictures, her rich honey hair flowed down her shoulders in loose curls.

He loved the one where she leaned back on the bed, the phone in her hand and a smile on her face, like she was laughing. Her green eyes were bright, and that smile could light up the whole fucking world. The clock by her bed read ten o'clock. Gavin remembered calling Hannah at just around that time a few nights before. He'd lost an important phone number. She'd teased him about his organizational skills.

This was how she looked when she talked to him? Half-dressed, plump lips welcoming? Fuck, he'd explode next time he had to call her at home.

Gavin flipped the photo over.

Don't let those perverted brothers touch you. You're mine.

Gavin shoved the photo aside and surged to his feet. Hannah was in danger, and he'd been getting a hard-on looking at evidence. What kind of man was he?

You know, that voice said. *You know exactly what kind of man you are, asshole.*

He was a man who had just shoved his half brother aside in one of the cruelest ways possible. He shoved everyone away. Now, he was going to lose everything if he didn't get his shit straight.

Not this time. By damned, he was going to make things right.

Gavin paced as he waited for Slade, a plan already forming.

* * * *

Hannah Craig stopped and stared as Dex Townsend walked out of Gavin's office and into the grand reception area she liked to consider her turf. Walked? Dex never walked. He strode. He swaggered. And now he charged out of the office like an angry bull.

She inched back into the hallway to observe him. She'd discovered that all of her men tended to put on a front when they realized she was in the room.

Her men. It was all she could do not to laugh at herself, but that was the way she thought of the James Gang—Gavin, Slade, and Dex. In her fantasies, they were her men, though she would never, ever tell them. But she'd fallen madly in love with them, and all three were way out of her league.

Now one of her men walked straight up to the wall across from her desk and scrubbed an angry hand across his head. He looked back at the door to Gavin's office as though he wanted to march back in and give his oldest brother a piece of his mind. Something definitely had Dex in a state. His handsome face was a mottled red and yet...she swore she saw a slight sheen of tears in his eyes. With a little huff, he pulled back his fist and put it straight through the wall. The drywall gave without a fuss, merely cracking and sending up a little cloud of dust. Dex yanked on his hand to pull it free.

It was time to bring that man down from whatever had him so mad or he'd start in on the furniture.

"I never did like that wall," Hannah said softly.

Dex turned, shock obvious on his face. His angry, red flush muted to an embarrassed pink. "Hannah. I didn't know you were here."

She smiled at him and walked in as though nothing at all was wrong. Life was what a person made it, her Gran had always said. It was time to make Dex's life a bit calmer. "I mean it. I'm glad someone finally put that arrogant wall in its place. I've slapped at it a couple of times, but it always just stands there."

He huffed a little laugh. "You're crazy, girl. You know that, right?"

The tension in Dex dialed down several notches.

"I have no idea what you mean. And you're one to talk. I'm not the one taking out my frustrations on a wall."

She set her purse down and looked around for the mail. Nothing. Gavin probably had it. She was going to have to have a discussion with the man about his priorities. A CEO looking at the mail. Hannah sighed. If she let him, he would make the coffee, too. Gavin James was a micromanager. She opened her calendar to get ready for the day ahead.

"Hannah, I'm sorry."

When she looked up, Dex was in front of her desk, six foot five inches of the hottest cowboy she'd ever seen forced into a business suit. Dex had the broadest shoulders and the deepest chest, but what got her every time was how often he showed off his big heart. He tried to hide it, but she knew he'd helped out more than one employee with money troubles or medical bills.

If she told him what was happening to her, he would move heaven and earth to fix the problem. More than once, the information had been right there on the tip of her tongue, but she held back. Dex had his own troubles, and she could handle hers. She was an independent, strong woman who wasn't going to panic because some idiot sent her a few letters. And called a couple of times. And had potentially killed her cat.

She forced a smile on her face. "You didn't hit *me*, big guy, so no apologies. Do you want to tell me what's going on with Gavin that has you feeling violent?"

She didn't want to bring him into her trouble, but she couldn't stay out of his. Dex and Gavin had a difficult relationship, to say the least. Slade was the bridge between the two, but he wasn't here, so it was up to her.

Dex took a long breath and then that "aw shucks" smile was back on his handsome face. "It's nothing, darlin'. Just a small difference of opinion. Put it out of your mind."

She looked over at the hole in the wall.

He flushed again. "I'll have that fixed."

The outer doors crashed open, and Slade rushed in. He was one disheveled hunk of male hotness. His dress shirt hung together by one small button at the hips. The rest fell open, exposing his hard pectorals and giving her a breathtaking glimpse of his ridged abdomen. She damn near swallowed her tongue. His inky hair sat slightly askew. And he looked rattled.

Hannah managed to smile without panting. "You are going to be a big hit in the board meeting."

He looked down at his clothes as though it was the first time he'd given it a thought. "I was in a hurry. Hannah, are you all right?"

"Fine."

She picked up the phone, knowing exactly what he needed. This wasn't her first rodeo, as the folks back in Two Trees liked to say. "Wendy, you have a code blue."

Wendy, Slade's admin, sighed. "Which part do I need to replace? Tie? Socks? That man is constantly wearing athletic socks with his dress shoes."

Hannah looked Slade up and down. He knew the drill, turning in a circle for her inspection. "Nope, Wendy. This is a head-to-toe fixer-upper."

She hung up the phone just as Slade got a look at her wall. He stared at it a moment before glaring at Dex.

"Seriously? Please tell me that wasn't Gavin's head. Where's his body? Do I need to call 911?" Slade asked the questions with a sarcastic edge, but Hannah heard his concern.

Dex simply shook his head. "No trouble at all. I'm going to call maintenance and get them up here to fix this. Then I have a few things to do. I think I'll skip the meeting."

"You can't skip the board meeting."

Dex shrugged as he moved toward the door.

"Watch me. I have more important things to do. And Hannah, you're having lunch today with me and Slade."

She glanced down at her calendar. "I can't. I agreed to have lunch with Scott."

"Who the hell is Scott?" Slade demanded.

"He works with the IT teams. He said it was important," Hannah explained. "I'm sure it has something to do with those installs I've been helping to coordinate."

Both men went very still.

"You're not meeting Scott anymore. You're having lunch with us, and we're going to have a long talk, the three of us." Dex's dark eyes held hers for a moment. He was so serious that her heart started racing. When his voice got deep and dark, it made her blood pound.

"Absolutely." Slade crossed his arms over his chest.

"Okay," she said. She hadn't sounded that breathy, had she?

Dex walked out, the doors slamming behind him. Slade shook his head. Even disheveled, he was a gorgeous sight. With thick, dark hair and a face that looked like Michelangelo sculpted it, Slade always made her sigh.

Gavin opened his door and stepped out. He radiated power. Unlike Slade and Dex, there was nothing less than perfect about his appearance. No suit would ever dare to wrinkle while Gavin James wore it.

He nodded grimly at her. "Good morning, Hannah. I need to talk to Slade, but I would like you to stay close to your desk this morning."

"Of course." It was an odd request, but one she could handle.

Slade disappeared into his brother's office. Gavin closed the door, watching her intently until it shut between them with an ominous thud.

And then Hannah was alone.

She reached into her purse and pulled out the number for the private investigator she'd hired two days before. He'd cashed her check but hadn't returned her calls. Maybe it was time to admit that hiring someone named Vinny who worked out of the back of a tarot reader's shop hadn't been the greatest idea. When he didn't answer, she left another message while e-mailing Scott to cancel lunch. After that, she called the local animal shelters to check if they'd found Mr. Snuggles. Her cat had been gone for days, and Hannah was beginning to fear that she was gone forever.

Her eyes teared up. She was going to have to take action and soon. She felt alone now that her three men were gone. It was a long time until her lunch with Dex and Slade. The office seemed big and empty. She wanted so much to call them back and tell them her trouble.

But why tell the busy men she loved—who couldn't possibly love her in return—that someone was trying to kill her?

Chapter Two

Slade's blood pressure rose as he looked down at the photographs in front of him. From listening to Dex and Gavin on the phone, he'd figured out that someone was stalking Hannah, but seeing the sick evidence in front of him was staggering.

Gavin walked around his desk and sank into the huge wingback chair their father had sat in for forty years. Slade would have burned the big reminder of the son of a bitch, but Gavin had kept it, even after he'd completely redecorated the office.

"They were addressed directly to Hannah," Gavin said, his voice clipped. "No return address. No postage."

"So this asshole brought the envelope into the building? It has to be an employee. No one can get past reception without a keycard."

Gavin went pale. Then he flushed with fury. "Goddamn it."

"Have you looked through the security tapes?" Slade picked up a photo of Hannah lying on her stomach across her bed, a book in her hand. He couldn't make out the cover, but he'd bet it was a romance. She always had one in her bag. And every copy was battered and dog-eared as though it had been through many a hand before hers. For her birthday, he and Dex had bought her a new eBook reader and loaded it with credit. The look of delight in her eyes had done strange things to his heart.

Now, someone was watching her. Stalking her. And from the messages on the back of several photos, the creep knew how he and Dex felt about her. And, Slade suspected, Gavin too. This threat seemed so surreal, but the proof was staring him in the face. Someone wanted to hurt Hannah.

Gavin frowned. "I don't have cameras outside my office doors. Maybe I should have listened to Dex about that. I'm sure he's is in the mailroom now, interrogating the employees." He sighed. "I think I should call in an outside firm."

"What happened between you two? He put his fist through a wall." Slade's stomach was turning at the idea of some asshole harassing Hannah, but he had to deal with his brothers' problems, too. Gavin would only be talking about calling in an outside security firm if things had gone terribly wrong between them.

"It's complicated." Gavin looked down, a sure sign that he was ashamed of something.

"How about I uncomplicate it for you? You took one look at these photographs and blamed Dex. Because he wants her badly, you leapt to the stupid conclusion that he was desperate or impulsive enough to become a peeping Tom. And his only choice was to call bullshit and walk out. Simple enough?"

Gavin's gun metal gray eyes flashed back up, but there was a weariness to them that had Slade backing off. "Almost spot on. I thought Dex was using the

21

photos to tempt me into joining the two of you in seducing Hannah. I know you want that, Slade. I can't do it. I just can't. Dex took offense to my mistake, and now he says he's quitting as soon as she's out of danger."

"And Dex leaving is all right with you?" Slade wasn't sure he wanted the answer to that question, but he had to ask.

Gavin clenched his fists. "No, it's not. Damn it, Slade, he's my brother, too. I have no intention of letting him walk out because of a misunderstanding."

"I was listening in, Gavin. Dex didn't misunderstand. You flat out blamed him."

Gavin sat back, raking his hand through his thick, chocolate-brown hair. "Okay, I'll rephrase. I have no intention of losing my brother because I was an asshole. Nor do I intend to allow someone to stalk my admin."

Slade bit back a smile. Despite the horrors of the morning, he sensed a little progress. Gavin had admitted that he didn't want to lose Dex. He was still calling Hannah his admin, but that would change, if Slade had his way. "Have you talked to Hannah yet?"

Slade wasn't looking forward to the conversation. Hannah was going to be terrified when she found out about these pictures. He stacked them, pulling out the least salacious one. They would have to show her so she grasped how serious this was, but he didn't want to embarrass her.

"Not yet. I wanted to talk to you first. We'll do our due diligence and call the police to report the threat, but there's not much they can do unless this bastard has actually committed a crime. They'll tell her to lock her doors and buy a dog."

Slade shook his head. "She's a cat person. I'm sure Mr. Snuggles will be hell on intruders. She'll purr them to death."

Gavin frowned. "Mr. Snuggles is a she?"

"Hannah was fifteen when she got her," Slade couldn't help but smile. "Apparently, she didn't think to look for boy or girl parts. The name stuck."

Gavin threw his head back and laughed. The rich, deep sound filled the room and made Slade realize just how much he'd missed his older brother's laughter. It had been so damn long since he'd heard it.

Gavin had tears of mirth in his eyes when he came up for air. "She has a transvestite cat."

"She says Mr. Snuggles is just gender confused." Hannah loved that damn cat. Slade knew he was going to have to learn to love the little furball, too.

"Such a silly, sweet girl," Gavin said, his gaze straying to the photos.

There it was, that smile—with a healthy hint of lust—that told Slade everything he needed to know.

"We have to protect her," Slade pointed out.

"I have a plan, and I hope you'll back me on it. It should keep Hannah safe and bring Dex back into the fold."

There was nothing Slade wanted more than that. "I'm listening."

Gavin hesitated. "You heard Dex say that he would take Hannah with him when he left, Slade. I know how you feel about her. Maybe you need to talk to him. I don't want Hannah coming between the two of you."

And just like that, Slade's cock got hard. An image

of Hannah between him and Dex assaulted his brain. She would be so small sandwiched by their bigger bodies. They would have to be careful, but they would get inside her, so deep that she wouldn't know where they ended and she began.

"Oh, she's going to be between us."

Gavin flushed slightly. "That's not fair to Hannah. She's not some club bunny for the two of you to fuck and forget."

Slade wasn't going to take this crap from his brother. He would never play games with Hannah. He'd known from the moment he'd seen her that she was different. "Dex and I love Hannah. We're not going to forget her; we're going to build a life with her. This isn't some one-night stand."

"Are you both insane? No one will accept that kind of relationship here."

"I'm not going to live my life by some societal dictate. And they will accept us. I have a billion-dollar trust fund. Let them talk all they like, but money opens doors. What would be unacceptable for a normal person is merely a quirk for the superrich." It was a harsh reality.

Slade and Dex had talked this out, hashing out plans over months to get what they wanted and protect Hannah from nasty gossip at the same time. Now if Gavin would just get with the program, their lives could begin.

"That's an argument for another time," Gavin conceded. "Now, we have to figure out what to do with Hannah. I was thinking that, perhaps, she needs a small vacation."

Slade frowned. "There is no fucking way I'm

letting her run off by herself."

"Of course not. But maybe Alaska would be a good place for her now. You did say you have to go see to some trouble there. River Run is isolated, and we own the whole damn town. All three of us can take Hannah and hide out while the security team figures this out."

It took all Slade had not to fist pump in victory. "Perfect. When do we leave?"

Gavin sat back in his chair. "Today. But I want to be clear. I'm only going to work things out with Dex. I'll help with Hannah, if the need arises. But that's it."

Slade wasn't fooled. His older brother could lie to himself, but Slade knew the truth. Gavin could more easily monitor the situation from Dallas. Since Slade had always been the go-between for Gavin and Dex, it seemed obvious that Gavin was coming along because he wanted to repair the relationship with Dex...and because he couldn't stand to let his two younger brothers have Hannah all to themselves.

Slade contained his excitement—barely. "Understood. I'll make the arrangements. Then we can talk to Hannah."

Gavin nodded as though happy with the decision. "Excellent. We'll have to convince her to go, you know."

Slade would have to convince her of more than just an impromptu trip to Alaska. He was going to have to persuade her—and everyone else—that this ménage relationship could work. To do that, he had to restore peace between Dex and Gavin. Then he had to talk Gavin into sharing Hannah with them. Hell, he also had to convince Hannah that taking on three passionate, dominant men would be a dandy idea.

"No problem, Gavin." Slade sounded way more confident than he felt.

But as he walked out of Gavin's office to start planning, he vowed to make it work.

* * * *

Dex parked his Harley about a block away from Hannah's apartment and started walking. His cell trilled, and he pulled it out of his pocket. *Slade.* Probably wanting to talk about Gavin. Dex growled. He thought about ignoring it, but did what he always did when it came to Slade. He gave in.

But that didn't mean Dex had to be nice about it. "What?"

"Well, I suppose I should be happy you're using words and not just grunting."

Dex had no comeback for that. Grunting was a perfectly acceptable form of communication in his book. It got the job done. So did growling, snorting, and just flat planting his fist in another guy's face. When he found whoever was stalking Hannah, he didn't intend to give the fucker a nice long lecture.

Slade's sigh came across loud and clear. "Damn it, Dex. Where are you? You have to set aside this crap with Gavin and get your ass back to the office. Hannah's in trouble."

"I know that," Dex practically yelled into the phone. "I'm going to her place. I want to see if I can figure out where the jerk has been hiding when he does his stalkarazzi thing."

"Maybe that will give us some clues about his

identity. That's a great idea."

"Yeah, well, it's what I do for a living."

When would his older brothers finally understand that he was damn good at his job?

Dex looked up and down the cracked sidewalks of Hannah's neighborhood. It was old, with a ton of mature trees, but he'd never liked her living here. Hannah's apartment was in a rundown fourplex. The paint was peeling, and one of her screens was propped against the side of the building. He'd bet it was the one to her bedroom window, and that fucker had taken it off. Had Hannah not noticed? The nearby tree would be a great place for this scumbag to hide and snap pictures. But what the hell was Hannah doing lying around her bedroom with the shades wide open?

"Look, you do your thing, but be back at the office by one. We're going to take Hannah to Alaska with us."

Dex stopped. "We are? Hannah wants to go to Alaska?"

"Not exactly," Slade admitted. "We're going to talk her into it. We'll say it's a business trip. But we can keep her safe there until the police figure this shit out and nail this guy. I really do have to go up there. I'm the head engineer. I'll convince her that she needs to take notes or something."

Dex knew he should stay here. He should be the one running the investigation. Damn, it meant Slade would probably sleep with Hannah. There was no way his brother would have such close access to Hannah and not claim her now that they'd decided she was theirs. But he trusted Slade. "Take care of our girl. You explain that I love her, too, but I need to find the

27

bastard who's stalking her."

Hannah's safety was more important than his dick, though his dick was protesting mightily.

Dex walked up the stairs to Hannah's apartment. They wobbled under him. Ratty old place. It reminded him of his last foster home. The house had been falling down around them, but his foster father spent every dime on beer, cigarettes, and the lotto.

He was going to get Hannah out of here. She didn't know it yet, but she wasn't coming back to this dive. She would come home with him and Slade. Dex refused to accept any other outcome.

"You're coming to Alaska with us," Slade said. "Gavin is putting the Lenox brothers on the case."

"He took me off? Without even consulting me?" Dex stopped right in front of Hannah's door, his heart sinking to his gut. He'd been hoping Gavin would apologize. Dex wouldn't accept at first, of course, but eventually he would and agree to stay on as Black Oak's Head of Security. The fact that Gavin had actually removed him was a blow he hadn't been expecting—and it was more painful than he'd imagined. It might have been better for all concerned if Gavin and Slade hadn't come looking for him in that foster home.

Dex thought about that day often. He'd been just about to age out of the foster system. He'd had no place to go one day, then the next, he was moving into this huge mansion with the brothers he'd never imagined he had. Starting over again was going to be hard, but he wasn't going to hang around to be Gavin's whipping boy.

There was a long huff from Slade's end of the

phone. "Dude, you're just like him, you know? Why does your brain always go to the worst possible place? Gavin wants you to come with us. He set this whole thing up to *include* you. Come on, this is our shot with Hannah. We're going to talk to her about the pictures when we get to Alaska. We need to break this to her gently, then assure her that she's safe."

Dex pondered that. At least if he was close to her, he could protect her. Maybe he and Gavin could work things out, too. Burke and Cole Lenox would definitely track down this scumbag threatening Hannah. "All right. I'll go. And I'll pack Hannah some clothes so she doesn't have to come back here."

"How are you planning on doing that? Do you have a key to her place?" Slade sounded miffed.

Dex tried the front door. It was locked, but just barely. He gave it a shove, and the door gave way. "I don't think a gnat needs a key to get into Hannah's. No freaking security at all. I'm in."

"I'll let Burke know he should watch her place and see if we can catch this guy. Do what you need and get your ass back here by one." There was a short pause. "This is all going to work out. I promise."

And that was Slade, always the optimist. Dex wasn't feeling so rosy. What if Hannah didn't want him? He'd live with that. But damn it, she was going to get his protection. "I'll see you then."

He hung up and looked around her apartment. Hannah had never invited him in, and he was wretchedly curious. The place was neat and feminine with yellow curtains hanging in the small kitchen. There was a single coffee mug drying on a mat by the sink and a dish for her cat's food and water on the floor.

With zero remorse, he went through the mail she'd stacked neatly on the counter, then pressed the button that started her answering machine.

Ms. Craig, this is Brenna from the South Side Animal Shelter. I'm sorry, but your cat isn't here. I'll call if I find out anything.

Her cat was missing? Hannah loved that damn feline.

Hannah, it's Preston. Look, we need to talk. Why would you call HR in? It was one kiss. You were coming on to me, and we both know it. Let's work this out, just the two of us. What do you say, baby? Maybe over dinner?

Dex clenched his fists. Preston Ward III was fortyish, balding, married, and Black Oak's dickwad Chief Information Officer. Not a chance Hannah would voluntarily kiss that asshole. He must have forced it on her. Now Dex knew whose name to put at the top of the suspect list—just before he broke the bastard's face. The machine beeped again and changed to a thin voice.

Hey, Hannah. I—I was, uhm, calling to make sure we're still on for tonight. I have the part to fix your laptop. It'll only take an hour. So call me and let me know when I can head your way.

Dex had no idea who that asshole was, but a file folder on her tiny desk caught his attention. He flipped it open, expecting to find some piece of work Gavin had given her, but his eyes turned stormy when he realized he was looking at a police report.

As he read it, his blood started to boil. Hannah wasn't going to be shocked by the photographs Gavin had found. She already knew someone was stalking her, and she hadn't bothered to mention that little fact to any of them. She'd just smiled and pretended like she hadn't received threatening phone calls and letters for the last four fucking weeks.

She'd called the police, who couldn't do a damn thing. But she hadn't asked him for help. She knew someone was after her, and she hadn't even installed new locks on her doors. What the hell was she thinking?

The Dom in Dex took firm control. He'd been gentle with Hannah. He and Slade had intended to introduce her slowly to submission. But when she allowed herself to be in danger? Slow was no longer an option. Hannah needed a firm hand now and was going to get a quick lesson in obeying her Masters.

He stomped into her bedroom and yanked a ragged suitcase from her closet. He tossed in a couple of pairs of jeans and shirts, a bathrobe, some socks, and a pair of sneakers. Dex pushed the bathroom door open and shoved her toiletries into the front pocket before striding back out.

Her eBook reader was sitting on the nightstand. He grabbed it, then opened the top drawer of her dresser. There was a mass of pretty, frilly panties in every color imaginable. Dex shut that sucker fast, gritting his teeth. The one thing Hannah wasn't going to need for the foreseeable future was underwear. In fact, she'd never need them again if he had his way.

He turned to leave, but paused when he heard a faint little whine. A single, small sound, like a baby sighing. Dex went to the window and opened it. There was that huge tree he'd noticed earlier right outside her bedroom window. The mighty live oak that gave easy access to her window, just as he'd suspected.

This was where the shitbag stalking Hannah sat. The branches were thick and would easily hold a man's weight. The foliage was dense. A stalker could hide here, and she wouldn't know.

The thought made Dex violent.

Rawwwwr.

Dex dropped the suitcase as he caught a glimpse of orange fur. Mr. Snuggles. Damn. Hannah's cat was stuck in the tree. Dex opened the window and leaned out, searching for the cat's hiding place. He found her clinging to a high branch. Dex sighed as he realized her fur was covered in blood.

Maybe Mr. Snuggles had gotten into a cat fight, which would be perfectly normal. But upon closer inspection, Dex didn't think so. Someone had tried to hurt the cat, and now she was clinging to life. And probably very terrified.

Dex sighed. He wished he hadn't taken off his suit coat.

He reached out for the nearest branch and hauled himself up. The cat hissed, but he moved in anyway.

Damn, the things he did for love.

Chapter Three

Gavin was surprised at just how nervous he was when Hannah walked into his office, notepad in hand. She didn't dress like an executive secretary. Ms. Rogers, his former assistant, had never worn her dark hair in anything less than a professional twist or bun. Her perfectly tailored business suits had shown off her trim figure, which she'd probably spent most of her off time honing. She would have been at home on the cover of a magazine. He could have kept ice frozen on her ass, too.

By comparison, Hannah wore a too-big skirt that couldn't conceal the erotic flare of her hips and a shapeless blouse that hid even less. Hannah had gorgeous breasts. She wore very little makeup, and her honey blonde hair fell in pretty, loose curls. She was lovely, but never flashy.

Why did his damn heart pound when she walked in the room?

"Hi, Slade. Mr. James. You wanted to see me?" Hannah asked with her sweet West Texas twang.

Thankfully, Slade could at least say words when Hannah was around since Gavin felt incapable at the moment. Slade rushed from his seat to show Hannah to hers. Naturally, it was right next to Slade's, so close their knees would almost touch, and Gavin was stuck behind his mammoth desk. Alone.

It was where he belonged, anyway.

"Have a seat, love," Slade said with a smile.

She didn't seem to mind the endearment. "Thank you."

She smiled up at Slade. Gavin forced himself not to move. Every instinct told him to get out from behind the damn desk and join them. Hell, he could pick Hannah up and settle her on his lap, and they could conduct this little meeting with his cock pressed against her ass. Maybe then she would start calling him Gavin. Although having her call him Mr. James in that so-sweet Southern way of hers as he rammed his cock up her pussy would be a turn-on, too.

Fuck. He had way more in common with his brothers than he would ever admit. Shifting in his seat because his cock was at full mast, he settled for what he hoped looked like paternal concern. "Hannah, we need to talk about something."

Her spine straightened, and she held her pen at the ready. "Yes, sir."

Sir. That would be a good thing for her to call him as he forced her down on his cock. Or she could call him nothing at all, unable to talk because she was so overcome with pleasure.

Or she could be silent because she killed herself after you neglected her. Yeah, that's more realistic.

"Are you all right, Mr. James?" Hannah sat forward, her eyes wide with worry.

Gavin forced the thoughts from his head. He wasn't going to act on them. Hannah deserved far better than him. He briefly considered staying behind. Slade and Dex could handle her in Alaska. But if Dex left with Slade now, Gavin knew the chance that he'd ever repair the relationship with his brother would be slim. Damn.

"I'm fine, Hannah. But I do have a problem you can help with."

Her smile practically lit up the room. "Of course."

Slade took over, his eyes bright with affection as he looked at Hannah. "We need you to come with us on a little business trip and play our girl Friday."

She put the notepad down and turned to Slade, delight plain on her face. She really did have a connection to Slade. Though they weren't touching, Gavin couldn't miss the attraction that connected them like an invisible thread. "Are we going to Houston? I've never been."

They had an office in Houston, near their refinery. It was a good bet that if they were going on a trip, it would be there. But that wasn't far enough away from Dallas and Hannah's stalker for Gavin's peace of mind. "No. We're going to our facility in River Run."

She turned to him. "Alaska?"

Slade was on the edge of his seat. "Yes. It's beautiful, Hannah. We have a house there with plenty of rooms. The view is incredible. I have to do some work up there, but I think we can find the time to show you around."

She bit her bottom lip. "How long would we be gone?"

Slade's gaze found Gavin's. They hadn't actually discussed that. In the hours since finding the photos, they'd made a lot of plans. They had canceled the board meeting. They had called private investigators Burke and Cole Lenox. The former Navy SEALs were already talking to Black Oak security about getting the keycard logs and security footage for the last twenty-four hours. Slade had made the arrangements to open the house in River Run and had the corporate jet fueled. Not once had they discussed how long they'd be gone. There had been an unspoken agreement that they would be gone for as long as it took.

"A few days," Gavin said with the smooth tones of a man who knew how to massage the truth. "You should be home on Sunday night at the latest."

Once they had her in Alaska and Burke had useful information, they could admit to Hannah why they'd really spirited her away. Until then, he didn't want her to worry.

She shook her head, blonde hair swinging. "I am so sorry. I can't be gone that long. I have a bunch of obligations. I'm supposed to have someone over this evening. My laptop is giving me hell."

"I'll have IT give you a new one." Gavin could solve that problem easily.

"I don't want a new one. I'm used to this one. Lyle said he can fix it, but he's only free tonight. And I'm supposed to go home this weekend to see my grandma. I'll tell Wendy to get ready. She would love to go."

Gavin didn't like to think about Hannah driving all the way to West Texas in her beat-up Chevy. That car was on its last leg, and most of the road between Dallas and Two Trees consisted of mile after mile of nothing. If she broke down—and the way her car sputtered, that was almost a given—she would be all alone. And it would be easy for her stalker to follow her and possibly drive her off the road.

Gavin's blood pressure rose with each potential hazard he imagined.

"We don't need Wendy," Slade insisted. "We need you."

She shook that off with a wave of her hand. "Trust me, Wendy has ten years' seniority on me. She'll be great. And she loves to travel. I'll give her a call. How long does she have before the plane leaves? She'll want to pack a bag."

"Hannah." Gavin tried to hold his temper in check. "The plane leaves in less than an hour. We've already placed your name on the passenger list with the FAA. And don't worry about packing a bag. We've taken care of everything."

Slade's hand came out to cover hers. "It's going to be fine. Your grandmother will understand. You can call her when we get there."

Hannah pulled back. "I can't just up and leave."

Gavin forced a placid smile on his face. "It's going to be all right. Let's talk about your other responsibilities, and we'll make sure they're handled."

The door to his office came open with a crash. Gavin looked up, ready to yell at the intruder.

"Dex?" Slade stood, staring with his mouth open. "Dude, what the hell happened to you?"

Dex was carrying a battered pink suitcase, but that was the most normal thing about him. His dress shirt was shredded and his arms covered in scratches, as though he'd gotten into a fight with a chipper-shredder and taken the worst end of it.

Hannah stood, and her notepad fell to the floor. "Oh, my…Dex, you're hurt! We need to clean you up.

Do you need to go to a hospital?" She frowned. "Is that my suitcase?"

Dex set the luggage down and turned to Hannah, his dark eyes laser-focused on his target. "Maybe a mental hospital, darlin'. As for the damages, well, let's say I got into a little tussle with your pussy. I discovered that it has claws, rather like her owner. But I won't make the same mistake twice."

"You found my cat?" Hannah's voice was a hopeful whisper.

"Found, fought with, and saved," Dex confirmed. "She's at the vet being taken care of. Now it's time for round two."

Dex strode up to Hannah and didn't hesitate. He bent and shoved his shoulder in her midsection, his bulky arm curling behind her knees. She was over his shoulder in an instant. Her blonde head came up, and she looked at Gavin.

"This isn't company protocol, Mr. James." She said it so primly. Gavin would have laughed if he wasn't so perplexed by his youngest brother's behavior.

Dex turned around so all Gavin could see were her perfectly shaped calves and a backside to die for. "If you two are done pussyfooting around, I believe we have a plane to catch."

"Dexter Townsend, you need to put me down right this instant! I am not going to Alaska."

Dex's free hand came out and slapped that perfect backside. The short smack resounded through the room right before Hannah's outraged yelp drowned it out. "I don't like to be called Dexter, darlin'. And you are definitely going to Alaska. Is the car here yet?"

Gavin wasn't sure if he should punch his youngest brother or congratulate him for doing what he and Slade had seemed incapable of. "Dex, you better set her down. You're going to scare her."

"Am I? Really? Why don't you look at the folder in the side pocket of her suitcase and tell me if she seems afraid enough. We'll be out in the car. And Hannah, if you give me any trouble, I swear, I will tie you up and leave you bound until we get to Alaska."

Gavin walked to the suitcase and pulled out the manila file folder. Hannah's head came up, and she looked to Slade for help.

"You have to stop him. I can't go, and Dex's caveman ways aren't going to change that. Now you tell your Neanderthal brother to let me down this instant or I am going to scream until the cops come."

Slade merely looked to Dex. "We should gag her, too."

"You jerks!" Hannah tried to kick, but Dex merely tightened his arm around her legs. "You let me down."

She was still yelling as Dex walked out the door, Slade following behind. Gavin thought seriously about taking off after them and forcing Dex to let her go. They couldn't just kidnap her. She could call the police.

Then he opened the folder and realized that Hannah had already called the police. Several times. His hands tightened as he read the incident reports. Hannah had known about her problem for over a month. And she'd never said a word.

Gavin closed the folder. He picked up the phone and quickly advised his private investigators. They would get all the reports and follow up on their end.

Gavin picked up Hannah's sad little suitcase. His own luggage had already been delivered to the airport.

He walked out of his office with a new sense of purpose. If Hannah didn't have the sense to protect herself, she'd just found three men who did. Gavin checked his apprehensions at his office door. He could handle this. He might not be good for Hannah, but maybe his brothers were. It would be an odd relationship, but he loved all three of them. He wanted them to be happy.

No, wait. He didn't love Hannah. He couldn't. She was going to be like a sister. That was all. He would get over this raging desire to have her underneath him.

He could hear her screaming as he walked toward reception.

Slade was right. She needed a gag.

* * * *

Hannah took a deep breath as the airplane finally leveled out.

Slade released his seat belt and stood. "I'm going to need a drink."

He walked down the aisle and opened a small door, revealing a surprising amount of liquor. He poured a couple of inches worth of scotch into three crystal glasses and passed them to his brothers.

They offered Hannah nothing. *Bastards*. She wouldn't curse anywhere but in her own head. It wasn't ladylike, her grandmother had taught her. But deep inside, she was using all kinds of four-letter words to describe the three men who had kidnapped her. *Jerks*. No, *kinky jerks*. She'd known that since the minute Dex forced her into the limo and opened his own small suitcase to reveal a rubber ball with ties. He'd threatened to gag her with it, and she'd since refused to speak.

Besides a ball gag, what else had the big cowboy packed? Probably some rope. She looked between Slade and Dex. She'd heard the rumors. They liked to share the same woman, and they frequented several exotic clubs like the ones in those books on her eBook reader.

But they weren't taking her needs into consideration. So she wasn't going to fantasize about them tying her up and having their rough and ruthless way with her.

God, what was she thinking? They would laugh their asses off if they knew how often she thought about the three of them. They would laugh even harder if they found out she was a twenty-five-year-old virgin.

"You read the file?" Dex asked as Slade passed him his drink.

Slade's face went hard as he looked her way. That wasn't good. Slade was the happy brother. Gavin was the brooder, and Dex the bruiser. Slade almost always had a smile for her. Now he scowled as he pinned her with his deep blue eyes.

"I read it. Are we in agreement about how to handle this?"

"I think the kid gloves are off," Dex said enigmatically.

"I think you burned the kid gloves when you hauled her out of the building kicking and screaming," Gavin said drolly. He took a long swallow of his scotch. "That poor IT guy just about fainted when you

41

shoved past him."

Dex gnashed his teeth. "Was that the fucker who offered to fix your computer?"

She itched to give them the cold shoulder, but clearly none of them would accept that. Something had changed. Her men were on edge, and her self-preservation kicked in. She folded her hands in her lap. She wished Lyle hadn't witnessed her abduction. What must he be thinking?

"Yes. Lyle is the head of the help desk. He'd graciously agreed to come to my house tonight to fix my laptop."

"Gracious isn't the word I would use," Slade said under his breath.

Her little laptop was currently in its bag, sitting on top of her suitcase in the overhead bin. How had Dex gotten her things? And how had he known Lyle was fixing her computer?

"You broke into my house." It was the only explanation. Lyle had left her a message on her machine this morning. She hadn't gotten back to him, and now it looked like she wouldn't.

He shrugged his big shoulders negligently. "Yeah. It wasn't hard. You don't even have a damn deadbolt."

She'd never really needed one and hadn't thought about it until about a month ago. "Well, now that I know you're willing to just barge in, I will certainly buy two or three."

"Don't worry about it," Dex said with a nasty smile. "You won't be going back there."

"What is that supposed to mean?" What the hell was going on?

Slade turned to her. "Besides, if Dex hadn't broken

in, he wouldn't have found your cat."

She softened. Her normally sweet cat must have gone through hell because she'd obviously taken a few swipes at her rescuer. "I really do appreciate that. Though, I would have liked to have seen her."

"The vet said she was going to be fine," Gavin said. "Do you have any idea who would want to hurt your cat? She had a knife wound in her gut."

She gasped in shock. Tears followed. "No. I don't know."

All three men growled. Hannah shrank back in her seat. Gavin held up the folder she kept by her phone, the one in which she had been storing all her evidence. She winced.

Dex leaned forward. "You want to amend that statement, darlin'? Because I'm done playing around, and the next lie that comes out of your mouth is going to earn you some punishment."

Punishment? "I don't like the sound of that, Mr. Townsend." *Liar.* She liked it way too much. She was pretty sure everyone in the Boeing could hear her heart pound. "And it's none of your business."

She had to put this on a proper footing. She couldn't let these men intimidate her. They were her bosses—or had been. She couldn't go back to work for them now, not after they had kidnapped her. Right? Her grandma's etiquette lessons hadn't covered this situation.

Dex stood up, but Slade held a hand out. "Why don't we get the full story before we start in on her?"

Gavin looked between the two of them, an oddly indulgent look on his face. "You really were born far too late, Dex. Genghis Khan could have used you."

Dex eased back into his seat. If the comment bothered him, he didn't show it. He simply grunted and nodded toward Slade, who turned to her, arms crossed over his wide chest. He reminded her of a prosecuting attorney about to slice and dice an opponent.

"How long have you known someone was stalking you, Hannah?"

The silky slide of his voice didn't fool her. He was pissed off. Maybe it was time to come clean. "About a month."

All three men huffed.

"Tell us." Gavin didn't ask. He simply commanded.

What would it hurt now? Her secret was out, and maybe they could help. Though she wouldn't admit it, it felt like a huge weight had just lifted off her shoulders. "It was phone calls at first. I would answer but no one was there, just a lot of breathing."

"Caller ID?" Dex asked.

"It showed up as unavailable. He called my home phone, not my cell." Hannah remembered being annoyed at first. She'd stopped answering the phone. "Then, after a week or so, he left a message, but in a weird voice."

Slade sat back in his chair, his hand going to the folder, fingers tapping against it. "According to the police report, he used a computer-simulated voice. Burke should be able to get a copy."

Hannah took a deep breath and forced herself to go on. "Then I changed my number and made it unlisted. He called me again two days later."

"Bastard," Dex cursed. "He must work for us."

"Agreed." Slade nodded sharply.

Really? She couldn't imagine which fellow employee would go to this much trouble to scare her.

"Hannah sent HR a notification when she changed her number. Besides the three of us, HR was the only one with a record."

"So it's likely someone with access to the HR files. We should have known something was going on when she changed her number." Slade cursed under his breath.

Dex nodded, then turned back to her. "How many friends have your new number?"

She didn't have a horde of friends, but she did have a few good ones. "Uhm, I told Wendy and Heather. Oh, and a couple of people from work."

"We'll need you to write them all down," Gavin said.

"I can do that," Hannah replied.

"What about Preston Ward, our CIO? You gave him your number after he kissed you?" Dex arched a brow at her.

"What the hell?" Slade stood, staring, his expression thunderous. "He *what*?"

Hannah flushed. "I've handled that. And no, I didn't. He must have gotten it from HR."

"Why didn't you tell me he'd come on to you?" Gavin demanded, looking none too pleased.

She looked at her boss—former boss—trying to understand the reason for this third degree. "You're the CEO. You don't have time for my troubles."

"Like hell," Gavin snarled.

Slade's mouth flattened into a thin line that Hannah couldn't help but think boded ill for her.

Dex speared her with another stare. "What else

haven't you told us?"

She confessed the rest. It was like ripping off a Band-Aid. Once she started, she just wanted to get it over with. She explained that this crazy man had somehow gotten her IM address and had started sending her long notes on her laptop about how beautiful she was and how much he wanted her. He'd called one night in a rage threatening to hurt her because she'd come home late. He'd asked if she'd been out with those perverted brothers.

"I think he meant you and Slade," she said, biting her lower lip. Gosh, she didn't want to offend them. "He obviously doesn't understand that we just work together."

Slade frowned. "I think he understands all too well."

Hannah frowned. What did he mean by that?

She pressed on. "Then Mr. Snuggles went missing, and I called the police again, but they said they couldn't do anything since cats run off all the time."

Dex pinned her with his steely gaze, making her feel like a bug he was about to dissect. "Yes, the cops can do very little in a situation like this, which begs one question: Why didn't you tell us?"

"It wasn't your problem. Y'all are very kind to me. It seemed like a crappy thing to pay back your kindness by pulling you into this mess." Hannah didn't mention that she desperately wanted them to see her as a capable woman, not a burden. "Besides, I didn't just call the police. I hired a private investigator."

She waited for praise. They would see that she had this handled and they would lighten up. Instead, they just stared at her. She tried not to but she squirmed in her seat.

"His name is Vinny. He came with great references." The psychic whose shop he worked out of had thrown in a free tarot reading.

"I think I'll stick with mine," Gavin drawled. "But Hannah, a private investigator isn't protection. You could be assaulted while your private investigator is digging into this."

Hannah reached for her purse, because she had an answer for that, too. Her hand met with cold metal, and she pulled out her brand new pistol. "That's why I bought this. See? I'm prepared."

Gavin turned a shade of white Hannah was certain no living human should ever be. Slade gasped, but Dex was on his feet in an instant, prying the gun away from her.

"Goddamn it, Hannah, the safety isn't even on. You could kill yourself with this fucking gun. What were you thinking?" Dex's voice resounded through the plane.

"Well, I was surprised that I managed to get through security." Thank goodness security in a private airfield was very different than a commercial airport. They had just driven up to the plane. "And I didn't know about the safety. Maybe I should have read the manual."

She noticed that Slade's eyebrow was twitching slightly. "Are you okay, Slade? See. This is why I didn't want to bring you all into this. It's very stressful. But I have it handled. You don't have to worry."

Slade closed his eyes. "Right now, I'm not worried that the stalker is going to get you, honey. I'm worried about what I'm going to do."

"What do you mean?"

He didn't reply. Instead, he reached across the aisle and pulled her over his knee. She gasped as her stomach hit his lap. "Slade, what are you doing?"

"I'm regaining my sanity."

"It's about damn time, brother," Dex said.

She forced her head up to look at Dex and Gavin. Both men stared at her, but neither moved a muscle to help.

"Do something!" she demanded of Gavin. She knew Dex would be no help.

"Oh, I'm going to," he assured, leaning forward to brace his elbows on his knees. "I'm going to watch."

Hannah took a deep breath. Nothing would ever be the same again.

Chapter Four

Slade's big hand slid up Hannah's calf. Shock ricocheted through her body. Tingles skittered across her skin. She fought not to shiver as his palm worked up, up, up her leg in a slow slide.

"Slade." Her voice shook. "What are you doing? We should talk about this."

"Time for talking is past, baby." Slade's voice sounded hoarse, utterly unlike the sunny man she knew. This man had purpose, and it wasn't to make her laugh.

Dex was on his knees before her. He gently threaded his fingers through her hair and pulled, lifting her head until she caught his eyes. "You gave up the right to talk, darlin', when you didn't tell us that someone is trying to hurt you. So now we're going to go over the rules. Rule number one, you never hide anything from us."

Rules? Hannah might have thought they meant rules of employment…but with Slade's hand making its way up her thigh, she didn't think that was the case. What was he planning to do?

She was so damned confused. Tears welled in her eyes. One minute they were her friends. The next, they

49

thrust her over their lap, touched her in the most
deliciously inappropriate way, and started talking about
rules. If this was a joke, she wasn't laughing. She
certainly didn't want to be the butt of it.

"Slade, let me up."

Gavin's voice broke through her panic. "Slade,
release her. She asked."

"That is not the way this works. You don't
understand, Gavin. Unless you're willing to rethink
your position, stay out of this." Slade's hand was right
under the cheek of her ass now, caressing her, lighting
up her skin. "I can't let you go, Hannah. We meant to
do this slowly, but that's no longer an option."

"Do what?" Her voice shook.

"Teach you to submit." Slade's voice was husky as
he bent to whisper in her ear.

"To us. Open your eyes, darlin'." The deep drawl
she knew well wound through Dex's words, but there
was an underlying note of command she'd never heard
him use before.

Shivering, Hannah did. She couldn't ignore that
voice. But when she looked into Dex's dark eyes, the
gravity there terrified her.

"Please don't do this to me. I'm not like the other
girls. I have…feelings for you. I couldn't handle being
your plaything." Her breath hitched, and she tried to
control her tears.

Hannah had stupidly fallen in love with the three
of them, but she wasn't naïve. They never kept a lover
for long. If she gave into her desires, she would have a
few days of sex-soaked bliss with them before they left
her behind for their next willing female. That would
break her heart into a million tiny pieces.

Then she would definitely have to leave her job—maybe even leave the city. Because no way could she be close to them every day, knowing they'd found another lover and were lavishing all their attention on her.

But maybe if she held them off now, she could move on one day, find some nice guy and have a decent life. She would never let that nice guy know she longed for these three men. Hell, she could never let *them* know how much she truly loved them.

Dex and Slade shared a glance before the middle brother caressed her thigh. "Thank you for that, Hannah."

For admitting that she was a lovesick idiot? "Please let me up, Slade."

"I won't do that, baby." He sounded as tortured as she felt. "I can't."

Dex leaned in, his face inches from hers. "Hannah, we know you're not like the others. We knew it the minute we met you. Do you have any idea how hard it's been to wait for you to get to know us? But that's over now, especially since we know how you feel."

Behind her, Slade pushed her skirt up to her waist. She felt the cool air on her backside and she shrieked.

"Just because I care about you doesn't mean I'll be your plaything."

Dex's jaw firmed, but he cupped her face tenderly. "Relax, darlin', and listen to me. You're not our plaything. But don't think for a second that you're not ours, Hannah. You are."

Ours? They couldn't possibly mean in any other way except to toy with and use. They would discard her when the fun and games were over because that's what they did with every woman. Hannah wanted to believe that she was different, but she'd be kidding herself.

She wriggled, trying desperately to force Slade to release her. "Let me go. Take me home. I swear I'll tell you if this stalker contacts me again. Just...don't do this."

"Calm down," Slade demanded. "There is no going back, baby. We're going to keep you in Alaska until you agree to be ours."

"Marry us, darlin'. That's what he means."

Marry? Her head was whirling. They wanted her to marry *them*? How was that supposed to work? Or was this "proposal" just one way more they played with a woman's heart? If so, she already couldn't take it. The yearning was too deep and haunting. Their leaving would create scars she'd never heal from. "Please, don't."

"Hannah, baby…"

"Stop talking, Slade," Dex snapped. "She's not listening."

"You're right. We just need to move forward."

Relief poured through Hannah—along with crushing despair. They'd release her, and she could go back to her old life, minus the job she loved. She'd carry on somehow. But since they hadn't really touched her, she'd get over her broken heart someday. Maybe.

Instead of letting her go, Slade pulled her underwear down around her thighs. Hannah gasped. Her bare bottom was on full display.

Dex stood over her, leaving her to stare at the blue industrial carpet. "Look at that beautiful ass."

"I told you it was gorgeous under all that crap she wears. Her breasts are going to be spectacular." Slade ran a palm over her backside.

Tingles danced everywhere he touched. Were they really talking about her sexually?

"The only thing that would make this gorgeous bottom look better is a nice shade of pink. How many?"

Slade continued his perusal of her ass. Hannah could feel the heat of his stare. "I think her offense was pretty damn grave, but she's a novice. She didn't understand the rules. I say twenty-five."

Hannah brought her head up. "Twenty-five? You—you're going to spank me twenty-five times? You can't..."

But Slade proved in the next instant that he could. His hand came down with a *crack*, and fire licked across her flesh. Horror and desire washed over her in equal waves. Hannah howled and bucked.

Dex knelt to her again. "Be still, Hannah. No fighting us. You take your discipline with grace or there will be more of it."

It seemed wrong, but desire swelled as Slade palmed her ass. Still, nothing could dampen her fury. "Gee, thanks."

Smack. Hannah stiffened and whimpered.

"No sarcasm," Slade growled. "But you can make that breathy little sound you just made, love. That went straight to my cock."

One smack. Then another. Hannah gasped, fists clenched. Slade didn't seem to notice. He simply went to work, his hand raining down blows on her backside. She bit her lip, forcing herself not to cry. Even if they thought she needed disciplining like a child, she refused to act like one.

Then something strange began happening. Heat permeated her skin. She cried out, her eyes still blurry from tears. The pain lingered, but it was being overtaken by a whole new sensation, a weird sort of pleasure she didn't understand.

"Fifteen," Slade called out.

He had been methodically counting every time his hand slapped her flesh with firm male gusto. As he dealt her ass another blow, he announced the sixteenth whack. Hannah drew in a sharp breath and tried to focus on Slade's voice telling everyone how many times she'd taken it.

Nine more and she'd be done. *Smack.* Eight more and this punishment would be behind her. Would that end the sweet heat and amazing floaty feeling taking over?

Hannah finally stopped tensing against Slade's hand. There was no use fighting it. Slade would have his way. Dex and Gavin would let him. They would spank her when she was bad. If it felt this good, she might be bad a lot.

With a sigh, she let go and melted into Slade.

"Fuck, I told you she was submissive." Dex's growl made the burgeoning ache right between her legs worse.

"Twenty-two," Slade called out, his voice deepening.

Since her neck didn't seem capable of holding her head anymore, she let it fall. She was languid, her whole body centered on the riot of sensations screaming across her backside. Three more smacks, then a pause. Followed by utter bliss. The mere cessation of pain was its own pleasure.

"That was beautiful." Slade's hands soothed now, pressing his palm into her skin in long, deep strokes down her spine and across her ass. Every touch reminded her that he'd been the one to bring her to this place. Hannah sighed as he leaned over and kissed each of her cheeks.

Heat flamed through Hannah again, and she couldn't say it was all embarrassment.

Then another brush of lips on her ass. Dex.

"So submissive. I can smell you from here, darlin'."

Hannah flushed at Dex's hoarse words, bringing her out of her relaxed state. Yes, she'd had a very unexpected reaction to Slade's discipline. She *was* wet. In fact, she was pretty sure she'd never been this wet before.

Cringing at Dex's words, she tried to arch and struggle to her feet.

"Hold still or I'll give you ten more," Slade said, his hand pressing down on her lower back. He didn't say another word or give an inch until she complied. Finally, when she had no choice but to lie still, he rewarded her with a caress as he slid her panties to the floor. "Good girl, Hannah. Now, spread your legs. We want to see how much you enjoyed your spanking."

Spread her...? Hannah was so embarrassed. He thought she would just show them what only her doctor had ever seen? If she did, they'd know that she enjoyed Slade's handiwork far more than she could have imagined.

"Every second you delay earns you more

punishment." Slade's voice had gone silky and dangerous.

"We aren't going to hurt you, darlin'. We'd never hurt you," Dex vowed. "But we're also not going to let you up until you understand that you're ours and you submit to us. Spread your legs so we can see your pussy. Now."

Hannah didn't want more spankings. Or did she? She shook her head. Maybe it was stupid of her, but she wanted their attention, just this once. She'd deal with the inevitable heartache later.

Besides, what had propriety gotten her so far? She'd always been a good girl. She'd followed all the rules and taken care of everyone around her. Her mother had floated in and out of her life, coming back only when she needed money. When her grandmother had been unable to work anymore, her mother simply started hitting Hannah up for it. Hannah's sister, Crystal, had been the same. She'd preferred boys and drugs to her little sister. In the end, she'd just preferred the drugs, and they had taken her life.

Still, being good hadn't made her happy or kept a stalker away. It certainly hadn't kept her from being lonely or helped her find someone to love.

She loved Dex, Slade, and Gavin. Maybe...if she could be the kind of woman they wanted, they would never leave. Maybe they really would marry her, and they'd all be happy together.

The thought was intoxicating.

"Hannah, I gave you an order. Last warning." Slade's hand tightened on her thigh.

"Give her a moment," Gavin insisted, speaking for the first time since the spanking had begun. "Hannah, they're serious. I know my brothers. Dex and I may fight from time to time because he's hot-tempered and pigheaded, but he's not a liar. Trust them, honey. They'll take care of you."

Gavin's words sounded a bit strangled, as though he'd struggled to get them out. But one thing about her boss: he never spoke less than the truth to her. Knowing that worked magic on Hannah's overwrought nerves and fragile heart.

The brothers really cared about her?

If she did as they asked—if she believed in them— she'd be taking a chance. But if she always played it safe, how would she know if she could find something wonderful?

Taking a deep breath, Hannah let her legs slide open.

* * * *

Slade's heart pounded. Spanking Hannah had been the single most erotic experience of his life. It had been everything he could have hoped for. Having her over his lap, her gorgeous ass in the air waiting for his discipline, made Slade feel like he was ten fucking feet tall. He'd spanked subs in the club he and Dex belonged to, but never had it felt like this. Those subs hadn't been his, and spanking them had been a fun game. Disciplining Hannah was important because she was their woman, and teaching her to look to her Masters was their responsibility and pleasure.

And when Hannah tentatively parted her pretty thighs, his heart swelled at the trust she placed in them. They wouldn't let her down.

God, this was the rest of his life.

He exchanged a look with Dex, who clearly understood just how important the moment was.

Slade let his hand slide over her cheeks then glide down to her pussy. Her wet cream coated his fingers, making them slippery. Hannah gasped at his touch.

He looked up at Dex, fighting a smile of triumph. "She's soaking wet."

"Show me."

Slade froze. The command hadn't come from the person he expected. Dex's face was just as shocked as Slade knew his was. They both turned to their oldest brother. Gavin wanted to see? Maybe they were closer to a breakthrough than Slade had hoped.

He grabbed Hannah by the waist before Gavin could change his mind. She tensed a bit, but he dropped a kiss on her shoulder, and she became a sweet bit of languorous femininity, trying to show trust in her men.

With minimal fuss, she allowed him and Dex to pull her off his lap then sit her on his thighs once more, her back to his front. Slade arranged her legs on either side of his knees so that when he widened his stance, he parted her thighs.

Hannah's blonde hair flowed down her back, tickling Slade's face. She smelled like peaches and sweet sex. Her head fell back against his shoulder. She was closer to him than he'd ever managed to get to her. The hugs he'd stolen before were nothing compared to the intimacy of holding her in his arms after disciplining her.

Enfolding her in his arms, he turned his chair and faced Gavin.

His brother's serious face tightened, his brows a deep *V* over rain-cloud eyes. He was perfectly still as his gaze fused right on Hannah's very slick pussy. Gavin clutched the arms of his chair with trembling fingers.

"Pretty, isn't she?" Slade couldn't resist baiting his brother.

Gavin swallowed in silence—but didn't look away.

Slade trailed his hands up her body. Hannah whimpered but didn't fight him, and her soft submission went straight to his cock and filled a place in Slade he hadn't known was empty. He'd been working to earn Hannah since that first night he'd entered a BDSM club. Now she was here.

With seeking palms he found her breasts, gorgeously round and soft. His thumbs grazed her stiff nipples through her clothing. She whimpered a little.

"It's all right. I just want to play for a minute," he whispered.

After a moment's hesitation, she settled back down.

"Don't try to tell him that you don't like it." Dex knelt between her legs. "Your lips can lie, but your pussy doesn't." He peered at Slade then shot a glance over his shoulder at Gavin. "She's coated in cream and getting wetter."

Gavin clenched his jaw, but he stubbornly remained mute.

"Dex," she protested. "Do you have to say it so bluntly? It's…impolite."

His brother grinned, the expression making him seem younger than his twenty-eight years. Dex never looked as open and young as he did when Hannah was making him smile. "Darlin', you have your legs spread in front of three men. We passed polite a while back."

Slade pinched her nipples again. "And we like you this way."

Her head lolled back on his shoulder. Even from his vantage, Slade could see the hint of a smile on Hannah's face.

She had entered the plane filled with self-doubt and no small amount of fear. Now she was relaxed, even somewhat happy. He'd given that to her, and damn if it didn't make him smile. He'd almost be happy, too, if he could just get the reaction he wanted out of Gavin.

Slade rolled Hannah's nipples through her shirt. He couldn't wait to get those breasts in his mouth. What would Gavin do then?

"Damn, darlin', you're so wet." Dex didn't hesitate. He put his nose right where Slade knew he wanted it. Hannah gasped as Dex inhaled loudly. "And you smell so fucking good."

She tried to dodge him, but Slade tightened his arms around her. If Hannah was concerned with the impoliteness of Dex talking about how good her pussy smelled, she'd likely have a problem with him diving in for a feast. But that wasn't going to stop him.

"Oh, oh." The breathy sounds that flowed out of Hannah's mouth told Slade that maybe they really had moved past simple courtesy. "That shouldn't feel so good."

"Yes, it should, baby," Slade encouraged. "It's going to feel even better when you have one of us suckling your breasts and one eating your pretty pussy.

It's going to feel so good then."

Dex dropped back beside Gavin. "She tastes like sunshine. Get her off. We want to watch."

Slade couldn't wait. He cupped her cunt. It was soft and slippery, swollen and pouting. His thumb went to the nub of her clit and caressed while he slid a single finger in. "You are so tight, love."

He groaned because he could feel her muscles clamping down on his finger. His cock protested. He wanted to be inside her so damn badly, but this was about her. She'd submitted beautifully and deserved to be rewarded. Besides, Gavin needed to see what he was missing.

Slade struggled to work a second finger into the tight clasp of Hannah's pussy. He doubted he could squeeze in a third. She was going to be so damn snug, but that was okay. He'd do whatever it took to maneuver his cock in and make her like it. Dex—and hopefully Gavin—would do the same.

As he felt his way around her cunt, he hit just the right spot. Hannah gasped. He pressed in and rubbed, rotating as he slid his thumb over her hard bundle of nerves. Her entire body stiffened. Her breath came even faster. She clawed at his thighs.

"Slade…"

"Feel good, baby?"

She nodded frantically, words seemingly eluding her.

"That's so fucking sexy," Dex purred as he moved in again and trailed a hand up her thigh. His gaze fused with hers.

"You have no idea. You've got to feel her." Slade pulled his slick fingers back, lavishing all his attention on her hard clit, paying close attention to the cues of her body. He kept her right on edge with soft, circular strokes.

Dex didn't waste a second before he slipped a thick finger inside her pussy. "Fuck, she is tight. You're going to be incredible."

As Hannah whimpered, Dex kissed the inside of her thigh and pumped another finger inside her, turning his wrist so his fingertips danced right over her most sensitive spot.

He and Dex didn't have to speak a word. They both knew it was time.

While Slade rubbed the hard little nub a bit faster, a bit harder, Dex prodded that spot inside her relentlessly. Hannah's back arched. As he worked his lips up her neck, her skin turned dewy and damp. She drew in sharp little breaths, one after the other.

"Give it to us, darlin'," Dex demanded. "Let go."

Immediately, she shot off like a rocket, bursting high. She shook, screaming her pleasure in his arms. He wished he could see her face, but he watched Dex, who looked supremely pleased. Slade could tell that Hannah in rapture was a beautiful sight.

He glanced at Gavin. Every muscle in his oldest brother's body was tense. Hunger darkened his eyes as he watched the explosive orgasm wrack Hannah's body until her mewls became whimpers, and she turned limp in his arms.

Still, Slade wasn't quite ready to let her go. He continued to brush her clit gently. Each time he did, her body spasmed with little aftershocks.

Dex withdrew his fingers and sucked them, closing his eyes with a moan. "That was gorgeous, darlin'. I can't wait to see it again."

"Oh my goodness. What was that?" Hannah asked in a desperate, breathy voice.

Slade turned his face in to breathe her scent, his lips scraping across her cheek and chuckled. She could be so adorable.

"That was a killer orgasm," Dex said with a grin as he stood, his hand on the button of his pants. "It's going to be even better when it's my cock inside you. Come on, baby. I want you to ride me."

Abruptly, Hannah sat up, pulled her skirt down, then glanced at him. Brows knit, green eyes uncertain, she looked away. Slade reeled back at the confusion on her sweet face and forced himself to sit up.

He turned her in his arms. "You've never had an orgasm before, baby?"

Hannah stared, blinked at him. "No."

The entire room froze.

"Darlin', what were those men thinking?" Dex scowled.

"What men?" Hannah asked, her eyes innocent.

The clues slid into place for Slade. "You're a virgin?"

With a pretty flush, Hannah scrambled off his lap, smoothing her skirt. "Yes."

He and Dex exchanged a quick glance. This changed everything. They'd been ready to introduce her to the pleasures of ménage at thirty-thousand feet, but if this was her first time, she deserved a real bed and an enormous amount of patience from them.

"Oh, I get it," she murmured. "You don't like virgins. Because I don't know what I'm doing, right?" Hannah backed away. "I don't know what came over me earlier. Let's just forget it happened."

Slade got to his feet. His cock was a hammer in his slacks, but it would wait for Hannah.

He took her hand and drew her closer. "Look at me, love."

She hesitated, then finally met his gaze. He could see the courage it cost her.

"No, we won't forget that it happened. And it's going to happen again. We are so honored that you trusted us with the truth. We hope you'll do the same with your body." Slade raised her hand to his mouth, palm up, and kissed her. "We'll take such good care of you."

Dex was right there, taking her other hand. "I promise. We're going to cherish you."

Tears filled her eyes, along with a spark of what Slade could only describe as hope. "You're not disappointed?"

"We're thrilled," Slade said. "Now, sit down, and I'll fix you a drink. You should rest."

He poured her a glass of Sauvignon Blanc. When he turned, she was sitting in her chair next to Dex. They had left a seat open beside her. That was his place, beside her. He passed her the glass and sat. Dex began to talk about her cat and how he'd rescued the fur ball. By the time he was finished with the story, Hannah was smiling into Dex's face. When Slade found her hand with his, she squeezed back.

Slade couldn't help the smile creasing his face. The moment was perfect with the singular exception of Gavin on the other side of the aisle. Alone. His gray eyes were stark, miserable. Slade didn't know what to say, but he figured he'd better come up with something fast.

Before he opened his mouth, Gavin shook his head and stared out the window.

For the first time it really sank in that Slade could gain a wife and lose his brother.

Chapter Five

The limo slid away from the tiny airstrip, its engine purring almost silently.

Gavin was well aware that it was utterly incongruous to have a limo in a backwoods town like River Run, Alaska, but his father had kept one for his infrequent trips, and it had seemed cruel to Gavin to fire the driver. The man had been with his family for almost fifty years, so when Gavin or any of the executives came to River Run, they were greeted by the elderly driver and late-model limo.

The vehicle seated six, not that they needed that much space. His brothers had practically sprawled Hannah across their laps. She didn't take up much room anyway. Nor, apparently could she walk. When the plane had touched down, she'd tried to stand, but Dex had been there, sweeping her into his arms. He'd passed her off to Slade when they reached the limo. Now she sat curled up like a sweetly rumpled, sexy kitten between them. The minute Dex had curled his arm around her she'd let her head find his chest and fallen asleep. Dex had closed his eyes, too.

Lucky bastard. Gavin doubted he would be able to sleep even in his comfortable bed. His cock was still hard hours after watching Hannah spread her legs and come for the first time. Gavin knew he'd never touch her…but in that moment, he'd felt so involved, sharing that brand new experience with her and his brothers. Fuck if he didn't want more.

He'd never given much thought to the whole Dominance and submission thing Dex and Slade were into, but watching Hannah's pretty backside turn bright pink under Slade's hand had flat out done something for him. He'd imagined it was his own hands holding her down, administering discipline. He would have turned her over and forced her to ride him.

But she was a virgin. God, he didn't want to think about that, about the fact that before too long, she wouldn't have her virginity anymore—and one of his brothers would be the privileged man taking it.

"Have you heard from the Lenox brothers, yet?" Slade kept his voice low, in deference to the sleeping pair.

Gavin was grateful for the reprieve from his dark thoughts. When he found Hannah's stalker, he would think of an excellent way to take more of his frustration out on the asshole. "They sent a text saying they have all the data. It will take them a few days to go through everything."

"We can always hope this sick fuck walked past a couple of security cameras with the package."

"Yes, we can hope."

Gavin watched the terrain slide by. It was high summer in Alaska, and the ground was covered in colors he never saw in Texas. Rich, vibrant flowers formed a carpet that led from the road to the flat, plain that seemed to go on for days. Even the grass was a lush Technicolor green.

"I always loved it here," Slade said, his gaze trailing to the mountains in the distance. "I felt free."

"We were certainly much freer than we were at home." Gavin knew his strict father thought that sending Slade and him up here every summer was some form of punishment. Stuart James had told his nine- and five-year-old boys that they needed to toughen up, and that Alaska would make them men.

His father really had been blind. What he and Slade had discovered in River Run was real kindness and affection for the first time in their lives.

"Marnie says her cabbage won first place at the fair this year." Slade smiled as he spoke of the woman who had met them at the airstrip that first day. Marnie ran the local tavern and knew how to handle roughnecks with ease. She'd also known how to deal with two scared boys.

He wondered if she would have any advice for one conflicted man.

Gavin turned away, staring out at the landscape. Honestly, he had no reason to be conflicted. He was realistic. The past had proven to him, in the ugliest way possible, that he couldn't put anyone fragile in his hands. He was too broken to care for Hannah like she deserved. Getting aroused by watching his brothers touch her pussy and bring her to orgasm didn't mean anything except he was male and healthy.

"You and Dex have barely said two words to each other."

Gavin realized that, but at least Dex had gotten on the plane with him. "Dex was far too busy with Hannah to speak to me. And we shouldn't pretend like he isn't here listening to every word we say."

Slade waved off that thought. "He's the soundest sleeper I know. A nuclear bomb could go off, and Dex would sleep through it. He told me that he grew up in some of the loudest homes imaginable, and he had to train himself to sleep through anything."

Gavin hadn't heard the stories, but he'd read the files the private investigator had compiled. Dex had grown up rough. His mother had been one of Stuart James's many girlfriends. She'd been a stripper. When she'd turned up pregnant, he'd given Roxanne Townsend a check for ten thousand dollars and told her to get an abortion. Roxanne had ignored the orders, but she'd died in a car accident when Dex was seven. He'd spent the next ten years in and out of foster homes until the day Gavin and Slade had found him.

"He looks up to you," Slade said.

Gavin doubted that. "He sees me as his boss."

Slade's head shook. "That's not true. He's only closer to me because we went to college together. Dad had just died. You were twenty-two, and you had to take the reins of a multi-billion-dollar company."

"And deal with a hostile takeover." A group of board members had tried to wrest control, thinking that Gavin was just a kid. He'd proven then that he could swim with the sharks.

Now he made sure they damn well knew he could lead them, as well.

"And Nikki died just a few months after that." The soft words landed with a thud Slade couldn't possibly have intended.

Gavin felt his whole body go cold. "We're not talking about that."

"Maybe we should. She's been a ghost in your life all this time, holding you back. You have to move on. You loved her, and she died. You can't blame yourself. Gavin, wouldn't she have wanted you to be happy? What happened was tragic, but not your fault."

Except it had been his fault, and it had cost far more of his soul than Slade could possibly know to keep that fact from everyone. *But you also kept all the nasty stuff out of the papers. You protected the family's good name. Too bad that was all you protected.*

He could still feel the cold air of the coroner's office as he received the news. Sometimes he had nightmares about that cramped, foul-smelling room. If he'd never gone, if he'd never known, would he have been able to move on? Could he have forgiven himself if it had only been Nikki he'd killed with his neglect?

"Clearly, you're under some misconception that I'm hung up on a sad event that happened a decade ago." Now wasn't the time to trot out the truth.

Slade sat back, obviously disappointed. "I hate it when you lie to me. But I appreciate your help convincing Hannah of our sincerity earlier. She needed to hear that Dex and I are serious about her."

He'd ached to include himself in that statement he'd made to Hannah about his brothers' intentions. That had scared him more than anything. "I know you care about her."

"I love her."

Gavin envied the unrelenting sureness of Slade's statement, but he knew he'd never be able to give his whole heart to another person now. "She seems to feel the same way about you two. Be gentle with her."

Slade's lips slid into a grin. "You think the

spanking was a little rough?"

He'd thought the spanking was absolute perfection. "It seemed to please her."

One eyebrow crept up on Slade's face as he stared at Gavin. "But it did nothing for you?"

"It relieved me to see that she handled it well." She'd been sweet and submissive and graceful. So unlike his typical women these days.

Sex had become an exchange for Gavin. He kept a companion, paid for her condo, and gave her an allowance. In exchange, she was his partner in social occasions and sex until he deemed otherwise.

The arrangement was good enough. It was all he deserved.

Slade's eyes narrowed, and Gavin was deathly afraid that Slade meant to continue this little interrogation. "How is Kristin doing?"

Kristin? He hadn't talked to her in over a year. "I think she got married, actually."

Slade's fingers drummed along the arm rest. "That's right. You've moved on to Tiffany. She's your latest...girlfriend?"

He said girlfriend in a halting way, as though he knew the words didn't fit, but couldn't come up with anything better. Gavin could. "She was my mistress, Slade. And she's no longer with me, either."

His current mistress, Brooke, was exactly like Tiffany, and the sort of woman he needed—cold, skilled, and efficient.

Slade rolled his blue eyes. "Mistress. That makes you sound like some freaking nineteenth-century lord. No one has mistresses these days."

"It's the perfect accessory for the modern-day

CEO."

"You're more than a CEO, Gavin. I wish you would understand that there's more to life than work." Slade's eyes drifted to the woman at his side. She twisted in her sleep, and her head rolled from Dex's shoulder to Slade's. His brother cupped her cheek and kissed the top of her head, practically sighing at the contact. "There's a lot more."

Resentment bubbled up in Gavin. Of course Slade thought there was more to life than work. He'd been in college when their world had nearly been ripped out from under them. Gavin was the one who had to deal with the fallout of their father's untimely demise. Slade had been in college, and Dex had followed him there for fraternity fun and games. Given the fact that Slade and Dex were only a few months apart in age, it was no surprise they had fallen in together. By the time Gavin had been able to come up for air, Slade and Dex had bonded, and Gavin was on the outside.

In the years that had passed, nothing had changed

"How about you work on your little engineering projects, and I'll run the company."

Slade frowned. "My 'little engineering projects?' You mean like the project that found a huge reserve in the middle of the Gulf? That billion-dollar project?"

Gavin was saved by the trill of his cell phone. He looked down at the caller ID. Burke Lenox. The man worked fast. He stared for a moment wondering what he wanted from this call. If the Lenox brothers had solved the crime already, then he and his brothers could turn right around and take Hannah home. Or he could leave and let her, Dex, and Slade have a romantic getaway. He didn't want to leave. He wanted more.

Damn it, he was tired of being on the outside.

But it wasn't going to change.

"You're right. I'm sorry about the engineering crack," Gavin said shortly. If he wanted to get back in good with his brothers, he needed to stop being such an asshole. He slid the answer button on the phone, and was surprised at how fast his heart was beating. "Lenox? What have you got for me?"

Burke's smooth voice came over the line. "Not much yet. Cole is going over the tapes. I think you're definitely right. This is an insider."

He'd known that. Part of him relaxed. He didn't have to decide yet what to do next. But Hannah was still in danger. "Run deep background checks on everyone. Human Resources would have done some of the legwork, but you have resources they don't."

"I'll start with anyone who has daily dealings with Hannah. This is a big company we're talking about, James. It could take awhile."

"I understand. I want you to be very thorough. Start with Scott in IT. The way I see it, he might be hung up on Hannah in a dangerous sort of way if he's suddenly demanding to have an important lunch with her. There's nothing so critical about the project she's coordinating that should require her to spend her lunch hour with him. And our CIO, Preston Ward III. He and Hannah had an...altercation recently."

"Funny that you mention him. The other reason I called you was to let you know you've got trouble up there in Alaska."

"Yes, there were some minor computer issues. It made a decent cover for us leaving, but it's nothing we're too concerned about."

There was a long pause. "I was in your office this afternoon. Apparently, your minor trouble became something major. I overheard Ward saying that River Run is in serious trouble, and he's headed up there himself with a couple of techs to fix it. You're going to love this. One of the techs is Scott. The other is the head of your help desk, Lyle."

Gavin didn't love it. It was the worst news possible. Preston was on his way down with two techs, and all three men were on Gavin's list of suspects. Any of them could be Hannah's stalker. Son of a bitch.

While in Alaska, Gavin had imagined that he could go fishing with his brothers in an attempt to reconnect, but maybe a good old-fashioned ass-kicking was the ultimate bonding experience. Because by the time the trio got here in the morning, he hoped they'd figured out the identity of Hannah's stalker. The asshole was going to have a welcome party he would never forget.

"Thank you, Burke. Could you find out what flight they're on? One of the admins should know. I want to be prepared."

"I just sent you an e-mail with that information. I'll keep digging, focusing first on the men you've mentioned. But something is off here; I feel it. Watch your back, James. I'll call back when I know more."

The line went dead, and Gavin immediately opened his e-mail.

"What's going on?" The expression on Slade's face told Gavin he'd figured out something was up, but he couldn't move because Hannah's head was on his chest. Otherwise, they might be wrestling over the phone. "What did he find out?"

Gavin scanned the e-mail. It was a copy of the incoming employees' itinerary. Preston hadn't wasted a minute. He and two others were coming in on the redeye to Anchorage, followed by a puddle-jumper they'd hired to get them to River Run. First Class for Preston, but he'd shoved the techs into coach. *Douche bag.*

"It looks like we're going to have company. Have you checked your cell lately?"

Slade flushed slightly. "I turned it off while we were in the air. I haven't turned it back on."

Because he was far too busy with Hannah. Work was going to come second for Slade from now on. Gavin could deal with that. He scanned through his e-mail, reading a group of them from the foreman at River Run, which had started minutes after Gavin's plane had taken off. "Don't feel too bad. I just started mine again. There was a system failure at the facility. They got it under control, but it needs to be looked at by an expert."

"I can be there in an hour," Slade said.

"A computer expert. It isn't an engineering problem. The system crashed, and now that it's back online, it's giving off some strange numbers. Ben Kunayak, the IT guy who runs our facility up here, thinks the system has been hacked. Preston decided it was serious enough to investigate in person. Scott and Lyle apparently volunteered to come with him."

"What the fuck?" Slade's voice boomed through the car. "How convenient."

"Exactly."

* * * *

75

When they reached the house, Slade caught him up on the Lenox brothers' call. Dex thought seriously about putting his fist through another wall. "That fucker is going to be here in the morning?"

Gavin nodded from his seat on the couch. Dex couldn't sit. All he could do was think about the fact that Preston Ward III had followed Hannah to Alaska.

"We can't say anything to Hannah until we know for sure, but he's not coming anywhere near her."

"Agreed." Slade walked in from the hallway that led back to the bedrooms. "I settled her in. She's not particularly happy that she lost her cell phone."

Gavin eyed Slade. "Lost?"

Slade pulled the small phone out of his back pocket with a grin. "It got lost in my pants."

Gavin sighed, the sound so familiar to Dex that he no longer winced at it. He was used to disappointing Gavin. But it was nice to know their oldest brother handled Slade the same way. "And why would her phone decide to hide in your slacks?"

Dex held his hand out, and Slade turned the phone over. Dex immediately started going through her recent calls. "Slade and I talked about it earlier. Hannah knows a lot of people. Maybe one of them is her stalker. But if she has this phone, she's going to answer it. She might even call her friends to let them know where she's gone. We can't risk that."

She'd had twenty damn phone calls in the last ten hours. Dex ignored the ones from Wendy and the other female office workers Hannah had befriended. There were several numbers from inside Black Oak that Dex didn't recognize, and Hannah didn't have contact names for their numbers.

"We need to keep Hannah's whereabouts quiet. Wendy is the only one who knows where she is. She's been with the company for over a decade. I would trust her with company secrets." Slade flipped open his laptop and started it up.

"And Wendy loves Hannah," Gavin offered. "She views her as the daughter she never had and has lectured me several times on the importance of taking care of Hannah properly. Wendy wouldn't give up her whereabouts. She knows the danger."

Dex sat down beside Slade, who had pulled up the company directory. "Who has extension 709?"

Slade's fingers flew across the keys. "Scott Kirkwood. He works in IT. That's the guy she was supposed to have lunch with today so he could talk to her about something 'important.'"

Dex remembered Scott. Short, scrawny. Pale hair to go with his pale face. When Dex had gone to the IT section to interrogate the little prick, he'd been out with a 'personal appointment,' according to his supervisor. Scott was supposedly both reliable and punctual, but the timing smelled damn fishy to Dex. "Send Burke his name."

"Already done," Gavin advised.

Satisfaction rolled through Dex. "Good. I'll bet we have dates and times on some of this damn stalker's actions. Maybe we can use those to narrow the list of suspects down and eliminate others."

"I think you should have this conversation with Hannah," Gavin suggested.

Dex turned to him. "We don't want to scare her unnecessarily. Once we know something, we'll bring her in and tell her everything."

"I understand not wanting to frighten her, but you can't pretend the problem doesn't exist when she's around. Isn't she our best resource on figuring this out? I mean, she does know who she speaks with on a daily basis."

"I don't want her involved." Dex flipped through her phone. "Extension 830?"

A few clicks on the computer, and Slade had the answer. "That's Heather Coleburn. She's in the business management office. She and Hannah have had lunch every Wednesday for the last year."

"She makes friends so easily," Dex murmured with a hint of a smile. She was a genuine friend, and some people took advantage of that. "722?"

Slade rolled his eyes. "That's Lyle. You know Lyle."

Dex knew him well. Lyle was the head of the help desk and a supposed computer genius. He just seemed like an unctuous prick to Dex. "Yeah. He left a message on her machine at home, I think. He was supposed to fix her laptop tonight. Maybe we should give his name to Burke."

Gavin shrugged. "Next time I talk to Burke or Cole, I will."

"Good. Now does someone here want to tell me why I didn't know that Hannah filed a sexual harassment complaint against our CIO?"

"I didn't know, either," Slade added.

Gavin's eyes hooded. "She told me it wasn't serious. He got a little handsy at happy hour a couple of weeks back. He and his wife are separating, and Ward was drunk. I talked to him yesterday, just after I found out. I told him I would fire him if he even looked Hannah's way again."

"And you didn't bother to mention this to either of us, why?" Slade asked, looking up from his computer.

Gavin's perfectly polished shoes tapped against the hardwood floor, a sure sign he was getting impatient. "By HR's standards, Hannah's complaint is confidential. The only reason I knew about it was Preston himself. He was worried HR would pursue the matter, and came to plead his case to me. Then I asked Hannah."

Dex wouldn't have let the asshole plead anything. "How could you let him get away with harassing her like that?"

"She took care of him. Broke his big toe by stomping on it. She's stronger than you give her credit for. You should be damn lucky you got the jump on her today, or you might have ended up limping like Preston." Gavin stood. "I'm going to bed. I suggest the two of you do the same. And while I agree that Hannah is fragile in some ways, I think you'd do well to remember that she is a very independent woman who has a brain."

Gavin stalked past them, heading toward the kitchen, slamming the door behind him.

"Give him a little time," Slade said. "He doesn't understand our relationship with Hannah."

"Well, he's not the only one," a soft voice said from the doorway.

Dex turned and saw Hannah standing there in one of the long, white terrycloth robes stashed in all the bedrooms for guests' comfort. Based on the flushed anger all over her face, he'd bet she'd been standing there for a while. "Hannah, you're supposed to be in bed."

She adjusted her robe. "Yes, you put me to bed and tucked me in. Clearly, you expected me to stay there like a good little girl. If that was your goal, you should have just locked me in."

"I thought about it." Dex got the feeling she wouldn't believe him if he lied. He'd given serious consideration to locking that door and knowing beyond a shadow of a doubt where she was.

"Oh, well, live and learn. Maybe you can lock in the next girl. I would like my phone back." She strode up and held her hand out.

"That's not going to happen," Dex said, snatching it up in his big fist.

"Hannah, love," Slade said, getting to his feet and cupping her shoulders. "You don't need that phone. You're safe here."

"Really? Who's going to keep me safe from your overprotectiveness?" she drawled. "I want my phone, now."

"You don't need it."

"I certainly do. How else am I going to call and make a reservation to fly out of here?"

Dex itched to mete out some discipline. But when he heard Slade's sigh, Dex knew his brother was going to try to gently talk Hannah out of her anger. That would be a mistake, in Dex's opinion. He took a moment to really read her body language. She was tense, her eyes narrow and tight. Her fists were clenched and every now and then she rolled them like she was digging her nails into the palm of her hand. Dex would bet that she was keyed up and itching for a fight…or something else that would take the edge off.

He was willing to give it to her.

"You're not going anywhere, Hannah." He said the words with implacable surety.

Her head came up, and she went toe-to-toe with him. Dex couldn't hold in a little smile. Her perfectly painted pink toes were so obviously wrong up against his worn boots.

"Don't you laugh at me, Dexter Townsend. I want my phone—now. I'm leaving, and you're not stopping me. I'm done playing whatever game you've cooked up. Oh, and I quit. Please let Mr. James know. As soon as you give me the phone, I'm going home. And by home, I mean back to West Texas."

Slade stood beside Dex, clearly no longer in the mood to reason with her. "If you think we're going to let you leave here when there's a stalker out there waiting for you, you're crazy."

Hannah thrust her hands on her hips. "You don't own me. I can come and go as I please."

"You're ours, and you're staying in this house if I have to tie you up." In fact, it would be Dex's pleasure. He would tie her hands to the headboard and place those shapely legs in a spreader bar that would leave her pussy on full display and ready for their use. Why hadn't he thought of that in the first place?

"So, I'm a captive here?"

Dex paused, then nodded. "That's accurate, darlin'. You're not leaving, and that's for your own good."

"This is how you're going to convince me you're better than the guy stalking me? Whatever you thought we started on the plane is over." She turned on her heel and walked away.

Slade's jaw dropped as they watched her. Dex had a sinking feeling they'd just fucked up big.

Chapter Six

Hannah fought to contain her scream. She stomped down the hall toward her bedroom, plotting the whole way exactly how she'd get the hell out of this mess.

She'd been so stupid. She'd thought because the brothers had shown her some affection, they really cared about her. But no. They'd spanked her and flashed her to each other. That wasn't affection, just perversion.

But then...Slade picked her up and carried her down the steps. That felt like affection, just like waking cuddled between them in the big stretch limo.

She pushed the images aside as she strode through the bedroom door. The room beyond was bigger than her apartment, and the bed looked like it was built to sleep a football team. She could only imagine what the brothers had planned to do to her there.

With a little bit of malicious glee, she turned the lock on the door. No way was she letting them in after they'd deceived her.

Now they'd find out what she was capable of.

She'd heard enough of their conversation to realize that Gavin alone thought she possessed a brain capable of independent thought. Slade and Dex...God, did they really think she was that needy? That stupid?

And where did Gavin fit into all of this? He hadn't touched her, but she could still hear his deep hypnotic voice telling Slade to turn her around so he could see her, still feel her boss's scorching stare right between her legs after her very first orgasm. And her last with them as well, because there was no way she was letting any of those men near her again.

"Hannah?" There was a tentative knock on the door. "Baby, we need to talk to you. Let us in."

Slade. That tender voice urged her to trust him. After he had stolen her cell phone and told her he had no idea where it was? No chance. "Go away."

"We can't," Slade said in that cajoling voice. "Hannah, I'm coming in."

She felt a rush of satisfaction as the doorknob moved, but the door stayed closed. They probably didn't think she was smart enough to lock it. "I don't want to talk to you."

Because they wouldn't talk, they would lie. They would tell her whatever it took to get her to open that door. She would fall for their sweet-talk. Then she would be right back where she started—sweet, trusting Hannah letting them lead her into trouble.

Fat chance.

She could see now that they didn't really want *her*. They wanted someone submissive, a trusting little toy, and they thought she fit the bill. Despite her virginity, she wasn't completely naïve. She'd read books, heard the rumors. They were Doms, and they wanted someone pliable who wouldn't complain when they tied her up, spanked her bottom, and used her in a million delicious ways.

She was not that girl. No matter how much some part of her wanted to be.

"Hannah, you open the door this instant," Dex demanded.

He was the hard-ass. She'd always known he was the one with the quick temper, but Dex's flare burned out quickly. Slade, however, would hold a grudge. He'd always try to persuade and cajole first. If that didn't work, he had no problem using force.

"What part of 'no' don't you understand? Is it the 'N' or the 'O' that's confusing?" she asked sweetly.

Seconds later, the door burst open, the finely crafted piece of wood no match for two Doms. What was left of the door hung on busted hinges. Dex prowled straight in, all caveman. Hannah forced herself to stand her ground. What now?

Slade glared at Dex. "I had a key, you know."

"You weren't fast enough." Dex stalked toward her. "You were going to stand in the hallway and sweet talk her all night."

Hannah thought about running, but one of them would catch her. Besides, it would likely incite their tempers. She needed to calm them down.

"Naturally. At least your brother has a modicum of civility," Hannah pointed out.

Slade crossed his arms over his chest and smiled.

"He was wasting time." Dex took her by the shoulders. "Hannah, you can't leave. I am willing to sit down and talk this out with you, but you need to understand that I will not allow you to step foot off these grounds."

"You don't own me, Dex. I already quit, so you can't stop me from leaving."

"Watch me, darlin'." His arrogance came off him in waves.

"I have to agree with him." Slade sent her an apologetic but implacable glance.

"And when I call the police?"

Slade smiled and proved he could be just as difficult as his brother. "There are no cops in River Run. There's a sheriff, but good luck getting him away from his fishing pole. This whole damn town is owned and operated by Black Oak Oil. No one here will help you leave us."

He was dead serious, and Hannah had to shove down her panic. "I will not be held captive."

Slade scrubbed a hand across his hair, frustration evident in the tense set of his shoulders. "Hannah..."

"If I'm not a captive, then give me back my phone."

A long sigh fell from Slade's mouth. "Whoever is out there knows your habits. He knows your friends. Promise me you won't call any of them."

She was done bargaining with them since all the compromises were heavily in their favor. "I won't promise you anything, Slade. I want my phone, and I want to go home."

"Can't you see how dangerous that would be?" Slade asked.

Was it really any more dangerous than staying with them? They'd probably use her for fun and games, tie her heart to theirs, then cut her loose when the fun ended. All their talk of marriage and forever was bunk, and she'd let herself believe it on the plane because she'd wanted to so badly.

"I understand that it's a risk. The only concession

you'll get from me is that I'm not going back to Dallas. I'm going straight to Two Trees to see my grandmother. I seriously doubt that anyone would follow me. Once I'm gone, this guy, whoever he is, will give up."

She had to believe it. Really, why would anyone follow *her*?

"And if he doesn't?"

She smiled, though she was aware the gesture didn't reach her eyes. "Well, then I'll know who he is. The first person from Dallas who sets foot in Two Trees will realize that I've purchased another gun. And I'll be ready to shoot."

"Hannah, tell me what went wrong. I get that you're upset about the phone. I really do think that a complete communications blackout is necessary until we catch this man." Slade sounded so reasonable she almost found herself agreeing with him.

"Maybe explaining that to me like I had a brain in my head would have worked." She could be reasonable. Or, she would have been, had they given her the chance.

Slade took her hand in his. She found herself turning her face up to him. He was so beautiful, with high cheekbones, a strong chin, and thick, dark lashes that framed blue eyes able to go from kind to hot in an instant. She wanted to run her hands through his inky hair and wrap herself around him. She wanted, in that moment, to be everything he desired—soft, submissive, cared for. She could just push the whole problem off in their laps and worry about nothing more than what she would have for breakfast the next day.

But she couldn't give up everything she'd worked

so hard for just for momentary comfort. As a girl in Two Trees, missing her absent mother and watching her sister self-destruct, she'd known then that a girl had to be able to take care of herself. If she let Dex and Slade have their way now and gave over her independence, they would grow bored with a clinging vine, even though they thought that was what they wanted. She couldn't build anything with them if they didn't respect her.

She took a step back and pulled her hand from Slade's. His face fell.

"Hannah, please. Can't we talk about this?"

She shook her head. "We could have talked earlier in the day. I would have listened. But now that I understand exactly what you want, I can't be that woman."

Dex's face had gone shock white. "What are you saying?"

"Aren't you listening? I'm saying I want to go home and I don't want either of you to call me. I don't want to see you again." She hated the words. She might regret them, but she would regret it more if she stayed and they walked away when the sex wore off.

Dex's face was a stony mask. "Message received. You're still staying here for a day or two so we can hunt down your stalker. If you want to call the cops after that, I'll take whatever they want to give me. I promise I won't touch you again. If we can't figure this out in a day or two, I'll let you go home, but you'll have bodyguards until this man is caught."

Hannah didn't like the tense set of his jaw. She wanted to soothe him, but forced herself to stand strong. "I don't like it, but I see the wisdom of your plan. No more than two days. After that, I'm leaving."

Slade's face was bunched in a sad sort of confusion. "Is this because I took your phone?"

"Not entirely. Let's call it a pattern of behavior."

"I didn't mean to scare you," Slade said. "Look, if you're regretting the spanking thing, we don't have to do it anymore."

"Stop." Dex put a hand on his brother's shoulder. "She's done. She doesn't want us. We can't force her, as much as we'd like to. It's against the rules. We never gave her a safe word, but if we had, she would have spit it out by now. It's not your fault. It's mine. I come on too strong. Gavin's right. I'm a fuck-up. Now let's go and give her some privacy. I'll start running those reports."

Dex turned back to her, his face so polite it tore at her heart. "Hannah, I swear we'll catch this bastard. We won't let him hurt you."

Slade's stare burned into her. "That's a promise. In the meantime, if you need anything, we're just down the hall. And here's your phone. Please, I'm begging you, don't call anyone."

He slipped the phone into her hand. She clutched it, her stomach in turmoil. They were leaving. That was what she wanted, demanded even. But she couldn't stand the defeat on their faces. Or the way Dex almost looked through her.

"You're not a fuck-up," she said gently.

Dex shrugged as if it didn't matter. "I am, darlin'. Your rejection isn't a big surprise. I guess, deep down, I knew you could never really want me."

Her heart hurt for him. She knew his background. Not a lot had worked out for Dex Townsend. "If you had talked to me, maybe we could have worked it out."

"I'd only make the same choices again. I'm like a dumb old dog. I'm never going to learn a new trick. I see you in danger, and I'll do whatever it takes to protect and shelter you."

"Hannah," Slade jumped in. "We really were trying to protect you, not take away your independence. I can see why you'd be upset, but this wasn't some ploy to trick or deceive or use you. We were trying to wrap you up so tight that nothing and no one could ever hurt you. We only wanted a chance to keep you, make you happy."

"I don't understand this. One day we're friends, and the next you're all over me?"

"We overwhelmed you, I see that now," Slade said. "The idea of a relationship with two dominant men would be daunting for most women."

"Relationship? You didn't even ask me on a date. You just went straight for the panties. No preliminaries."

The righteous scowl on Dex's face made her take a step back. "No dates? No preliminaries? You think that I just woke up this morning and decided I wanted you and took you?"

It had sure seemed that way, but his tone suggested something much different. "Didn't you?"

"So all the lunches and dinners don't count?"

He and Slade had taken her out at least once a week for almost six months. "Those were about business."

"They were excuses, Hannah," Slade said with a sigh. "You're not our admin. You're Gavin's. When we decided we wanted you, Dex and I decided to go slow, ease you into this. It's not exactly a traditional relationship."

It wasn't, but she'd been crazy about the entire James Gang from the moment she'd met them. Something had fallen into place the first time she'd been in a room with all three.

"Aren't we fucking smooth?" Dex said, bitterness dripping. "She didn't even realize we were interested."

Only because she was brutally inexperienced. Hannah hadn't dated much in high school. She'd gone to the local college, but by then her grandmother was ill. She'd never had much time to herself, even since coming to Dallas. She was usually busy with work. Now she thought back over the last year and could see some signs she shouldn't have missed.

"You remembered my birthday."

"Of course we did," Slade replied. "We planned it for weeks. We've already started planning next year's, though I will admit it was going to be better than a little cake and a couple of presents."

They'd given her the eBook reader she'd been coveting, and she loved it. Maybe they'd paid more attention to her as a person than she'd thought. "I liked my party."

They had thrown it for her at one of Hannah's favorite diners. It wasn't really their speed. When she'd gone after work for a down south, home-cooked meal, they'd been waiting for her. If they'd had nothing but seduction on their minds, it would have been more advantageous for Slade and Dex to take her some place quiet and upscale, get her alone and tipsy, then whisk her back to their lair. Instead, they had invited her friends, sipped iced tea with her, and smiled all evening. When they'd walked her to her door, neither had asked for a "nightcap." Instead, they'd hugged her, kissed her forehead, watched her walk into her apartment, and left.

"I'm glad you liked it, Hannah." Slade sent her a sad smile.

She bit her lip. "I don't understand what you see in me. Or maybe I'm afraid I do, and I don't like it."

"What do you think we see in you?" Dex asked.

"A quiet submissive? Do you like me because I do what I'm told?"

Dex almost choked, and Slade slapped a hand over his face, howling.

"You don't do what you're told, Hannah. Didn't I ask you a couple of days ago to stock my office with Cokes?" Dex asked.

Hannah winced. He had. "Yes."

"And what did I get?"

"Green tea is very healthy." She'd expected him to complain more, but when she'd smiled at him, he'd just said thank you.

"It's disgusting," Dex replied.

"And he drank every single one," Slade countered. "How about the time you took the keys to Dex's motorcycle and my car after we had a beer at the office happy hour?"

"Yep." Dex nodded. "I still have that written down in a note for future punishment."

Fine. So she wasn't always obedient. "I gave them back when I knew you'd be sober. And I only did those things because I was trying to protect you."

The second the words were out, she wanted to take them back.

Slade sent her a sly glare. "Doesn't that sound an awful lot like the reason I took your phone, Hannah?"

"It's not the same," she argued.

"Why not?" he shot back. "You said that you were trying to protect us. Well, we tried to protect you."

"I did it because I didn't want you to get hurt."

Slade crossed his bulging arms over his big chest. "Still not seeing how it's different."

Were they both dumb? "I wasn't just looking out for my sex toy."

"Baby, we're not either. I could have one of those in the next five minutes if I just wanted to get laid. Dex, too. We're in it for way more than sex. If you haven't figured that out yet, tell me how we can prove it to you."

"Once you kidnapped me, forced me to come to Alaska with you, and lied to me, you made that impossible."

They stared at her. She could feel displeasure coming off them in waves. This was how a relationship with them would work. Everything would be a fight. They would always want to control and protect her.

Hannah could handle them. She wasn't really afraid of being steamrolled, but of herself and how much she wanted them. How much of herself she'd be willing to surrender in order to keep them.

"I refuse to believe that," Slade insisted. "So we screwed up. You've already stopped caring for us?"

No. Never.

"You have to understand that I'm not fragile." It was a bit of a revelation. She'd always thought of herself as quiet. But that didn't mean she wasn't strong.

"If you think we don't know that, you're wrong."

Slade smiled again, as though he knew she was coming around.

"Hannah, darlin'…" He started to reach for her, then yanked his fist away. "We never meant to imply that you aren't strong and smart."

Dex, for all his arrogance, required a softer touch. He didn't believe in himself yet. Didn't think he belonged. But she could help him. After he answered a simple question.

"Why?"

His brows lifted in confusion. "Why?"

"She wants to know why we want her. I believe she's under the mistaken impression that we selected her almost at random simply because she's pretty and submissive." Slade nearly read her mind.

When Dex looked at her again, his face was gentler than she'd ever seen it. "I remember the day you walked in the door. You were wearing a denim skirt to a job interview."

She flushed. She'd only been off the bus from Lubbock, which didn't even bother to stop in Two Trees, for a handful of hours. "So I wasn't fashion forward. And I was interviewing for a mailroom job, if you recall."

"Oh, I recall. I watched you wait in the lobby. There was another woman interviewing for the same position. I listened to the two of you talk. Do you remember what you did?"

He'd seen that? "It was nothing."

"Bullshit. You got up and told the receptionist that you were no longer available for the job because the other applicant had three kids and a husband who'd just walked out on her."

"She was going to get kicked out of her apartment. I couldn't take that job away from her. I knew it was down to just the two of us. If I hadn't been very sure she would get the job once I bowed out, I wouldn't have left. Besides, I never made it to the door because the receptionist..." She frowned. "Wait, you called her. You told her to stop me."

"He ran all over the building trying to find me," Slade said. "When I came down and talked to you, I realized that I wanted you as much as Dex did. You smiled at me and started talking about your cat, and I was a goner. I scrambled to move enough people around to secure you a junior admin position. A month later, when Gavin's admin quit, we moved you where you belonged."

Dex took a long breath. "I don't think you're just some submissive to put in our bed. I admire the hell out you, Hannah. You're feminine and giving and sweet, things I didn't grow up knowing a whole lot about. I learn from you every day. In fact, I think that I became a better man the minute I laid eyes on you."

Hannah gasped. That wasn't desire on his face, in his voice, but true, genuine love. Tears welled up, then rolled in hot streaks down her face.

"You made me see a future," Slade murmured, taking her hand in his. "I had everything money could buy, but I was a hollow bastard who only thought of the next conquest, whether business or pleasure. You taught me about making someone happy, not because I expected something in return, but just to see the smile on their face. That was all you, Hannah."

She sobbed, bit her lip, and looked at them with her heart in her eyes. Goodness, she'd misunderstood them completely. She'd let her insecurity get in her way. Did she really want to let her best chance at happiness walk through the door because she was afraid?

Dex turned to go. "But if we aren't what you want, Hannah...we'll protect you until this is settled, then we'll leave you."

He was heading for the door? Slade stood, watching, waiting and hopeful. Dex had obviously missed her signs. That's okay. She would rather show him.

Hannah walked straight up to Dex and grabbed his elbow.

He turned, eyes wary. "Hannah?"

Dex spoke her name like a question, but Hannah only answered by standing on her tiptoes and staring straight into Dex Townsend's gorgeous eyes. "You two spanked me, but neither of you bothered to kiss me. I'm waiting."

He hesitated, frowned. Then her words hit him, and he wrapped his big hands around her face, his gaze delving into hers. The care he saw shining there made him wilt with relief. "That was a mistake on our part. We'll fix it now."

She felt Slade slide in behind her. His hands grazed her hips, and she felt the sweet stirrings of arousal.

"Tell me you've never been kissed, Hannah." Slade's breath was hot against her neck.

She was caught between two hard bodies, and she couldn't stop quivering. "I've been kissed Slade. I'm a virgin, not a nun."

"Who kissed you?" Dex asked, his mouth hovering

over hers. He was right there. So close.

"Brandon Powers kissed me at the church social behind the elm trees. He used his tongue. I didn't like it." There had been a few other boys. She'd dated a little in high school and once in college, but it had been hard. Her family had demanded so much of her time. She'd been asked out a couple of times in the year since she'd moved to Dallas, but she'd always said no. She'd told herself it was because she was too busy, but she knew the truth. She'd been waiting for these men.

"Hmm, do you think we can change her mind about kissing, Slade?"

Slade's hands ran up her torso, dangerously close to her breasts. "Let's try and see what happens."

Dex's lips touched hers, and she realized this wasn't going to be some sloppy precursor to the main event. His mouth played with hers, skimming before pulling away. He nibbled at her lips, heating her up, making her want so much more. Over and over he pressed their mouths together, while Slade kissed her ear. Who could have guessed her ear was so alive with nerves? Slade was making every one of them light up.

Hannah opened her mouth. She wanted Dex deeper.

"What do you want, darlin'?" The deep chuckle that rumbled from Dex's chest told Hannah that he already knew.

"Kiss me."

"I am." He began that maddening play at her mouth again. Tantalizing, but never fulfilling. "You still don't like kissing?"

"Her nipples like it." Slade skimmed her breasts, his fingertips dusting over their hard tips.

Hannah gasped and tried to catch a breath, but sensations rushed through her, wild and electric. She'd never known anything like it. Lord, she ached for more.

"I'm not kissing her nipples. At least not yet," Dex pointed out. "I'm kissing her pretty mouth."

"But not with your tongue. I want your tongue." Her cheeks heated at the words, but darn him, she was done waiting.

"Well, if that's what you want." Dex tightened his grip on her and took control of the kiss. He parted her lips with his own and his tongue slid in, dancing against hers. Her knees went out from under her as her entire body melted. Yep. She liked kissing. A lot.

Dex teased her while Slade let his hands wander everywhere. He pushed back her borrowed robe. Cool air floated over her skin, which was quickly replaced by a breath-stealing burn when Slade pinched her nipples.

"Brother, I believe it's my turn." Slade's low growl made her heart skitter.

Dex kissed her one last time then turned her to Slade. "Never let it be said I don't know how to share."

Hannah felt deliciously languid. This was exactly what she craved. Now that she was in the moment, she felt safe, cared for. These two men might be overprotective, but she understood now. They cared for her as much as she cared for them. And she reveled in it.

Then Slade's mouth covered hers, and he proved that he knew how to kiss just as well as his brother. He dominated her mouth, his tongue plunging and caressing, keeping her under his body, under his spell, and under no illusions that she wouldn't be giving all of her herself to them tonight.

Dex tugged the robe off her shoulders and down her body. Suddenly, she was naked between them. Her nipples rubbed against the cotton of Slade's dress shirt. Dex's rough denim abraded her tender backside. The heat built between them. The musk swirled. With the gentle touches and drugging kisses they gave her as they passed her back and forth, Hannah drowned in sensation.

"Do you have any idea how long we've wanted this?" Dex whispered against the back of her neck, making her shiver all over.

Slade feathered his lips across her jaw line and worked his way down until he found the pulse in her neck. "Or how badly?"

"I've wanted this, too." Hannah echoed back. "I think, deep down, I secretly waited for you."

In fact, she'd waited her whole life to feel this connected to another human being. The fact that she was surrounded by two of the men she loved so much felt right. The only one missing was Gavin. But she put him from her mind. For tonight, it was about her, Dex, and Slade.

"And we're happy you waited, love." Slade pressed his forehead to hers. "Are you sure you're ready for us?"

"We can take it slow, baby." Dex ran a hand down her torso, toward her aching sex.

"I want you. Both of you." That husky tone sounded nothing like her own voice.

Slade hunched over briefly and swept her into his arms. She felt delicate against him. She looked over his shoulder to find Dex following them, his hands on the buttons of his shirt. She watched as he shrugged it off and tossed it aside, revealing the kind of cut chest and abs she'd only seen in magazines. Dex's body was big and muscular, covered in sun-kissed skin that she wanted to run her hands over. She could touch him, hold him. Give herself to him.

Slade strode to the big bed dominating the room. He tossed her lightly on the mattress. Hannah's eyes widened as Dex kicked off his boots and shoved his denims off his hips. He was obviously not a great believer in underwear. His cock sprung free, big and thick with a bulbous, purple head. Dex's body was a thing of beauty.

Slade shucked his clothes, and Hannah watched, unblinking. His wide shoulders and so-ripped chest had her dropping her jaw. As his pants fell to the floor, her gaze slipped down to his cock. She felt her heart stutter. Long, thick…oh-so ready.

Honestly, she didn't know which way to look. Both men were gorgeous.

"Darlin, we're going to go easy because it's your first time, but I believe in beginning as we mean to go along," Dex said, his Texas drawl thicker than ever.

Slade stood beside his brother. "What he means, love, is that you're going to obey us in the bedroom. We can talk about most of the other decisions, but here, we are your Masters. All you have to do is trust us, darlin'. Can you do that?"

Hannah blew out a nervous breath. She was naked with two men who wanted her utter and complete obedience. She shivered at the thought of all the things they could do to her. Even so, she knew they would never hurt her physically. If she wanted this relationship to work, she had to believe they'd never meant to hurt her emotionally. And she had to believe in herself.

She nodded.

"Not good enough," Slade murmured. "Give us the words. This has to be a conscious choice on your part. Can you obey and give yourself over to us?"

"Yes." The word was barely more than a breathy murmur, but they heard it.

A sexy smile split Dex's face as he reached for her. "Then spread your legs, darlin'. We want to see our pussy."

Hannah took a deep breath to quell her nerves and let her legs fall open. She knew she wasn't the most beautiful woman ever, but she felt that way when they looked at her, attention rapt, eyes hot.

"We're going to have to set up a schedule for training and maintenance. I'll call the spa when we get home." Slade stared, his eyes going straight between her legs.

"Training? Maintenance?" What were they talking about?

"Shh," Slade commanded. "No talking. It's nothing you can't handle, baby. I have faith in you."

She closed her mouth. Oddly, she took their word that whatever they had in mind, she would have no problem managing it. They sought her submission now, but as long as her voice was heard outside the bedroom, she could give them what they needed.

"Absolutely. When we talk about training, we're talking about teaching you to be our perfect submissive. We're going to train your body to accept pleasure and dominance, while you learn to please us in return," Dex explained. "We'll introduce you to bondage and some forms of exotic play."

To someone with so little experience, it all sounded ridiculously over her head. But this was Dex and Slade. They would take care of her. They would open a whole new world for her.

"And the maintenance refers to a regular waxing regimen we'll insist on for that pretty pussy." Slade's lips curved into a wicked grin. "It's going to be so pink and pretty."

"We can always shave her in the morning. I would do it tonight, but I don't want to wait."

If anyone would have asked her in the past how she felt about altering her body in such a personal way to suit them, she would have balked. But now it sounded so simple. They weren't asking a lot, and it pleased them. Pleasing them made her happy.

Slade got down on one knee. "Do you understand what he's saying? Soon, we're going to take you into that shower and spread your legs. I'll hold you down, and he's going to shave that pussy of ours until it's ripe and bare and pretty as a peach."

"A-all right." Her voice shook almost as much as she did. She wanted to say it was nerves, but Hannah knew better. Excitement coursed through every muscle until she shook.

"But don't think I won't taste her just the way it is. Slade, you got to spank her. It's my turn to play."

Slade climbed onto the big bed and wedged himself behind her. She could feel the hard line of his erection against her spine as he pulled her back, his chest to her back, cradling her in his arms. He caught her ankles with his legs and spread her wide, kissing her temple, her neck, as Dex climbed between her thighs.

"He's going to eat your pussy, love. He's going to make a feast out of you." Slade's voice had gone dark and deep, seducing her with words. "I'm going to watch and feel every shudder and twitch you make."

Her breath caught. Her womb clenched. She could hardly wait.

"I love the way you smell." Dex took a deep breath, letting his nose touch her labia. Hannah felt so vulnerable, and somehow that excited her even more. She loved the way Slade's body wrapped around hers, anchoring her. In other circumstances, she would be horribly embarrassed by what they were doing to her, but now it seemed right.

And then she wasn't thinking about anything but the slow slide of Dex's tongue rasping against her flesh, lighting up every one of her nerves. She tried to arch, to demand more, but Slade's grip tightened.

"No, Hannah. You be still. Take what Dex gives you."

He licked his way up her swollen folds slowly, followed by a torturous flick over her clit. She gasped, every sensation so stirring. He made her dizzy. He made her feel alive. She writhed between the two men, wondering how she'd ever survive such pleasure.

"Let him lead, Hannah," Slade insisted. "If you misbehave, we'll tie you down. We're fully equipped here. We can bind your hands to the headboard and strap down your torso, but my favorite part will be fitting your legs to the spreader. I'll make sure you're comfortable, but you won't be able to shift even an inch. Your pretty thighs will be so wide."

Hannah moaned as Dex continued to nibble on her pussy. He pulled one soft fold into his mouth, sucking briefly, then the other. He was devouring her like a sweet treat. His tongue slipped in and out, plunging deep, as if he couldn't get enough. There wasn't an inch of her he didn't taste. The orgasm built inside her. Now that she'd had one, she recognized the sensations. And she longed for it.

"Please, Dex."

Slade's hands went straight to her nipples. He pinched them with a punishing little twist. Hannah gasped as that tiny bite of pain opened a livewire straight to her pussy. Arousal jolted her, hovered, like it played on a knife's edge.

"That got her juices flowing, brother." Dex chuckled, the vibration resonating against her sensitive flesh.

"She's not allowed to talk." Slade pinched her again, making Hannah mewl. "Next time, I'll put these incredibly sensitive nipples in clamps."

"We should have them pierced. Hmm..."

Hannah started to say something, but Dex nipped the nubbin of her clit between his teeth. She whimpered as he toyed with her, gently biting and laving.

"I like that thought. Dainty little bejeweled rings." Slade's tongue traced the shell of her ear. His fingers still played with her breasts. "We can run a chain through them and tug when we want to arouse her. You'd never get me off you then, baby."

Even the thought made her tremble. But all they needed to do to arouse her was to walk in the room. It had always been that way.

She bit her bottom lip to keep from pleading again. She wanted to come. She was so close. And Dex merely toyed with her, pulling away when he knew he'd driven her close to orgasm.

As she tensed and cried out again, Dex eased away to lave her thigh. "We'll need to begin her training as soon as possible. She has zero discipline. She's almost gone off three times since I put my mouth on her."

Slade tsked behind her, as if she was a naughty school girl. "That won't do. We can't have her coming every time we touch her."

"I thought that was the point," Hannah groused, and then hissed as Slade tortured her nipples once more. This time the punishment was accompanied by Dex's short slap to her pussy, which had Hannah bucking. But Slade's iron grip wouldn't allow her to move. He forced her to lie still and take it.

"Your orgasms belong to your Masters," Slade explained. "Just like your body belongs to us. We're going to teach you to accept pleasure and to discipline your responses so you can come on command. Would you like that, love? Would you like for us to look at you during one of our office parties, and with a simple touch or one word be able to get you off? You'll be so well trained that no one will know what's happening besides you and your men. We'll always be close, always willing to bring you pleasure."

"And to receive it," Dex added. "I can picture that party. After we make our girl come a few times, we'll find a nice place away from the crowd so we can lift your skirts. Then you'll take our cocks. You'll know to keep quiet or everyone will hear you. Everyone will know just how well we're fucking you."

She hadn't thought she could get aroused merely with words, but her sex clenched and spasmed. It felt so good—far beyond anything she'd imagined. She wanted everything they were offering.

"But I think since she's a novice, we can forgo the rituals tonight. It would just delay the good stuff." Dex's tongue came out to lick at her clit.

"Agreed. I'm very eager to get my cock inside that cunt, but I'll leave the actual deflowering to you, brother. I did get to spank her first, and you were the one to find her."

Dex groaned. "Let's get her ready."

Dex's fingers poised at the entrance of her pussy. He gently worked one inside her. Then another. Hannah fought not to squirm as he filled her, his rough hands oddly gentle, but providing friction that sent her even closer to the edge. It felt so good, even as he stretched her, scissoring his fingers, and it burned. What would it feel like when he was inside her? And Slade, too? She might be a virgin, but she wasn't naïve. If they intended to share her, she knew what that meant. They would fill her front and back. What would it feel like then? A wave of heat scorched her at the thought.

"She's still so fucking tight." Dex shoved his fingers in a bit farther.

Slade held her closer and ran his tongue up her neck. "I'll bet. She's going to have the tightest pussy we've ever fucked."

She was going to be their last one, too. A savage possessiveness was overtaking her. They thought they were the barbarians, but maybe she could be one, too.

Hannah reveled in the passion she felt. Love had been a quiet thing before this moment. Her feelings for her grandmother had been a gentle camaraderie. Loving her mother and sister had required sacrifice and patience. But this, oh, this required a kind of trust she'd never given. It challenged her courage…yet it was as natural as breathing. She was allowed to be greedy in her love for them. Hannah grabbed it with both hands and held it to her heart. These men were steady anchors, and for the first time in her life, she felt certain that she could fly.

"Come for us, baby." Dex growled the words, then sucked her clit between his lips. His fingers moved in time, curling up and finding some sweet spot Hannah hadn't known existed. Sensations piled up under her clit, inside her body, building, converging. The orgasm rushed over her like a tidal wave, sure and powerful, drowning her in need and leaving her gasping for more. Her body jerked, but Slade continued to hold her tight, utterly safe in his arms.

"That was so beautiful." He kissed her temple with a sweet affection that softened her after the violent orgasm.

"And she tastes so good. She came all over my mouth." Dex dropped a similarly gentle kiss on her pussy, before looking up at her through the thick fringe of his dark lashes. "We want you so badly, Hannah. Let me make you ours."

Her lips curled into a shy smile. "Yes."

Chapter Seven

Dex looked up at Hannah, and his heart constricted. She was the most beautiful thing he'd ever seen. As she rested against Slade, her soft honey hair spread out across his brother's chest. She arched and slowly blinked, revealing slumberous green eyes. Her lips parted; her mouth relaxed. Hannah looked so well loved. He and Slade had put that look on her face. That fact made him proud—and hungry to do it again.

And she'd said yes. She'd invited him into her untouched body. Dex's cock swelled, and he'd been pretty damn sure he couldn't get harder than when Hannah's cream pulsed from her pussy onto his tongue. He'd been wrong. Now, his entire body was hard, excruciatingly aware of what he was about to do. Still, he hesitated. God, he wanted to get it right.

Hannah's lips curved up invitingly. She reached out and touched his hair. "Just love me, Dex."

That was his Hannah. So giving. He loved her wild and wanton side, but her soft heart pulled him to her every time. "I love you, Hannah."

She should know that the man who claimed her body first was mad about her. Dex looked up at his brother, who stared down at Hannah with desire and joy. The second man who would claim her adored her, too. They would wrap her in their love. She wouldn't want for anything.

Dex got to his knees, his cock standing straight up his body. He stroked himself a few times, enjoying the way Hannah's eyes widened. He reached over to the nightstand and pulled out a condom.

"Someone was sure of himself." Her words were sassy, but she kept watching the way he rolled the condom over his rock-hard erection.

He didn't want to put that fucking condom on. He wanted to take her bare, to spend himself deep inside her body, but he didn't have that right yet. When they were married and settled, he and Slade would talk with Hannah about starting a family. Until then, his caveman urge to fill her with every drop of his seed would have to wait.

"We were sure of the three of us being right together," Slade clarified.

Dex settled himself between her legs. Her pussy still glistened with moisture from her recent orgasm.

Slade palmed her luscious, round breasts, thumbing her nipples until she moaned. "You're so precious, baby. We're going to make you feel so good. So loved."

Dex wanted to show her just how much. Taking a calming breath, he lined his cock up to her pussy and watched as he began to sink inside that warm, sweet body.

Tight. God, she was so tight. He'd never been in a pussy that gripped him and threatened to rip his control away so immediately. It was a gorgeous sight, his big cock disappearing into her pussy. Dex gritted his teeth and forced himself to take her inch by inch, slowly plunging inside, gritting his teeth as he gave her time to adjust.

When she whimpered, fingers clasping Slade's thighs, his brother kissed her mouth, his tongue rolling in slow and deep, while Dex's dick sank down, thrusting past her barrier.

Hannah stiffened, and Slade thumbed her nipples, his lips soothing against her ear. "He's almost in, baby. Just a little more and you're ours. It'll be all pleasure then. Take a deep breath."

She did, and relaxed enough for Dex to delve in another inch.

"You're so big," Hannah moaned, wriggling.

He paused, cupping her cheek. "I'm doing my best to be careful, darlin'."

"It's okay. Just give me all of you."

Fuck, that turned him on. Heat sliced through his belly, fired through his balls. She was going to get all of him. No way could he hold back now.

With a grunt, Dex tilted his hips up and shoved deep inside her pussy. After a second of resistance, her flesh parted like melted butter, and he finally sank in all the way to his balls. Hannah gasped, holding Slade tightly.

"You're ours now, Hannah," Slade murmured, tilting her chin up and fisting a hand in her hair for another possessive kiss.

Dex held himself still, watching her soften under his brother's mouth. While Dex filled Hannah, their mate, completely with his cock, he took a moment to enjoy the feeling of rightness. But she constricted like a hot, silken vise on his dick. He wouldn't last long.

"Help me, brother," he said, desperate for her to find pleasure in the act.

Slade's hand left her breast and trailed down to her clit, gently pressing. Hannah's eyes widened. Her breathing shallowed.

"Please." She spoke the one plea Dex couldn't refuse.

Slade smiled. "Her clit is hard and so wet."

"And she's clamping down on me. I don't know how long I can hold out." Dex withdrew almost entirely, then thrust back in.

The walls of her pussy sucked at him, clung, shoving him ever closer to release. He set a gentle pace, unwilling to let himself go just yet, though every muscle of his body screamed at him to fuck her until neither one could see straight. Instead, he eased in and out, so slowly that his eyes nearly rolled into the back of his head from the pleasure. Damn it, he was close. His spine was tingling. His balls drew up.

"Hannah, darlin', come for me."

"For us," Slade whispered, his fingers continuing to circle her clit. "Now, baby."

Dex pressed up, his cock as deep in Hannah's body as he could go. She clutched at him, her nails digging into his arms. He welcomed that bite of pain. He loved Hannah submissive, but this time he wanted her wild.

He got his wish when he poured everything he had, that he was, into each and every stroke, sliding in and up with a slow force that had her wrapping her legs around him. Then she clawed at Slade, who took her mouth in another fierce kiss and swallowed her whimpers. Dex gripped her hips and shoved in again.

But deeper wasn't deep enough for him. Never would be. She took him completely, passing her passion onto Slade through their frantic joining of lips.

God, desire had never seared Dex so much that the pleasure was its own kind of pain. He and Slade had shared women—lots of them. He'd never felt this urge to keep one close forever. Nothing had ever felt so right. He'd never felt so...complete.

She pushed up against him, fighting for her pleasure. As her pussy gripped him in rapid pulses, she cried out, her face contorting beautifully as she looked up at Slade as if silently begging for mercy. His brother had none, rubbing her clit in an insistent rhythm. Neither did Dex as he pounded her like a piston. She screamed and clenched down on him like she never wanted to let him go.

Fuck, it was coming. *He* was coming. And he couldn't wait another second.

Dex plunged in again and let himself go. A shout tore from his chest. His back bowed as every drop of come erupted from his body with unstoppable force. The orgasm felt like it went on forever.

Finally sated, his shaking arms gave way, and he collapsed onto Hannah, utterly surrounded by her softness. Dex rested his head against her breast, listening as her heartbeat gradually slowed. She smoothed back his hair. This was what he'd longed for all of his freaking life. Unconditional acceptance, peace. Love.

"Would you really have let me go home?" Hannah's voice was breathless.

Slade chuckled. "Yes. We would have let you go home, but you would have taken two bodyguards with you."

Dex smiled. Hannah's nipple stood all pretty and pink, inches from his mouth. He lifted up long enough to kiss it. "Exactly. If you went home, you had to accept the protection we gave you. But that deal isn't available anymore. You're staying with us, Hannah. There's no going back."

She continued to stroke his hair, and he had to bite back a satisfied groan. He was the Master, but right now, she was the one with all the power.

"I realize that. I was just surprised that you'd let me go home with two men...wait, you were going to be my bodyguards, weren't you?"

Dex looked up, and she wore the cutest pout on her face. He grinned at Slade. "She's a smart one."

Slade nodded. "We had already cleared our schedules."

"You two move fast," Hannah groused. "You had a plan in place before I even walked out of the room."

"We had to. We'll never take chances where you're concerned." Dex rolled off her and quickly disposed of the condom. She didn't need to get crushed under his weight. And he had the feeling his brother was about to stake his claim in a far more physical way.

"Before you say anything else, I need to tell you something," Hannah said, sitting up in the middle of the bed cross-legged. Her blonde hair fell in loose curls around her shoulders, cascading down her arms. He'd thought she was beautiful before, but sitting here, naked, her skin glowing, she was nothing short of a goddess.

"What is it, baby? We'll always listen." Slade sat

up behind her, cupping her shoulders and angling her to face him.

She hesitated, as if uncertain how to proceed. "I love you both. You know that. But…I'd be lying if I said I didn't have feelings for Gavin, too. I don't really know how this kind of relationship works. Or how you want it to work. I won't jeopardize what we have. I promise. But I want to be honest."

Dex shared a long look with Slade. Despite the differences he and Gavin had, Dex didn't want to lose his brother. And he feared he was. But Gavin belonged with them—and with Hannah.

Dex had only briefly known the Gavin who existed before Nikki's death. He'd been serious about work, but had made the time for his brothers in those days. Gavin had been the one to pay for Dex's college and offer him a place in the family. They might argue from time to time, but Gavin was his brother. Dex had always assumed they'd work through their issues someday and truly be a family.

"We should probably talk about that, darlin'." Dex clasped her hand.

Slade brushed her hair from her cheek and took over. "Gavin is in love with you, too, Hannah. I can't tell you how happy it makes me to hear that you have feelings for him. We want him to share this happiness with us. His past hasn't always been an easy one. We'll have to move slow with Gavin, but I think he'll be worth it."

If Hannah had been in love with any other man, Dex would rip the bastard's heart out in an instant. But if Hannah could save Gavin from whatever dark path he stalked down alone, Dex would lock them in a room together and not let them out until Gavin stopped lying to himself about his feelings.

"Three men." Hannah shook her head. "I guess that when I go wild, I really go wild."

Slade twisted on the bed and was on top of Hannah in an instant. "Another reason we love you. I think it's time you went wild again, love."

He reached for a condom and spread her legs. Dex watched, his own cock hardening again as Slade captured her mouth, eased inside her pussy, then possessed her so completely that she screamed, sobbed, and finally sighed contentedly in his arms.

* * * *

The wall behind him thudded in a mocking, insistent rhythm, and Gavin wondered if his brothers were trying to set a world record for how many times they could fuck the same girl in one night. He'd given up trying to sleep hours before and now sat in the darkness, staring sightlessly out the window, listening to their erotic slaps and moans. There was no doubt his brothers were having the night they had longed to share with her for a year.

He might have grinned, but they had Hannah, and they weren't just fucking her. They were making love to her, bonding with the woman they wanted to spend the rest of their lives with.

Despair crashed through him. Once again, Gavin felt just how completely he was on the outside.

Swallowing a curse, he strode across the room, unable to listen to their passion anymore. Though their voices were muted, he knew what they were saying.

His brothers were telling Hannah that they loved her. And Hannah loved them back, giving herself to them, proving her devotion. She had waited for love, and what she'd given his brothers tonight was a precious gift.

Goddamn it, he'd wanted to be a part of that.

Gavin slammed the door behind him. They were mere feet away. The door stood right there. Five steps and the turn of a knob, and he could be with them. Would she turn him away? Would Dex punch him in the face? Gavin actually doubted both. For all he and Dex misunderstood each other, they shared the same desire to love Hannah thoroughly.

And Gavin couldn't forget the way she'd looked at him with desire in those pretty green eyes while he'd watched her come. She'd welcome him, he was almost certain.

That knowledge was killing him.

Gavin stayed on the other side of the door. From here, he could love his family at a distance, take care of them without worrying that he'd get too close, drag them into his shit, and destroy their lives. It was for the best.

But he would be forced to watch as Hannah married Slade and Dex. He could picture her, so lovely in her wedding dress, her eyes glowing with happiness. Eventually, the babies would come. Hannah would make a wonderful, nurturing mother. Not being a part of that felt like someone stabbing him in the heart and dragging the blade through his chest. He yearned so badly to give her at least a sliver of that happiness, to see her wear his ring or bring his child into the world.

But she couldn't know that. Ever.

Gavin walked into the great room. The bay windows stood open, revealing the beauty of the Alaskan starlit darkness. It was truly nighttime here in a way that was impossible in Dallas. The twinkling stars wove together to create a blanket of diamonds overhead. The sight would fill Hannah's eyes with wonder. It would move her.

He'd never brought a woman here. Never wanted to. Hannah was the first woman he'd ever thought about sharing much of anything with. Then again, she was the first woman he'd ever really loved.

For hours, he'd sat in his darkened bedroom, listening to her moans and cries of pleasure, hoping that he could find the jealousy that would rip her from his heart. All he'd managed was to adore her more for opening herself so completely to the men she loved. Envy pierced Gavin. He should probably be appalled at the thought of sharing a woman with his brothers, but somehow it made sense. If they were all truly together, they would rely on each other, take their family unit to the next level. When Hannah frustrated him, his brothers would figure her out. She would always be taken care of, no matter what. Someone would always answer her calls, hold her when she cried. She wouldn't be left alone like Nikki had been.

Nikki. God, if his brothers knew what Gavin had done to her, they wouldn't be so interested in sharing Hannah. Slade would be appalled. Dex would threaten to kill him if he so much as looked at Hannah. Gavin figured he'd deserve it.

Behind him, he heard a firm knock and a familiar deep voice. "Gavin? Is that you?"

Slade. Speak of the devil.

"Were you expecting someone else?" Gavin quipped.

His brother turned on the light to reveal a frown. He'd pulled on a pair of jeans, but wore nothing else. His hair was mussed as though Hannah had run her fingers all through it. His brother wore an unmistakable air of satisfaction on his face.

"Well, apparently half the damn company has followed us to Alaska. You never know. They might just show up on our doorstep."

"Well, Preston might be that obnoxious, but I talked to Marnie. He checked in an hour ago and has been complaining about the accommodations ever since. She promised to call me if he leaves the lodge."

Slade's face broke into an easy grin. "I can imagine he's not used to dealing with anyone like Marnie."

"She told him that if he didn't like his room, he should feel free to take a hike. I believe she put him in 108."

Slade's laugh boomed through the room, making it seem alive when just moments ago it had felt so lonely. "Chester will love Preston. Tell me she didn't fix the window. Tell me that old moose still sticks his head in at six in the morning, looking for treats."

Gavin felt his own lips turn up. He'd missed this place. Chester, despite being a moose, was known to walk into any establishment with a door big enough to accommodate his bulk. Long ago, a man had stayed with Marnie in room 108. He'd thought it was funny to have the moose greet him every morning, so he'd trained Chester to seek treats. Though the man had moved on, the people of River Run continued the tradition. Preston was in for a rather rude awakening.

"Gavin." Slade sobered as he sat in the chair nearby. "You don't have to be here alone."

His brother's soft words made his gut clench. He attempted to maintain a placid demeanor. "I prefer the solitude, Slade."

"No, you don't. Come on, man. Talk to me. I don't know what's going on in your head. Hannah has feelings for you. She admitted it to me and Dex. She wants to be with all of us. You're the only one maintaining distance, and I don't get it. I know you love her."

Gavin's irritation rose like a kettle getting ready to boil over. "Do I need to put it in the plainest terms possible? I'm not interested."

"Bullshit. This is about Nikki. She's dead, and you feel guilty for being alive. I never understood why you'd waste your emotion on her. I can't keep this a secret any longer. I overheard her telling one of her trailer-trash girlfriends that she was only interested in your money and your position. She didn't love you. Damn it, Gavin, she came onto me just before she died, when she thought she was losing you. I had planned to tell you, but when she died, it didn't seem right to pile that knowledge on top of an already tragic incident. Now I wonder if I made the right decision. You've damn near buried yourself with her. I can't stand to watch a ghost drag you down any more."

Cold filled Gavin's gut. He'd known most of that, but it didn't change anything. What right did his younger brother have to throw this shit in his face? He might have started the relationship with Nikki with the best of intentions, but the most they had ever had together was good sex. He'd never intended to marry her, never been in love with her. He hadn't even cared when she'd threatened to kill herself.

Do what you have to, Nikki.

His own cold words echoed in his brain. All he needed to keep him away from Hannah was to think about the past. He didn't deserve another chance after Nikki's demise. And especially not after what had happened to...

Gavin didn't dare finish the thought. Instead, he turned to his brother, eager to strike back. It was the only way to end his constant beating at Gavin's well-built defenses. "Hannah is a lovely girl, Slade. I am very happy that you and Dex have finally gotten between her legs. If you want to marry her, hell, I'll pay for the wedding, but she's not for me. I need someone with more style, more polish. Can you imagine me inviting investors over? She's a sweet thing, but she wouldn't last a minute with society matrons. They would eat her alive. Sure, I'd enjoy fucking Hannah, but marriage and kids?" He scoffed. "I can't possibly build a life with her."

A little gasp from the doorway froze Gavin's heart. He turned, and Hannah stood in the hallway, Dex by her side. She was wearing a robe that couldn't quite conceal the gorgeous bounty of her breasts. Dex's arm came around her middle, pulling her to him. Even in the low light, Gavin couldn't mistake his hard eyes and furious snarl.

But Gavin couldn't take it back, no matter how much it hurt to cause Hannah pain. It was better this way. They were all better off without him. He could plainly see that if he didn't end their hope now, they would never stop hounding him to get over Nikki and build a family with Hannah. And it might be cowardly, but he much preferred that they hate him for maligning Hannah than know the truth. Perhaps one day, when they were older, they'd forgive him for a few cruel words. They'd never forgive what he'd done to Nikki.

"I am sorry, Hannah," Gavin managed to say in an even tone, though his heart wrenched. "I didn't intend to hurt you."

Her lips trembled as though she was holding in some strong emotion. Pride obviously won because her chin came up. "What you just said tore my heart out. And you're wrong. I can hold my own with anyone. I would have made a great wife. You won't find a woman who would have been a better mother to your children. But if all you're looking for is someone to keep your social calendar and look pretty at company parties, then I don't want you. I suggest you find another admin, Mr. James."

God, he'd planted the knife in his own chest, but with her words, she'd just turned it. But that was for the best, too.

She turned her face up to Dex's. "I think I lost my appetite. I just want to go to bed. Could we do that?"

Dex didn't hesitate. He pulled her closer, his big arms cradling her, protecting her from the world. "Of course, darlin'. You go on. Slade and I will be down in a minute."

He kissed her forehead, and she walked down the hall, as regal as any princess. She was right. She would make a hell of a wife. Now, he would never marry because the only woman he wanted was one he could never have.

The instant Hannah walked around the corner, Dex turned on him. His fists were balls of fury. Slade stepped between them, but Gavin almost wished he hadn't. Letting Dex beat him might provide some small atonement. It would sure as hell be better than living with Hannah's face haunting his dreams.

"You're a despicable son of a bitch," Dex snarled his way.

"You're surprised?" Gavin tossed back. He felt like burning down everything. Something nasty had ahold of his gut. If he destroyed everything, maybe he could finally be alone with his guilt.

"Shut up," Slade snapped at him, bracing both hands against their youngest brother's chest to prevent a pending assault. "Dex, he didn't mean a fucking word of that."

"Stop talking for me." Slade's insistence on his innate goodness was starting to grate on Gavin. No matter what he did or said, Slade simply wouldn't let him be. "I meant everything I said. Hannah is fine, but my position is all about image, and I can't take a little country girl as my bride. If the two of you want to saddle yourself with a girl who has a community college education and no real manners, then good for you."

Dex paused. His arms came down, unwilling to continue the fight. That disappointed Gavin.

"Slade's right. You're full of shit. I know you love that woman. What the hell are you hiding?" Dex demanded.

Gavin's stomach turned. The last thing he wanted was Dex checking into the past. Slade would wait, never imagining that his brother would keep something from him. For Dex, trust came hard. He'd dig up everything.

"I'm not hiding anything. I've stated plainly that I don't want a relationship with Hannah."

Dex glared at him. "You don't want to marry Hannah. You're far too interested in your corporate image, right? Well then explain this to me, Gavin. As Black Oak's CEO, there isn't a woman more involved in your life or your business than your secretary. You've allowed Hannah to plan your parties, act as your hostess. She's always handled herself perfectly. You've said it yourself. So don't give me this crap. She's practically been your wife in every way but one. Now you find fault with her? There's something else going on, and I intend to find out what it is. Do you want to save me the trouble?"

"Fuck off, Dex. And stay out of my business." He charged.

Slade slapped a hand to Gavin's chest to ward him off. His eyes narrowed as he pushed back, then glanced Dex's way. "Let's go and take care of Hannah, brother. Gavin has some serious thinking to do about coming clean because I think he's definitely hiding something. If he is, we'll find it. And there will be hell to pay."

In silent unison, Dex and Slade strode toward the bedroom, where Hannah was probably crying.

Gavin flipped off the lights again and slumped down into the nearest chair, completely weary. He had to find a way to distract them from digging into Nikki's death. He could handle rehashing it; he did that nearly every day in his head. But he couldn't handle their censure, their disgust, when they learned the truth. Fuck, no matter what he did, he was going to lose his brothers. He'd already lost Hannah. He wouldn't have her cheery smile to look forward to any more. No longer could he fool himself into thinking that someday he'd find a way to be with her. That dream was over.

It was always over. It was over the minute you hung up the phone and left Nikki to die.

He sat for the longest time and finally managed to fall asleep. His dreams were filled with visions of Hannah and her teary eyes.

It seemed like an instant later when he felt his phone vibrate, and came awake. There was a horrible pain in his neck. He'd slept at an odd angle, but he hadn't been able to make his feet move to his bedroom. It had been one thing to listen to Hannah's cries of pleasure. He wouldn't have been able to handle her tears.

The phone chirped again. It was, as always, close to him, tucked into the pocket of his pants. Work was the only place where he hadn't heinously fucked up, and he meant to keep it that way.

With a heavy sigh, he pulled out the device to find a text. He looked at the clock. It was almost eight in the morning. Light flooded the room, and Gavin wished he'd closed the curtains. He could smell coffee percolating somewhere in the kitchen.

When he pulled up the text, he didn't recognize the number.

Stay away from Hannah. I know everything, Mr. Hot Shot. You can't bury it. If you don't let Hannah go, I'll release all the documents related to your girlfriend's death and take you down.

Gavin stared at the words, reading them again, dread drumming through him. After the longest time, he stood and walked toward his study. He didn't need coffee. He needed a lot of mind-numbing alcohol because his fucking past was finally going to catch up with him.

No way would he turn Hannah loose so this creep could get his hands on her. He would never give up her future to protect his past.

He loved her, and she'd never know how much. She'd never know that he'd willingly sacrificed everything for her.

Chapter Eight

Slade walked into Black Oak Oil's Alaska offices feeling like a new man. He'd left Hannah at the breakfast table, spooning a bit of sugar into her coffee. He'd kissed her forehead and told her he'd be back soon. It had been the perfect picture of intimacy. A man and his wife parting ways for the day.

Of course, Dex had kissed her, too. Maybe not totally conventional, but it worked for Slade.

"Do you want to kill Ward, or do I get the honors?" Dex asked.

He smiled at the threat from his hotheaded brother. Slade could always count on Dex to offer up a good, old-fashioned ass kicking to anyone who deserved it. "How about we figure out if he's the one who's been stalking Hannah before we bury him somewhere?"

Dex sighed in disappointment. "I hate it when you're logical."

The site office was small and underwhelming compared to the corporate offices. The place was utilitarian with white walls and concrete floors. Somehow, Slade felt more at home here than he ever did at corporate. He loved fieldwork and had been behind a desk far too long. He preferred roughnecks and spending time on platforms. He felt perfectly comfortable with the employees at River Run, but it was obvious, even from a distance, that Preston Ward III didn't feel the same.

"This is not protocol." Preston's voice rang through the small building. It was worse than nails on a chalkboard.

Dex's eyes rolled. "Be sure to call me if you change your mind and need someone to kill the son of a bitch. I'm going to get an update from Burke and Cole. Then I'll do a little snooping of my own."

Slade nodded. He would handle Preston better than Dex, and they had both agreed it was past time they figured out what was eating at Gavin.

After Dex walked toward the main office, Slade wound his way to the small group of IT cubicles. Preston Ward stood in the middle of the room, incongruous in his thousand dollar suit, staring down his Harvard nose at the squatty man with the mop of black hair and a face that proudly proclaimed his Inuit heritage. Ben Kunayak ran this place. He was shorter than Preston, but given the mulish set of his mouth, he was also meaner. Slade thought seriously about just stepping back and letting Ben do their dirty work, but then he wouldn't get the necessary information—or the satisfaction.

Two young men had joined Preston from corporate, both obviously IT employees. Slade thought he recognized the thin, sad-looking, brown-haired man as Lyle Franklin, the head of the help desk. Lyle stood with Preston, but the other twenty-something man, a pencil pusher dressed in a checked shirt with pale hair and fingers flying over his keyboard, sat behind his laptop. Crap, Scott Kirkwood. The little punk who'd tried to have an "important" lunch with Hannah. *Bullshit.*

With a sigh, Slade let his presence be known.

"Slade, thank god you're here. You need to fire this man this instant." Preston pointed at Ben. "He's rude to his superiors and obviously has no understanding of Black Oak protocol or regulations. I believe the men up here have been using company computers to access pornography."

That's what had Preston's panties in a twist? Slade snorted. Of course. These were a group of roughnecks in a city where men outnumbered women five to one and reliable Internet was tough to come by. He would have been shocked if they weren't accessing online porn.

"This employee has been allowing it to happen." Preston's fingers tapped against Ben's desk in a rapid, irritating accusation. "In fact, he's all but defended the practice."

"I've found at least four machines with restricted IP addresses in their browsing histories." Lyle Franklin had a thin face and obviously believed in sunscreen. "I don't think bugs caught from porn sites are the actual reason for our shutdown, but they could certainly cause problems in the future. It shouldn't be allowed."

So now the corporate IT department had become the morality police. *Great.* Slade had the urge to fire all three of them. If he got rid of them, he'd almost certainly be cutting off whatever access this stalker had to Hannah. But that wasn't going to make the son of a bitch go away, and Slade wanted to nail this bastard for good.

"If Internet porn isn't the problem now, let's focus on what is." Slade turned to the IT executive. "Preston, I'm sure that Lyle and Scott can figure it out."

He might not trust any of them with Hannah, but he knew from experience that they were more than competent at writing code and keeping a system safe. They'd do their jobs. And if either of them was Hannah's stalker, they'd want to do whatever necessary to maintain professional ties to her.

But Slade's money was on Preston.

"Already done, sir," said Scott. "It's weird. I isolated this virus. It's nasty, but I can fix it in a couple of hours."

"Excellent." The sooner Scott fixed the problem, the sooner Slade could ship the corporate men back to Dallas. Until then, he had to watch these three like hawks. Once they left Alaska, Slade could breathe a sigh of relief, let Burke and Cole do what they did best, and focus on Hannah.

"We'll have things up and running in no time," Scott assured.

"Go make it happen." Slade shot Scott a nod, and the IT guy scurried off to work. Ben and Lyle took the hint and followed. Soon, the trio looked deeply entrenched in their computers.

Slade nudged Preston into an adjacent room. "Let's talk, Preston."

"Lyle and Scott are very good at their jobs. They'll fix the mistakes arising from that native idiot's lax adherence to policy."

God, Preston just didn't know when to shut up. "Glad to hear it. But that's not what I want to talk about. I'm hoping you'll congratulate me on my engagement."

Preston shot him a bland smile. "Congratulations. I had no idea you were seeing anyone. What is the lucky young lady's name?"

"I believe you know her. Hannah Craig."

Preston's smile instantly faded. "You're marrying Gavin's secretary?"

Slade took a step in and lowered his voice. "I am. Would you like to explain why you molested my fiancée?"

Preston swallowed once and then again. "I didn't molest her. It was nothing."

"It doesn't sound like nothing to me, especially when you leave messages after calling her new, unlisted phone number and telling her to withdraw her HR action against you while calling her 'baby.'"

He had the good sense to look sheepish. "She's a cute thing. I guess...I misread her signals."

"I can assure you, if you were reading Hannah's signals, she wasn't giving you any green lights."

Preston held up his hands in defeat. "Since my wife and I separated recently, I haven't been myself. I-I was looking for comfort in the wrong place. I didn't hurt her. And she broke my toe."

"I will break way more than that if you even look at her again. When we get back to Dallas, we're going to have a long discussion about your employment with this company."

"Goddamn it, you can't fire me. I didn't even know the girl was dating the boss's brother."

"So that made her fair game?"

"I thought she might be amenable. There's a rumor that she's sleeping with all three of you. I figured that if she was working her way through the executives, why couldn't I have a turn?"

Before the last word was out of Preston's mouth, Slade's fist was flying. He connected to the middle-aged executive's ruddy face with a satisfying thud. Preston hit the ground and immediately started whining. A thick line of blood dripped from his nose.

Slade crouched down and got in the man's face. He was pleased with the fear in the other man's eyes. "You're fired. I want you on the first plane back to Dallas. Your secretary can clean out your office. If I catch you on Black Oak property again, I will have you arrested. If I see you near our fiancée again, I will have you killed. No one will ever find your body. Is that understood?"

Preston hobbled back with a nod, and Slade had to wonder if this coward would climb a tree to take pictures of a woman. It didn't seem like his speed, but Slade wasn't about to underestimate anyone's desire for Hannah. He knew firsthand how it burned, how it made a man crazy. Even if everything didn't add up perfectly, Slade still didn't want the bastard anywhere near his woman.

He heard footsteps behind him and turned to find Dex sauntering up. His younger brother stared at Preston, who whimpered and tried to cover his face.

"Punching him feel good?" Dex nodded with malice at the other man.

Slade smiled. "Imminently satisfying."

"Perfect. I'll let the receptionist know to book him on the first flight to Anchorage and to make sure his ass travels in coach." Dex started to walk away, then stopped short. "Oh, and I came in to get you. We have a conference call with the Lenox brothers in five minutes."

As Dex left, Lyle rushed through the door, then knelt to help his former boss to his feet. Lyle pulled Preston up, and the rolled-back cuffs of his shirt sleeves slipped up, revealing wiry arms covered in scratch marks. Slade suppressed a smile. The quiet ones always had the freaky sex lives. He wondered who would have scratched the hell out of a twerp like him.

Slade turned toward the door, but before he could leave, Scott, the blond tech who had supposedly identified the problem, stopped him. "Sir. Can I talk to you privately?"

Slade hesitated then opened the door to a small conference room. "What is it?"

If Scott said a word to him about Hannah, Slade swore he'd lay the prick out flat, too.

"It's about the bug, sir. Like I said, it's a nasty virus, but fairly common. Mr. Ward thinks it's Internet security issues from the porn, but it's not. It looks like someone uploaded this bug directly on to the system. Someone who had access to our software wanted this system to fail and at a very precise time."

Slade felt his body go cold. Then he paused. Believe Scott or not? Too early to tell. He needed more information. "When was it uploaded?"

"I don't have a firm time right now, but the bug crashed the system around eleven a.m. yesterday."

Right around the time the corporate jet took off with Hannah, himself, and his brothers, on their way to Alaska. Lyle had seen Dex carry Hannah out the door. Since the guy was still hovering protectively around his former boss, Slade could guess that Lyle was Preston's bitch. He would have told Mr. Harvard that Hannah had been whisked away. Ironic how perfectly timed that virus was. Preston was definitely smart enough to write the code to crash a system. Hell, depending on Lyle's loyalties, the little asswipe might have helped his former boss.

Slade marched into the IT cubicles, pinning a hard stare on Lyle. "Thanks. Get back to work. Fix that bug."

"Yes, sir," he said, then watched Slade drag a sputtering Preston away.

Building security joined him to walk the former CIO out. Slade vowed to sic Burke and Cole on him the second Preston's feet touched Dallas ground again.

* * * *

After finishing her lunch and finding some halfway decent clothes, Hannah explored the house. She was never again letting Dex pack for her. He hadn't brought along a single pair of underwear and refused to tell her where to buy some. She was commando under her cotton skirt. Bras, it seemed, didn't make Dex's list of necessary items, either. Her silk blouse brushed against her hard nipples making her so aware of her body and all the ways it ached. Now that she'd had sex, she couldn't seem to get it off her mind.

She peered into each room. Last night, Slade had recounted a few stories about this place and his time with Gavin here as kids. Now she was fascinated by this grand log home and its remote majesty, which skirted a placid little lake framed by snow-capped mountains in the distance. The sky was such a bright blue that it almost hurt her eyes. She'd never seen anything like this.

As she wandered into the office, Hannah peeked out the window at the grounds. Everything from every view seemed vibrant and alive. There were a couple of golf carts at the back of the house that she'd been informed by the staff she could use to get to the stables. She definitely wanted to see those before she left. She was a West Texas girl, so horseback riding had been part of her upbringing. Dex and Slade had promised to take her on a ride sometime this week. She was far too sore today since she'd spent her whole night riding hungry men.

Hannah felt her face flush at the thought. The night before had been perfect—with one exception: The terrible incident between her and Gavin.

Dex and Slade had sworn that Gavin hadn't meant a word of his ugly speech and that he was wrestling some inner demons. Perhaps. Gavin might be very corporate, but deep down, the man had a heart. She knew about his mistresses. And she knew that he had too much to give to be happy with such a cold arrangement forever. But right now, he didn't seem inclined to change the status quo, and his inner demons were winning. That made her reconsider her decision to be with Dex and Slade. She couldn't be the reason their family broke apart. Those brothers needed each other, and unless Gavin figured out how to conquer whatever ate at him, Hannah seriously feared she'd only stand like a wall between the younger two brothers and the eldest, squarely dividing them.

When Gavin had claimed she wasn't good enough, the barbs struck too close to home. Hannah had cried while Slade held and rocked her, assuring her she was everything they all needed. He'd teased her that he'd be a mess without her organizational skills. Dex would be a constant bull in a china shop without her calming influence. Even if Gavin wasn't admitting it, he needed her for her heart. Slade had insisted that if Gavin truly found fault with the way she represented him or Black Oak, he would have fired her long ago. Hannah knew Gavin never let any situation go unaddressed if he thought changes were due. But even if he was lying to her—and himself—she'd still be between him and his brothers.

Next, Dex had drawn a bath for her, complete with bubbles. They had led her back to the huge bathroom with a whirlpool—then made her forget everything. She'd felt like a princess as they worshipped her, passing her back and forth, washing her body and her hair, assuring her that she was perfect for them. That given time and patience, Gavin would come around.

Then Slade held her while Dex shaved her pussy. Afterward, both men had taken turns lavishing her newly bare flesh with affectionate tongues. For a few blissful moments, she had forgotten all about the ache Gavin's words had caused.

This morning had been the same. They'd cuddled her and loved her before they'd begun her training. She'd knelt before them, Dex patiently explaining the slave position while Slade had been preparing her for something else.

Her bottom clenched around the plug he'd lodged deep in her backside. It was a continual reminder of everything they wanted from her. Everything she ached to give them.

But now, Hannah found herself alone. Gavin crept back into her mind.

She wandered into the hallway and heard the haunting sound of a piano being played with deft hands. Gran had loved music, and Hannah had studied well. This piece, a sad etude by Chopin, was one of her favorites.

As she sought the source of the sound, she peeked into a parlor they'd passed on the brief tour Slade had given her the night before. Now, Gavin sat at a huge black grand piano, his fingers working the keys like a master. Of all the things she'd gleaned about her former boss, Hannah hadn't known that he played the piano, much less so beautifully. Music filled the space, the poignant melody battering her heart. Dumbstruck, she stopped, stared.

A bottle of vodka sat on the piano, and it looked like Gavin had made his way through most of it. She glanced at the clock on the wall. One o'clock in the afternoon. She'd never seen him drink more than a few sips of a vodka and tonic, and never in the middle of the day. What had him imbibing now? The fight with his brothers? His usually perfect, dark hair was unkempt, his charcoal gray pajama pants wrinkled. He hadn't bothered with a shirt at all.

As he played each note, every muscle of his shoulders, biceps, and chest rippled, bunched. Hannah had never seen Gavin James's bare chest. She clasped her hands to keep them to herself. Like his face and persona, even the way he handled the keys, everything about him was strong, commanding. His wide shoulders were capable of making a multi-billion-dollar company thrive for a decade. They also looked equally capable of dragging her under him, then holding her down and taking...

No. She would not let him exploit the small-town girl he'd sworn wasn't good enough for him.

But as his body swayed with the music, he clenched his jaw furiously. With one hand playing the next series of notes, the other reached for the bottle. He took a long, deep swallow.

Gavin looked...tormented. Had she done that to him?

The playing stopped suddenly with an abrupt clash of keys, and he straddled the piano bench, his gray eyes red rimmed, almost accusing. She doubted he'd slept much last night. "Hannah. Just who I wanted to see."

There was a little slur in his angry voice that made her wince.

"I'm sorry to disturb you. I'll go." She began to back out of the room, but his voice held her.

"Bullshit. You'll never go away, my pretty little Hannah. That's the problem. You don't even go away when I sleep. You're always there. And now it will be so much worse because you'll be near, but with Slade and Dex. I'll have to hear them fuck you every damn night, listen to your whimpers of pleasure. Now, I won't ever be rid of you."

Tears started to blur her eyes. It was worse than she thought. Never mind that he didn't want her. He didn't even like her. If he had this much contempt for her because she wasn't good enough for him, he probably felt the same about her relationship with his brothers. No doubt, he wished they'd settle down with some well-bred society women.

As much as she'd loved last night, Gavin's words proved that staying with Slade and Dex would tear apart their family and shred their brotherly rapport. And they'd end up hating her for it. She couldn't risk that. She had to put their needs beyond her own.

"You will, Mr. James. I know you need your brothers. So I won't be the wedge that drives you apart. I love them too much for that. And I know you don't feel the same way, but I care about you, too."

He rose from the piano bench slowly, his every move predatory. His stormy eyes pinned her in place. Even from across the room, she sensed the menace in him. "You care about me?"

Hannah's breath hitched. Fight or flight? She had to decide. Everything about Gavin, from the set of his broad, naked shoulders to the dangerous gleam in his eyes, told Hannah that something nasty brewed inside him. Definitely, she should run. Yet she couldn't make her feet move.

Fight it was.

"Yes, Mr. James. I care about you." She took a step toward the angry, inebriated male.

At six feet three inches, Gavin towered over her. She should definitely run from the room, screaming. Yet all she could think about was taking him in her arms and soothing his hurt. This was her last chance to fight for the future she wanted, to try to heal this proud, strong man. If she couldn't somehow stop him from drowning in his own pain, then she feared all was lost. If she failed, at least she would have the comfort of knowing that she'd given it her all.

"And you don't want to come between me and my

brothers?" He stalked toward her. He didn't wobble or hesitate, merely strode forward with dangerous grace.

"I don't."

Brow raised sardonically, he moved closer. Hannah fought the urge to back up and stood her ground. He needed to stop lying to himself and understand that she was right for all of them.

Gavin invaded her space. This close, she could feel the heat of his body, smell the vodka on his breath. She knew it should turn her off, but her body was singing.

"I think you're a little liar, Hannah. I think that being between me and my brothers is exactly where you want to be. I heard you last night. I heard your every cry and moan. You liked being between Dex and Slade. Tell me something, Hannah, did they fuck your pussy? Did they shove their cocks into that tight, virgin cunt?"

His challenge, his language, his aggression—none of that should turn her on. But it did.

"Yes." She hated the breathless way the word came out, sounding not strong, but submissive.

"Did you like the way it felt? Did they hold you down, make you take every inch? Pound you?"

She nodded as her pulse leapt. Her breathing turned unsteady. She didn't trust her own voice.

He moved closer, his body a wall of warm, muscular flesh. "And did my brothers fuck your ass, too, Hannah? Did one of them tunnel into your tiny hole back there and make you howl?"

"No. They said I needed to be prepared."

His eyes flared. His hands twitched at his side, coming out as though he wanted to touch her, but he forced them to behave. In the end, he lost. He grabbed her arm and dragged her against his body, her chest against his. Her head snapped back, and she looked directly into his eyes, gleaming with unslaked desire.

"I know my brothers, Hannah. Did they shove a plug up your pretty virgin ass?"

Hannah looked away, feeling a flush crawl up her face. God, she could feel the plug even now, and Gavin's words made her so aware of her body. Slade had promised her the pink plug was small, but it felt huge. She clenched around it again, as she had all day, lighting up nerves she didn't know she had.

Gavin took her chin in his hand and forced her to look up at him again. "Tell me what my brothers did to you, Hannah. Don't be shy. Tell me how it felt when they pushed that plug against your ass for the first time. Did you shiver when you felt the cold lube against your warm, puckered skin?"

She fought her embarrassment, wanted to look away. Gavin wasn't going to let her. And this was too important to simply give up. Gavin wasn't acting like a man who didn't care. He might not like the fact that he cared, but he wanted her. She could feel it. If details would bring him to his knees, she would give them.

"Yes. It was very cold. Slade's fingers warmed it."

"Did he play with you, then? Rim your rosette with his fingers?"

"Yes, for a long time. Then he pressed in, so deep. I gasped. I'd never felt anything like it." It had been an odd sensation. "I didn't like it at first."

His fingers stroked her chin. "Only at first? Then you changed your mind, didn't you?"

"Yes," she whispered.

"I'll bet. I think that, after a while, you liked Slade

putting his fingers up your ass. You liked it a lot. In fact, I have no doubt he kept at you until he figured out exactly what you like. Until you came, isn't that right?"

Hannah shifted, trying to back away, find a little breathing space. Gavin wasn't having any of that.

"Answer me," he demanded, gripping her tighter.

"Yes, I came."

The truth relaxed his body, but he fired his next questions out at her just as rapidly. "Because he also played with your pussy with his other hand? Because Dex sucked those pretty nipples that are poking through your silk blouse at me right now?"

"Because Dex used his mouth down…there."

Understanding flared hotly across Gavin's face. "So Slade shoved his fingers up that virgin ass to get you all ready? Did he tell you how much he loves anal sex?"

Hannah knew she couldn't help the shock jolting across her face.

"I didn't think so. Yeah, nothing our middle brother loves more than to bend a woman over and shove his cock straight up her ass. Every day. More than once a day, if she'll take it." A little smile smeared across his mouth.

"Slade ordered me to spread my legs, bend over, and present my backside." She remembered how insistent Slade had been and how obeying him made her feel like the sexiest goddess. But the way he'd stripped her of control had left her vulnerable, trembling. Excited.

"Exactly. Did you obey, or did he have to spank you?"

Yes. Gavin had liked watching her spanking. No

matter what he'd said before, he was interested in her. Hannah couldn't help but remember the conversation she'd overheard between Dex and Slade about Gavin. They believed Gavin was hiding something.

"I obeyed, Mr. James. I felt scared and vulnerable, but I did it. I placed my hands on the bed and presented my ass."

His eyes tightened, and his breath became ragged. Hannah glanced down. Gavin's cock tented his pajama pants.

"Then Slade plugged your ass?"

"Yes. He worked the plug in. He kept playing. He pushed it in and out, gaining a bit of ground each time. I thought it would never end. The sensations were so different."

"You mean it turned you on all over again?" His narrowed eyes warned her not to lie.

She flushed. "Yes. Slade pushed and pulled until the plug slid home. And I got...aroused again."

"Was Dex still eating that sweet little pussy? Because you know Dex loves pussy. Between the two of them, they are going to keep you constantly busy and sated, sweetheart, front and back."

"Dex didn't stop until I was boneless and wrung out. Until I almost couldn't catch a breath. Then he talked to me about all the things he wants to teach me."

Gavin stroked down her throat before his hand settled on her nape. "Like what?"

"How to suck his cock." Dex's words still heated her skin and made her tremble. While Slade had played behind her, Dex had leaned in and whispered to her. "He wants to teach me how to take his cock in my mouth and swallow him down."

His hand tightened around her nape, the slight pain cutting through her system. The pain heightened her arousal to almost unbearable heights. Her nipples were so hard she could feel her blouse chafing them.

"Sir," he growled. "You call me Sir when we're alone. I won't allow you to respect me any less than my brothers."

She brought her gaze up to meet his. If there wasn't any room for disrespect, then there wasn't any room for shame or shyness, either. "He wants to teach me to suck his cock, Sir."

One hand tightened on her hair. The pain tingled across her scalp. "They didn't force you to fellate them, then?"

"No, Sir."

He pulled on her hair, forcing her to her knees. Hannah hesitated only an instant before sinking down. As her knees hit the plush carpet, the plug shifted in her ass. She had to clench to keep it in. It was a constant reminder of Slade and Dex. Even if they weren't in the same room, it marked their possession of her in a real, physical way.

"You care about me?" Those words ground out of his sneering mouth again. He looked slightly cruel, but she could hear the want behind his words.

"I care about you, Sir."

Gavin had been alone for too long. She wasn't sure why, but he needed this. Needed her now.

He loosened his hold on her hair. His hands went to the waistband of his pajama bottoms. "So you say now. I wonder how you'll feel after."

"After?" Hannah's heart started racing.

"After you've had a little taste of me, sweetheart.

Open your mouth. I want what my brothers haven't had." His cock sprung forth. He was his brothers' match. It was big and gloriously hard.

No matter what he said, he definitely wanted her. He was on the edge. She could sense it.

With a secretive smile, Hannah leaned forward toward Gavin's cock.

Chapter Nine

What the hell am I doing?

Deep in his alcohol-rattled brain, some scrap of common sense screamed the question at Gavin, pounding at his consciousness. All of that fled the instant she lowered her tongue toward his cock.

He'd intended to scare her, push her away. But Hannah hadn't run. Instead, she'd answered every one of his questions with that sweet West Texas twang that made him hard. She'd told him how she'd submitted to Slade's fingers and Dex's mouth. Fuck, Gavin could picture it, could see himself there, watching, with her tongue lashing his dick. Though he teetered on the knife's edge, he knew he should push her away.

Instead, he pushed for more.

"If you're going to learn how to suck cock, then by God, I'm the man to teach you."

She stared up at him with big, green eyes and nodded. Fuck, she turned him on.

"Now what, Sir?" she breathed.

"Lick the head." God, he was a bastard, but he was going to enjoy every second of this.

Her pink tongue peeked out from her lush, berry lips. Gavin's cock twitched and strained toward her as if the fucking thing had a mind of its own. It was wrong, but his cock wanted Hannah. Who was he kidding? His soul wanted Hannah, too. Only his brain knew better.

Tentatively, she leaned in. He felt her breath on the swollen head. Every muscle in his body tightened. The wait was pure torture. Gavin knew his brothers had thoroughly debauched Hannah last night, but when she looked up at him with that innocent stare, all he could think about was that he'd be the first man on her tongue.

She licked him slowly, like an ice cream cone on a summer day. Then she eased back, waiting, uncertain.

"More, Hannah. Lick the whole head. Pull it in your mouth." She'd responded so beautifully to commands before, he hardened his voice now. He made it deep and unrelenting.

Almost instantly, that little tongue ran all over the sensitive head of his dick. Gavin gritted his teeth as fire sizzled up his spine. Desire scalded him.

Sweet Hannah was so submissive, so willing. He'd never had the urge to have a woman call him Sir or itched to spank her ass and watch it turn pink under his hand. Hannah changed everything. Gavin could envision her tied up and so trusting, waiting for him. She would be a beautiful sight.

Hannah worked his cock over with little butterfly licks and kisses. She trusted far too much. She wouldn't trust him at all if she knew who he was deep inside. And his brothers would never forgive him.

Fuck, he shouldn't do this to her. The command to stop her perched on the tip of his tongue, but then Hannah swallowed him down, nearly to the back of her throat. He hissed, groaned. It felt so good. He'd had women give him head more times than he could count, so why did Hannah's untutored mouth send him reeling? He looked down at his cock disappearing into her virgin mouth. Her eyes were closed, her face almost beatific.

He'd waited so long to touch her. The minute they'd met, Gavin had known on some level that her goodness and light was the perfect reflection of his terrible, dark soul. If he were a better man, he might have deserved her. If he were a better man, he would move heaven and earth to make her sublimely happy.

But this stolen moment would be the only time he'd ever touch her.

"Take more, baby. You can take all of me. Work it in." Gavin gentled his voice, but tangled his hands in her hair, grabbing fistfuls. Long and soft, her hair made the perfect handle to grip as he fucked his way deeper into her mouth, forcing his way in inch by delicious inch. "Breath through your nose, Hannah. You can handle this."

Her hands found his thighs, fingers gripping almost desperately. She trembled as she parted her lips wider to accommodate his short strokes. He sank another inch into her hot mouth.

"Touch my balls."

She didn't hesitate, cupping, rubbing. He shuddered. His balls were tight against his body and felt so heavy with come. Every ounce was meant for her. All the reasons he shouldn't be here fell away. She sat on her knees before him, touching him, accepting him. Hell, she'd opened her mouth and welcomed him. For this precious moment, she belonged to him, was his to do with as he pleased. No amount of guilt or self-loathing could keep him from taking her in every way he wanted.

Ruthlessly, he pressed even deeper into her mouth. Hannah tried to roll her tongue over his cock, but there wasn't any room in her tight, hot mouth. His balls drew up, so damn close to orgasm. But if he would only have this once with her, spewing down her throat, though hot, wasn't how he wanted to go.

With a grimace, he pulled from her mouth.

Hannah fell back. She panted, dragging oxygen into her lungs, as she stared with uncertain eyes. "You didn't finish."

"I'm not going to go easy on you. My brothers had all night. Did you think I would settle for a quick head job then send you on your merry way? Not a chance, baby. Take off your clothes."

Hannah rose, her body shaking. She held his eyes as she unbuttoned her blouse with trembling fingers. Slowly, almost uncertainly, she revealed her creamy skin, inch by inch.

When she peeled the blouse off her shoulders, he sucked in a stunned breath. God, she was fucking gorgeous. He'd said she wasn't worthy of him, but it hadn't been true. Looking at her now, he knew exactly how much he'd lied. Hannah was magnificent, with dainty shoulders, a trim waist, and large breasts topped with tight, pink nipples begging to be sucked. Everything a man could hope for.

And she belonged to his brothers.

She could belong to you, if only you would reach out, trust her. Stop everything and tell her your story. Ask for forgiveness.

He couldn't risk it. She would know—and loathe—him soon enough. The press would tell everyone, and life as he knew it would be over.

Her blouse fell to the floor.

"No bra?" he choked out.

Hannah shook her head, blond curls caressing her pale shoulders. "Dex didn't put one in my suitcase." Her hands went to her skirt, but she stopped when he reached out and cupped her breast, brushing her nipple with his thumb. It peaked, flushed. Hannah's breast fit his hand perfectly, every inch soft and silky.

"Did my brother neglect to pack your underwear as well?" Gavin could just imagine Dex's sinful glee.

"I'm not allowed to wear panties anymore unless your brothers choose it."

At her implication, Gavin nearly swallowed his tongue. "You're not wearing any now?"

"No, Sir."

Fuck. Every word out of her mouth made him harder. He stood back, stepping out of his pajama pants, then tossed them across the room. He stood naked before Hannah. She looked at him, her gaze taking him in, and she gasped. Then she met his gaze. No way he could miss the desire burning there.

When she reached out to touch him, he thrust her hand away. "I didn't give you permission to touch me. Present me that ass. Show me that plug. Now."

He wanted to see exactly what Slade had pressed deep inside her, how she clenched around the plug to keep it lodged. He wanted her to bend over and show him how wet and swollen her pussy was because of it.

Hannah pushed the skirt down her hips, revealing lush curves. She had an hourglass figure that made his mouth water. Her teeth bit into her lower lip, eyes wide with hesitation as she removed the garment and left it on the floor. She turned away and leaned over, but had nothing to hold on to, so she bent and braced her hands on her thighs. Her ass was gorgeous and round, the cheeks a perfect upside down heart. But he couldn't see what he wanted to see.

"Lower, Hannah. You bend lower and use your hands to spread your cheeks."

She mumbled something he couldn't quite hear.

"What did you say?" He drilled her with a hard stare.

"Nothing, Sir."

With zero hesitation, Gavin swatted her ass. He loved the sound, the sting, the way her skin pinkened. "Don't lie to me. What did you call me?"

"I called you a bastard, Sir." Her voice sounded high-pitched, thin.

He spanked her other cheek, watching as she turned pink there, too. God, he could get used to dominating Hannah. "You don't use that language around me."

"Then don't push me."

"I will always push you." He would push her right out of his life. He was just that stupid, and it was the right thing to do. But he wasn't going to deny himself this one moment with her. He would hold it close to his heart for the rest of his life. "Now do as I told you. Hold your cheeks apart."

He couldn't mistake her reluctance, but those hands came up and slowly pulled the globes of her ass apart. There it was, peeking out, a little pink plug shoved tight inside her. Gavin got to one knee and peered closer. That plug would prepare her to take a cock up her ass. She could also fit one in her pussy and another in her mouth. He and his brothers could possess her body all at once.

No. That wouldn't happen. He couldn't risk her and allow it to happen.

"Tell me something, Hannah." He touched the plug then palmed her ass, loving the way she quivered. "Do you still care about me?"

She drew in a shuddering breath. "I love you, Gavin."

Her breathy words finally broke him. He couldn't take another second of waiting. He needed to shove himself inside her, be surrounded by her. He just fucking needed her.

Gavin hauled her into his arms and carried her to the piano—the nearest flat surface. Hannah gasped as he set her bare ass down on the keys. They made a discordant sound, but her breathy cry as he shoved his cock between her legs was music to his ears.

As she curled her fingers around his shoulders and clung, Gavin drew her closer. He could feel how wet she was. She might think he was a bastard, but she wanted him all the same.

Hannah didn't hesitate. She wrapped her legs around his waist and pulled him in when she should be pushing him away. His cock nudged the entrance to her pussy, but he held back. He needed more than to simply fuck her. He needed to connect with her.

Gavin thrust his hands in her hair and tugged, pulling her mouth beneath his. He covered that pretty, red bow, her lips swollen from sucking his cock. God, she tasted sweet. His tongue delved deep, and she accepted. No, she submitted, allowing him to pillage and plunder. Nothing but soft, sweet whimpers came from her throat as she held on, her body writhing restlessly against him.

He couldn't get enough. He kissed her mouth, her nose, her chin, and her throat. She tasted sweet on his lips. His brothers could take her as many times as they wanted, but her innocence would remain. She would always taste sweet, always have a pure heart that pulled at him. He kissed her again, possessing and ravaging, but his cock demanded more. He probed her slick, soft folds then pressed in slowly.

He watched as her lovely, bare pussy accepted his cock, clamping down in welcome with every inch he gave her. Gavin pressed in farther. Fuck, she had the tightest hole he'd ever been in. Her pussy sucked at him, drawing him in, holding him deep. She wrapped her arms around him like she never wanted to let go.

When her head fell back on a moan, exposing her throat, he kissed the fair skin there. He couldn't get enough of the taste of her. He nipped at her shoulder while his cock stretched her cunt.

Finally, he thrust completely in. She felt so fucking good wrapped around his dick, Gavin didn't know how he was going to survive.

A warning bell went off in his head, but Hannah's soft moans and softer kisses across his jaw drowned out that insistent voice screaming at him that his world was about to go to hell. The trouble was, hell felt really good right now. In fact, hell felt perfect.

Gavin took her hard, holding nothing back. Right now, she was his to fuck and fill, arouse, plunder, and consume. She was his to hold and love.

God, he loved her.

"Hannah." Her name was a benediction. He pulled on her hips, sealing them together, fusing their bodies until he couldn't tell where he ended and she began. He thrust harder, deeper, faster, wanting more and more of her—everything, in fact. Heart, soul, future…everything he'd never wanted from any other woman. She made his heart nearly fucking burst.

Hannah nodded, gasped. "Gavin."

Her voice sounded frantic. Her pussy clenched down on him even tighter. He had to work to withdraw, then shoved his way back in ruthlessly.

"You ready to come, Hannah?"

"Gavin." She grabbed at his short hair with desperate fingers, her green stare so wide and needy. She looked at him as if he had the power to destroy or fulfill her.

"Tell me, Hannah," he demanded as his own orgasm roared closer. "Do you need to come?"

She nodded frantically. "Gavin!"

Her mouth opened wide as she came and screamed his name. He could feel the muscles of her pussy pulsing hard, milking his cock until he couldn't hold off a second longer. His balls drew up painfully. He thrust in to the hilt one last time, captured her cry of pleasure with his mouth, then orgasm slammed him. He poured everything he had into his Hannah, the feeling so good it had to be a sin.

In fact, it was a sin. Oh, God. He hadn't worn a condom.

The voice he'd ignored had been trying to warn him. He'd fucked Hannah, his brothers' woman, without protecting her. He'd fucked up again.

His stomach turned. His vision blurred.

Way to go, ruining another woman's life. And your brothers will really love you for killing this one.

Self-loathing boiled in Gavin's blood as he withdrew roughly. Muttering an ugly curse, he turned away. The jarring notes of the piano, followed by soft footfall, told Gavin that Hannah hopped off the piano.

"Gavin?" She touched his shoulder tentatively, softly. With concern.

He didn't fucking deserve it.

Everyone knows how great you are to your lovers. You use them and forget them. You do nothing as they lay dying. What a great guy.

"What's wrong?" Hannah angled herself in front of him, her eyes searching.

He just glared. What the hell could he say?

She backed away, reached to the ground for her blouse, and started to cover her breasts. She knew something had gone terribly awry.

Gavin wanted to hold her. The words were perched on the tip of his tongue. *I love you. I'll take care of you always.* He could say them. He would even mean them.

His cell phone chirped, reminding him that his time had run out. There would be no white picket fence for him.

But what if Hannah could forgive his past mistakes? What if his brothers understood? But what would any of it matter if he couldn't forgive himself? He didn't have any right to drag her into the scandal that was about to hit. If the stalker held true to his threat, the papers would soon get the full story on how he'd covered up the facts surrounding Nikki's death, and they would hound him and anyone near.

He had to push her as far away from him as possible, even if he had to make her hate him.

"Everything's fine, Hannah. But I'm done. You can go now."

Gavin retrieved his pajama bottoms and slid them on, eyeing the last of the vodka, before he forced himself to walk away. He couldn't look at the confusion on her face for another second. She'd been sweet and giving, and if he was a better human being, she might have been able to make him whole.

"Talk to me. Please, tell me what's wrong."

Gavin resisted the urge to go to her. He couldn't touch her again or he would weaken. He had to be strong for both their sakes. "There's nothing wrong, Hannah. I told you yesterday, I would love to fuck you. I did. It was okay. Now I'm done. You're an attractive girl, but I don't want a second round. I'm used to more experienced lovers."

"More experienced?" The words fell from her mouth with a dull thud. Her eyes lost their light.

His heart fell, but he managed a casual shrug. "One night with my brothers didn't teach you much, honey."

It was a lie. He was so used to lying, it came easy. The truth was, he would dream about having her every night for the rest of his miserable life. If he could ever work up the will to fuck another woman, it would be Hannah's face he saw. He would never forget the way she clung to him, the way they fit together.

But he would also never be able to get this broken-hearted Hannah out of his head. This Hannah wasn't smiling. This Hannah groped around for her skirt in an attempt to hide from him.

She dressed in utter silence, with her back to him. He wished she would just walk away. He wouldn't be able to handle the quiet dignity she would surely toss his way any moment. Still, he forced himself to stand there and wait as the guilt poured in.

Hannah turned after smoothing down her skirt, but it wasn't quiet dignity on her face. No, pure feminine fury reigned.

"You're a jerk, Mr. James. I never would have expected this from you."

He had to keep being a jerk. "What, Hannah, are you going to play the scorned woman now? I never lied to you."

"You've never told me the truth either. Why did you hire me?"

Because he wanted her close. He wanted to bask in her light. "It was a favor to my brothers."

Her eyes narrowed, sharp intelligence clear in their depths. "I don't think so. Dex and Slade could have just as easily pursued me without bringing me into your office. And why did you keep me as your executive admin if I was just 'okay'?"

Why was everyone questioning him? Why wouldn't they just leave him the fuck alone?

Because he deserved whatever shit rained down on him. God, he'd taken her without a condom. If she was pregnant, it would kill him. No, if she was pregnant, Dex and Slade would kill him.

"I told you before that I didn't have a problem sleeping with you. You have a certain charm, both in the office and flat on your back. But I won't give up my social standing to marry a girl so utterly lacking grace and upbringing."

Her lips curled up in a cynical smile. It was the first he'd ever seen on her. Gavin swallowed down a throat full of bile. His Hannah had learned a lot in the days since he and his brothers had kidnapped her, not all of it good.

"Right, I'm just a country girl without manners or education. I'm nothing but a good time to a man like you. Rest assured, I won't forget that again."

It made him sick, but Gavin nodded. "Good. I hope you won't make a fuss with my brothers."

"That won't be a problem." Her shoulders sagged. Her cynical smile fled, and tears welled in her eyes. "I won't cause any trouble between you and your brothers. We dumb country girls at least know better than to mess with family."

She started to walk out of the room, her head held high.

"What does that mean?"

"Piss off," she snapped, without even turning back to him.

"Where are you going?" he demanded.

"It's none of your concern."

"Stay in your room until my brothers get back." He couldn't see her again.

She still didn't turn back to him. "I don't need to follow your orders any more, Mr. James. You're not my boss. You're not even my lover. You're just a jerk who used me."

That summed him up in a neat little package. Pain slammed through him, but he swallowed it down. "This jerk thinks it would be best if you remained in your room."

"What you think doesn't matter anymore."

157

He laughed, a humorless sound. "I guess you don't love me after all."

"You're wrong." She sighed and kept walking.

With two words, she dismantled him. Gavin staggered back to the piano, clutching his stomach. He felt fucking eviscerated. He grabbed the bottle of vodka and drained the last of it, staring at the piano. He'd never be able to play again without seeing Hannah there. He'd never be able to come back to this house without aching for her all over again.

He was a miserable bastard, and it was only going to get worse. But he knew what he had to do, the only honorable thing he could do. He picked up the phone and dialed his lawyer's number.

Maybe someday Hannah and his brothers would understand.

* * * *

Hannah walked through the house like a zombie, her feet shuffling across the hardwood floors. The events of the past days played through her brain as she made it to her room. She'd been briefly happy here, but that was over.

She took off her clothes and started the shower. God, she felt dirty. Funny how she could be with two men and feel like an angel, but Gavin had made her feel slutty and cheap.

After washing away the evidence of her mistake, she climbed out and dressed the best she could. With tears blurring her eyes, she packed her things and closed her suitcase. She opened her laptop. With a few keystrokes, she found the phone number to the charter service that flew from River Run to Anchorage. She could find a flight home from there. In a day or so, she would be back in Two Trees. Maybe she could pick up the pieces of her life.

If she could find a way into town.

Next, Hannah pulled up her word processing program and typed out a note to Dex and Slade. After searching the nearby study, she found no evidence of a printer, so she left the computer open so they would find her goodbye.

Hannah cried as she dragged her suitcase behind her and searched the whole house futilely for car keys or the driver. Neither were anywhere to be found. Darn it, she needed to be gone before Slade and Dex returned. They wouldn't understand. They'd convince her that Gavin was like a lion with a thorn in his paw— snarling and mean, but really just hurting deep down. They'd convince her that she could heal him. But Hannah knew better. If she remained, she would just cause trouble between Gavin and his brothers.

God, she'd miss these men, and she would never love anyone half so much again, but she couldn't break up a family.

Why had she thought she could be involved with three men? She hadn't been thinking at all, at least not with her brain. Her heart and nether regions had proven that they couldn't make a halfway decent decision between them.

She wandered into the great room where she'd confronted Gavin earlier. If only she'd listened to him. She'd been so sure he was hiding something. Maybe he was, but nothing she'd done had cut through his protective walls. He didn't want her help or her love.

She stared out the window, wondering how far the walk was into town when the golf carts caught her eye.

She smiled for the first time. Country girls might not be polished, but they knew how to make do.

* * * *

She pulled her golf cart into a parking space behind the Angry Moose Saloon, Grocery, and Lodge. It was the biggest building in the tiny little town. Made of large logs, it resembled a huge cabin. Two burly men walked out of the saloon doors and stopped in their tracks when they saw her.

Both of them towered over Hannah. They stared openly at her, and then the one wearing a hat walked right back into the saloon without a word.

Fabulous. Everywhere she looked today, she found a man willing to be rude to her. She lifted her chin and walked through the saloon's double doors.

The Angry Moose was unlike anything she'd ever seen. The walls were covered with animal heads. These people took their hunting very seriously. Moose, bears, deer, even a gopher, all had heads hanging on the wall, a testament to human prowess with a shotgun.

A quick image of Gavin's head on the wall sprinted through her mind. She shook her head. Violence wouldn't change anything. It wouldn't make her feel better. Maybe it would assuage her for a moment, but she still loved him. In fact, she loved all three of them. The ache from leaving the James Gang behind was going to last forever.

She clutched her suitcase and walked to the bar, ignoring the crowd of men who stopped to stare at her.

What was going on? They acted as if they'd never seen a woman before.

A young man with dark hair and Native American features stood behind the bar. His eyes widened as she approached.

"Miss, can I help you? Are you lost?" He leaned over. "Do I need to call the sheriff? He's not exactly effective, but he's better than nothing."

Hannah frowned. "Why would I need the sheriff? I just need to find Billy."

Billy Harris ran the small charter service that would take her from River Run to Anchorage. From there, she was on her own. But she could find her way back to Texas.

The young man's face fell. "Uhm, are you Harry Crag?"

She shook her head. "Hannah Craig."

The bartender winced. "Sorry. Billy isn't really great with names when he's plastered. Unfortunately, that's most of the time."

Out of nowhere, a stranger's hand gripped her arm. "Don't worry about nothing, Harry. I'll have you out of this hellhole in no time."

She could smell the liquor on the man's breath. This was Billy, her pilot?

Hannah turned to the bartender. "Can anyone else take me home?"

The bartender frowned and pointed behind her. Hannah turned. Every man in the bar stared at her. Most had moved way too close for comfort.

"I can take you home," a deep-voiced man with faded jeans and a naughty smile said. She got the distinct feeling he was not talking about Texas.

"I should take her home, you old coot. I'm way closer to her age." A man who looked barely old enough to drink pushed to the forefront.

Hannah eased back—and felt the hard edge of the bar at her back. She swallowed. This could get ugly.

Chapter Ten

Dex walked into the house, an unaccountable sense of confidence clinging to him. Despite the fact that the conference call with the Lenox brothers hadn't yet yielded the name of Hannah's stalker, Dex had a feeling that they were close. Of course, now they had another problem, a corporate saboteur. Someone had purposefully uploaded a virus to their drilling sites' computers. Dex had already put out a call to their other drill sites to lock down their systems and accept no updates until further notice.

"Hey." Slade walked in behind him, through the kitchen doors, and into the mud room. "Since we got all the crap settled with the computers, I was thinking we should show Hannah around a bit. She's probably too sore to ride a horse today, but we could climb in the Jeep and take her up into the mountains."

"Yeah, good thinking." Then he frowned. "What about Gavin?"

Big brother was another problem they were going to have to solve. Hannah loved him. Slade would miss him. Hell, if he was really honest with himself, Dex didn't want Gavin left out, either, despite the awful lies he'd snarled at Hannah last night. If they allowed

Gavin to pull away this time, it would likely be permanent. Dex knew it deep in his bones.

"What do you mean? Are you asking if we should we invite him along?"

Dex shook his head. "No, we need to figure out what's eating at Gavin and how to stop it before we let him anywhere near Hannah again. What do you know about Nikki and the night she died?"

Slade zipped a sharp stare his way. "Not much. Nikki was really beautiful. You know, one of those girls who just catches everyone's attention."

"I remember." Dex tended to steer clear of women like her. Anyone who needed that much attention typically didn't know how to give it back. "Society girl, wasn't she?"

"Yes. The worst kind. Her family had fallen on hard times, and she was willing to screw her way back to the top."

"Starting with Gavin."

Slade shook his head. "Hell, no. She'd worked her way through a bunch of men before she got her hooks into him."

"Gavin has always been so smart. Why would he let someone like her get close?"

"It was a difficult time for him," Slade said slowly. "Our father was gone. We had just found you. Gavin got lost trying to save the company. I let him."

"You were barely eighteen." Dex remembered that time as the greatest of his life. He'd found brothers who'd seemed to embrace him, and he'd started college. Until Gavin and Slade had shown up, he'd been pretty sure he wouldn't see a college campus unless he was cleaning it. Many rich families would have never contacted him, much less welcomed him with open arms and offered to pay for his education.

But those years had been hard for Gavin. He'd barely graduated from college himself when he'd been forced to delve into the shark-infested waters of corporate life. If their father hadn't stubbornly held onto the majority of the stock, Black Oak Oil would have likely been savaged and broken up.

Gavin had saved it for his brothers. Yeah, he owed Gavin.

"I remember Nikki, but only a bit." Dex flushed. He hadn't wanted to admit this. "She came on to me one night."

"Join the club. What kills me is that Gavin wasn't in love with her. I think he liked the sex. She was very passionate. They fought constantly. At the time, some demon in him craved that drama. Maybe it took his mind off everything else." Slade shrugged. "I don't know."

And Dex could just bet that Nikki had made up for all that arguing in bed. "I remember a couple of breakups. They always seemed permanent, but the next week she'd be back."

"She always managed to lure him in again. But finally, he'd had enough and decided to break with her for good. Two days later, she died from an overdose. The police report says it was an accidental suicide—a cry for attention—but Gavin hasn't been the same for the last decade. I don't get it. He isn't pining for her." Slade shook his head. "Maybe he feels responsible, but he didn't shove a bunch of pills down her throat."

Sometimes it didn't take having an actual hand in something to make a man feel guilty. Dex knew that.

He felt guilty about his own damn birth. His mother had been sweet, but not too smart. She'd had to work two jobs to try to support him after her lover had shoved a ten thousand dollar check her way and told her to get an abortion. When he was a kid, he'd often thought she would have been better off if she had. If she'd followed Stuart James's instructions, she wouldn't have been working late in a bar. She wouldn't have been in a car that broke down. She wouldn't have been hit by a passing drunk driver.

Dex shook it off. His mother had loved him and done her best to provide. She wouldn't want him to feel guilty for anything. Maybe that's why Dex could let go of the guilt and Gavin couldn't. If Nikki could see Gavin's torment, she'd be eating it up.

"We have to talk to him, convince him to let this go," Dex insisted. He was going to make this right with his brother and give Hannah the complete happiness she wanted and deserved.

Slade smiled and put a brotherly hand on his shoulder. "I can't tell you how much that means to me, man. Yeah, let's find him and have a chat. Then we'll all take our girl out and show her the mountains."

Hannah would look beautiful lying back on a field of green grass. It had only been a few hours since he and Slade had cleaned her up and begun preparing her ass. His dick got hard at the memory of Slade sliding that pink plug deep inside her. Her eyes had widened, and a breathy moan had oozed from her throat. He'd almost come in his jeans right then and there. If he and Slade hadn't made the agreement to let her recover during the morning, he would have pulled her close and seen just how tight her pussy would be when her ass was filled.

He glanced down at his watch. Four p.m. He smiled. They had really only agreed to leave her alone for the morning.

"You're thinking what I'm thinking." Slade grinned. When it came to Hannah, they were always thinking the same thing.

They rounded the corner that would take them to the bedroom they shared with Hannah when they saw him.

Gavin stood in the doorway, his eyes haggard, staring at them. Dex had never seen his brother look so disheveled and distraught. Something had gone terribly wrong. How much had he heard? Had their discussion about Nikki put him in this state?

"Gavin, what the fuck?" Slade grabbed the empty bottle of vodka in his brother's hand. "What is wrong with you? Did you drink all of this today?"

"Yep. I came looking for another, but I didn't want to interrupt your brotherly chat."

Slade stopped, cursed at the haunted look in their big brother's eyes. "Tell us what happened."

Gavin's lips quirked up, but he radiated pure self-loathing. "Everything. Some of it was so long ago. But no matter how deep you bury it, that shit always comes back to haunt you."

"If talking about Nikki is upsetting you this much, I'll back off," Dex vowed. Gavin needed to heal, but he wasn't willing to hurt his brother to force the issue.

Shaking his head, Gavin stepped carefully across the room. His defeated mien contrasted sharply with the sunny kitchen table. "It doesn't matter. The entire ugly story will be out in the papers by tomorrow."

Slade slid Dex a long, worried look as he sat down beside Gavin. "The whole story about Nikki?"

Gavin nodded, eyes squeezed tightly shut, torment clearly wracking him.

"Did you kill her?" Dex asked calmly. "Have they dug up evidence? Is there time to make it go away?"

Gavin turned to him with a solemn frown. "Would you really cover it up?"

"In a heartbeat," Dex replied. "I would be pissed that you hadn't come to me in the first place. If you have a body to hide, you call your brothers."

"I sometimes wonder if you consider me a brother at all. I haven't been close to you. I accused you of behaving impulsively."

Dex managed a smile. "In the past, I have behaved impulsively. You had to bail me out of jail more than once in college."

Slade grinned. "At least you're not fighting in bars anymore."

"I got a text from Hannah's stalker." Gavin's words turned the conversation on end and stopped Dex's heart for a painful second.

"What? When?" He couldn't get the words out fast enough.

"About eight this morning."

Before they'd confronted Preston.

Slade glanced his way, then back to Gavin. "From what number? Let me see."

Gavin shook his head. "Nothing you can do. I just forwarded the whole text conversation to the Lenox brothers. They're working on it, but this guy isn't stupid. The number will be from an untraceable, prepaid cell. The gist of his little message was that he knew my secret, and he's going to tell the world unless we release Hannah."

"How does he even know we have Hannah?" Slade asked. "Unless it's Preston, then he knows from Lyle because the pipsqueak saw you carry Hannah out of the office yesterday."

"True. Slade fired Preston, Gavin. The guy is a prick who treated Hannah like shit."

Gavin shrugged. "The firing of our CIO is the least of my worries. This shit that's going to come out will tear us apart."

"We need to find out now if Preston made it on that plane back to Anchorage or if he's still hovering around here," Dex told Slade as he made a mental note to call the Lenox brothers ASAP to track down Preston's current whereabouts.

Gavin's shoulders slumped. "You really think Preston would stalk her? He's been in her face a lot. Why the sudden subterfuge?"

Who knew why a psycho did anything, Dex thought darkly.

"Until we know who the stalker is for sure, let's focus on keeping Hannah close and protected," Gavin suggested. "The rest of it is over and done. The fucking past is going to come out, and I've made suitable arrangements to deal with the fallout."

"What kind of arrangements? How bad is this story?" Slade grabbed Gavin's shoulders. "Is our stock going to take a hit? I don't understand."

"I'll explain. I'd rather you hear this from me than the press. And the stock won't take a hit. I've made sure of it. I'll be stepping down as CEO Monday morning. I've split the stock our father left me between you and Dex. My lawyer is finalizing the details now."

"What?" Slade exploded, standing and staring in disbelief.

Dex had always wanted a piece of the company his absentee father had built, but only because he'd wanted to be on an equal footing with his brothers. He sure as hell hadn't wanted it this way. "Call him back and tell him to unfinalize it."

"I won't," Gavin said, his voice taking on a grave finality. "This is what's best for the company and what's best for the two of you and Hannah. You'll think so, too, in a minute."

"I doubt that." Slade crossed his arms over his chest. "You're the heart of Black Oak Oil. You make it run."

Gavin barely managed a shrug, as if lifting his shoulders was too much effort.

"Tell us. Just spit out what's going to hit the press so we can deal with it." Whatever he was about to confess had been a festering wound poisoning his oldest brother for years.

Dropping his elbows to his knees, Gavin hunched over and stared at the floor. "I did kill Nikki, but worse, I killed my own child."

Dex slumped into his chair, the truth hitting him. Compassion welled up. He might not have been raised with Gavin, but Dex knew him. Guilt about Dex's rough childhood had brought Gavin to his unknown brother's door in the first place. Thinking that he'd been even a tiny bit responsible for his own child's death would crush him.

Gavin locked stares with Slade, then Dex. Clearly, he was braced, waiting for condemnation, rejection.

Hatred.

Dex reached out and put a hand on his. He said the words he'd never said before—to either of them. "I love you, brother. We'll get through this."

* * * *

Gavin pulled his hand back. Of all the things Dex could have had said, this shocked him most. He turned to Slade and saw the same look of concern and compassion on his face. No anger. No horror or exclusion. They simply waited for him to tell the story.

"Did you hear what I said?" he asked incredulously.

Slade nodded. "Yes. I heard. I'm going to tell you the same thing Dex said. I love you, and I'm here for you. Just get it all out so we can deal."

Their faces were grim, but they hadn't walked out on him. They'd shown solidarity, offered support. *Fuck.* His brothers had told him that they loved him.

Dex sent him a solemn stare. "I take it Nikki was pregnant when she decided to down a bunch of pills. How is that your fault, Gavin?"

"Let me enlighten you." He hated the nasty edge to his words.

Gavin had known this would be hard, but their seeming acceptance made it harder. What if they heard the details and decided that he was a murdering prick after all? He scrubbed his raw eyes with the heels of his hands. Then they would finally understand. None of that changed the fact he owed them the truth before the press splashed it all over the front page.

"Nikki and I had a volatile relationship, as you

know. It was interesting at first. A nice diversion from all the other shit in my life. We had some hot sex. She loved to fuck, and I enjoyed obliging her. For a while, it was worth all the drama. Then she got demanding. I found myself in this constant state of making up and breaking up with her. I have to admit, the more we fought, the hotter the sex became. It was damn good. And when the former Black Oak board was trying to eat me alive, I needed the release." He shrugged. "I got addicted to the sex and the anger. They made me forget work for a while. Our parents were dead. We didn't have a lot of other family. You two were in college, far away…so Nikki became a fixture in my life. I never planned to marry her. I knew she was bad for me."

"But she was there and we weren't." Guilt ravaged Slade's face. He shook his head, his shoulders slumped.

"Hey, you two had to go to school," Gavin rebuked. The last thing he needed was Slade or Dex feeling responsible. "This fiasco was all my doing. I was an adult."

"You were twenty-two, Gavin," Dex growled. "Most twenty-two-year-olds are drinking beer and trying to figure out where to get a job. They aren't dealing with multi-billion-dollar companies and hostile takeovers. They aren't trying to keep everything together."

"Stop trying to justify this, Dex. Being young doesn't absolve me of anything."

The liquor was wearing off. He needed more to get through this, but he felt sure his brothers would object at the moment. After he told them the rest, though, they might decide they didn't give a damn after all and let him drink himself to death.

"You're not fucking perfect. Don't expect yourself to be," Slade insisted.

"Perfect?" Gavin scoffed even as his stomach threatened to revolt. This was the part he'd dreaded. "Hell, I wasn't even close. When I decided to break this perverse cycle Nikki and I were in, I told her we were done for good. I made the break clean. I got a new phone. I told the security at the office and the condo to keep her out. She still managed to get my number. And she'd call, leave these long messages begging me to come back because she needed me. Then she told me she was pregnant."

"Had she ever told you that before?" Slade asked.

"She'd had a couple of scares, even though she claimed she was on the Pill. And I always used condoms with her."

But with Hannah he hadn't. He hadn't even thought of protecting her. He'd just lost himself and flooded her with every ounce of his seed. God, his brothers were going to hate him—and they had every right to.

Gavin sighed. "Nikki had tried to get me to marry her twice before by claiming that she was pregnant."

"So when she announced it this time, you didn't believe her for good reason." Slade sat back in his chair.

"I also didn't believe her when she said she was going to kill herself because I'd heard that before, too." Gavin's stomach turned again. "She called. I was at a party. I didn't even bother to step outside to talk to her. She asked if I even cared about our baby. I told her there wasn't a baby. She said she'd taken some pills.

She'd threatened suicide before and hadn't followed through, so I didn't alert anyone. I didn't lift a damn finger."

Dex's face softened. "This isn't your fault. You couldn't have known she was serious."

"I should have guessed or done something, just in case. Instead, I told Nikki to do what she had to do. Then I hung up on her. An hour later, her sister called me to tell me that she was dead."

"Damn it, Gavin, you didn't force her to take the pills."

"But I didn't even try to save her." Gavin stood and kicked the chair across the room. "She really was pregnant, a few weeks along according to the coroner. He kept it quiet for me."

Slade winced. "You are not going to want to hear this, Gavin, but how can you be sure the baby was yours?"

He'd asked himself that question a million times. "Does it really matter? If I had taken her threat seriously, that child would be alive today."

Dex shook his head. "You would never have intentionally hurt her or that baby. I know it."

"You're obviously missing the fact that through my negligence, I killed both a woman and a child."

"No," Slade said in an even tone. "You didn't. You broke up with a woman who wasn't stable, and she decided to go off the deep end. She needed help, man."

"I didn't give it to her. Damn it, you two are not listening to me." It was maddening. "I left her there. I let her die."

"She chose to take the pills herself. She didn't care

about the baby in her belly. She didn't call for an ambulance. She didn't want to live. That's not your fault." Slade stood and began to pace, his hand running through his hair. "You've seriously wasted years of your life over this?"

"That was my child!" Gavin yelled. Years of anger threatened to bubble to the surface.

"She took the kid down with her," Dex said quietly. Gavin couldn't mistake the sadness in his brother's eyes. "And that's what you're grieving most of all. I know. And I am so sorry."

Slade's hands rested on his shoulders. "I'm sorry, too. I wish you'd told us sooner. We would have done anything to help you through this."

Gavin pushed them away. "Don't."

Dex frowned. "Don't what, give a damn? Don't get pissed that you've wasted years of your life over something you couldn't control?"

"Don't forgive you? That's what you're really upset about it, isn't it?" Slade challenged. "You don't want us to forgive you."

Gavin sat for a minute, his thoughts racing. Slade's words hit him squarely in the chest. He didn't want forgiveness. He'd held the pain in for so long. The thought of releasing it terrified him. He'd hidden behind it, used it as barrier to keep him from everything that could hurt him again. He'd used it to push people away.

Like Hannah.

He hadn't loved Nikki. He'd had some vague affection for her in the beginning—and nothing but contempt at the end. That hadn't seemed abnormal to Gavin. He'd watched his mother and father's utterly loveless relationship and decided he was incapable of true devotion. He'd held onto that lie until now, even in the face of his feelings for Hannah.

Fuck. He wasn't afraid of what he would do to Hannah. He was scared of what he *felt* for her—and how vulnerable that would make him.

She could die or walk away. Hannah could love his brothers more than she would ever love him. Any of those scenarios would demolish him.

"You're right. Forgiveness is scary. Your loathing would have been easier. And now I've fucked up again." Gavin let his head fall to his hands.

Regret, deep and cutting, sliced through him. He'd allowed his own fear to push Hannah away. She'd offered him everything he could have hoped for, and he'd acted like an animal.

"Because you pushed Hannah away with insults?" Slade clapped him on the shoulder. "You're human. You make mistakes. An apology fixes things most of the time. You'll do better in the future. But now, it's long past time to forgive yourself. There's a woman in this house who loves you. Don't push her away again because you're scared. Do you have any idea how precious she is? She has a heart big enough for all of us."

Gavin shook his head. "Not for me. Not after what I did earlier. God, she'll never forgive me. Neither will you."

Dex's face got hard and unrelenting. "What happened with Hannah?"

This might be worse than telling them about Nikki. "Hannah found me shortly after I'd talked to the attorney. I had been drinking for a while—hard."

Slade slapped at the bottle. "Obviously."

"Did you hurt her?" Dex demanded.

Filled with shame, Gavin nodded, reluctant to say the words that might really sever his relationship with his brothers. He had only started to understand that he wasn't responsible entirely for what had happened with Nikki. He couldn't say the same thing of Hannah.

He hadn't known until this moment how much he'd needed his brothers' support and comfort. Now it might all be gone. But he owed them the truth.

"I didn't hurt her physically," Gavin choked. "But I tore her heart apart."

"Spit it out," Slade insisted.

"I was trying to push her away. I thought it would be easier on everyone if she hated me."

"The way you've been hating yourself?" Slade asked pointedly.

God, put that way, his behavior sounded pathetic. "I love her. I couldn't stand the thought that she would find out what I had done and look at me like I was a monster."

Slade's eyes rolled. "You don't know her at all. She would have hugged you and told you to forgive yourself. She would have understood."

"He knew that, deep down. But like you said, he wasn't ready to forgive himself. Now..." Dex loomed over him. "Tell me what you said to her."

In that moment, Gavin figured out why this relationship with Hannah had a chance. They would keep each other in line. When one of them was cranky and difficult, the other two would set him straight. They would all be there for Hannah and each other. They would be a family.

If he could find the courage to be a part of it.

"I called her graceless and classless. I told her that she wasn't good enough to be my wife."

Gavin had been prepared for the fist that flew his way. He wasn't prepared for just how hard his youngest brother hit. Gavin's head flew back, the pain in his jaw a welcome wake up call.

"Don't ever say that about her again. It's bullshit, and you know it. Understand?"

Gavin nodded. "I didn't mean it, Dex. I love her. God, I love her so much. I think she's perfect."

Dex pointed an accusatory finger at him. "You're going to make it up to her. You're going to treat her like a princess. You're going to apologize, and if she wants you to kiss her feet, then you're going to get down on the floor and kiss them."

Slade cut in. "Exactly. And you're also going to tell that fucking lawyer to stop whatever it is you have him doing."

"Damn straight. I'm going to go find Hannah. We're going to talk this out. You better be ready to grovel." Dex turned and stomped out of the room.

Slade calmly got up and walked to the fridge. He came back with a bag of frozen peas and handed it to Gavin. "Put that on your face. Is anything broken?"

Gavin moved his sore jaw. "I don't think so. But it hurts."

"Be glad you weren't standing up. I've been in bar fights with our shitkicker baby brother. He's mean. He might have kicked you in the balls." Slade's head shook affectionately. "But he's always quick to forgive when he gives a damn about you. I think you'll find Hannah is, too."

"Oh," Dex said. "That's better."

Gavin picked up the keys to the Jeep and handed them to Slade.

It was time to get their girl.

Chapter Eleven

Hannah stared at all the unfamiliar men at the Angry Moose crowding in on her with expressions ranging from curiosity to downright hunger. What the devil was she going to do?

"You boys take a big step back now," a firm, feminine voice rang out.

An older woman, her steel gray hair in a braid that ran almost to her waist, stepped out. The roughneck who had stared at Hannah outside the bar stood at this woman's side wearing a sheepish expression.

"Tobias, you little traitor!" The biggest cowboy in the group growled, but the woman hushed him with a single glare of her brown eyes.

"The first one to make a move on the young lady loses bar privileges."

Every man in the bar took a big step back. Hannah grinned. Apparently, her charms weren't as coveted as a cold mug of beer.

She breathed a deep sigh of relief as the older woman walked forward wearing a friendly smile on her face. The woman was slender but built solid, a fact underscored by her no-nonsense blue jeans and standard flannel shirt.

"You, young lady, look like you could use a drink."

Hannah took a seat on the nearest stool and peeked at her inebriated pilot, still happily snoring. It didn't look like she was going anywhere for a while.

"Yes, please."

Twenty minutes and two tequila shots later, she grinned at Marnie. "I want another one."

"Are you sure?"

Hannah pondered that question. *Probably.* After all, she'd spent the last few days biting off way more than she could chew. Did she want just one James boy? No, that was too simple. Two? Bring it on! Three? Well...three had proven one too many. Would a third tequila shot put her over the edge, just like that third man? It didn't matter. She might as well have another drink—one for each James brother.

"Yeah, I'll take another." She slapped firmly at the bar, missed and hit her own thigh. She probably didn't need more alcohol, but the tequila made her stomach feel warm and tingly. And that made her think of those men again, being naked and entwined with them, bringing her the kind of pleasure that even romantic fiction hadn't adequately described. She missed them, wanted them. She needed more tequila to drown that out.

Marnie shrugged and reached under the bar. She came back up with a shot glass filled with amber liquid. Without a second thought, Hannah picked it up and slammed it to the back of her throat. No feminine sipping for her this time.

Unlike the first two she'd had, this drink lacked bite. It was silky smooth and sweet. She put the empty glass down and stared with a frown. "I don't think this is tequila. I like this one, Marnie. I could drink this all night."

She'd probably have to. Glancing at the pilot again, Hannah asked, "Do you have any idea when Billy might be sober?"

It was rude to make her wait while he slept off his vodka. She'd planned a grand exit. She was supposed to be halfway to Anchorage by now. She couldn't sit here much longer or the brothers would find her. What would happen then? She shivered in anticipation. *No, you're supposed to be leaving them forever, not thinking about all the delicious ways they could punish you.*

Marnie leaned forward. "You're in trouble, girl. Why don't you tell me about it? I have a feeling this is about my boys."

"I'm sorry, ma'am. I don't know your boys. I just flew up from Dallas yesterday with my boss—well, my former boss—and his brothers. I haven't exactly seen much past the bedroom, if you know what I mean."

Had she just said that out loud?

Hannah felt herself flush. Where had her manners gone? Fled in a haze of alcohol, she suspected. Except she didn't feel very drunk. Tipsy, maybe. She picked up the last shot glass and sniffed it. "Hey, is this apple juice?"

Marnie merely poured another. "Now see, it sounds like you have met my boys. Gavin and Slade would be just the type to hide a woman away. And though I didn't have a hand in raising Dex, he's become like one of my own, too. He can be a caveman when it suits him."

"Perfect." Hannah downed the drink. "I flee, and I run straight into their surrogate momma. If you're not going to help me get drunk, will you at least get me a cup of coffee?"

A rustling against the beat-up hardwood floors sounded behind her. Hannah sighed. The men of the bar had been watching her every move since she'd walked in. Initially Marnie had scared them, but Hannah had heard them whispering. Now, they began belting out offers.

"I'll buy you a drink, ma'am."

"Me, too. One of them fruity drinks, if you want," added another.

"I have some of that fancy beer back at my place. We could get...comfortable and drink a few."

Wincing, Hannah turned. The dozen or so roughnecks had closed in. The big, burly men in faded jeans and flannel shirts, clearly used to hard work if their battered boots were any indication, hovered. If she hadn't already given her heart away, she might have found these guys attractive. But not a one could hold a candle to her men.

Except Gavin, Slade, and Dex weren't her men anymore.

Hannah smoothed back her hair. "I appreciate the offer, gentlemen, but I've had enough of men to last me a lifetime. And Miss Marnie is probably right, I really don't need more alcohol. I could, however, use a general store. Is there one around so I can pick up a few necessary items?"

Her head spun a bit. Hannah felt a deep gratitude to Marnie for cutting her off while she could still stand. She wasn't used to drinking, except the occasional

Shayla Black and Lexi Blake

glass of wine Slade ordered for her.

"The store is next door. What do you need?" Marnie asked. "I'll have someone pick your items up."

"Well, I need some underwear, for starters. Dex didn't pack any. He said I wasn't allowed to wear them, but now that I've left, I'll wear anything I like. And I like underwear."

She heard the men behind her erupt into a rumble of chatter. She turned to find some of them texting. Others blatantly talked amongst themselves.

"The new girl ain't wearin' no underwear."

Hannah held her head high and glared at the man who'd made that statement. He had to be at least six foot five and all of twenty-one, but neither trait excused him from using double negatives, at least not in Hannah's book. "It's more correct to say that I am not wearing any underwear. It's also rude to point that out." She turned back to Marnie. "I would also love a bra."

"I told you she didn't have no bra on. I can tell."

Hannah glared over her shoulder at yet another man. He was smaller, but seemed to have his height-advantaged friend's trouble with grammar.

"Sorry, ma'am," he said, a flush turning his skin a dark brown. "I meant to say that you haven't got a bra on."

She shook her head, resolved to ignore him and the others.

Marnie set a cup of coffee in front of her. Hannah picked it up, wondering if she could pour it down the pilot's throat instead. Time was running thin.

The older woman grinned, mirth lighting her dark eyes. "I can see why my boys are interested in you.

186

You can handle yourself, girl. But I'm sorry to tell you that unless you like boxer shorts in an extra large, you're out of luck. And I definitely don't stock bras, although the way some of these men have gained weight, a few of them might need a little support."

"It's my thyroid, Marnie," a particularly large man said as he crossed his arms and hunched his shoulders as though trying to hide his chest.

Marnie's eyes rolled. "Roughnecks. Suddenly, they're so sensitive. Now, which of my boys is giving you trouble? I bet it's Gavin. Unless you're leaving over the underwear thing. Then I'd say that's either Dex or Slade. I like my briefs, to tell you the truth. I don't think I could give them up."

Hannah could probably live without the underwear, though she'd intended to fight them on the bra issue. She also needed to figure out how to get the plug out of her bottom. It was still there, a subtle reminder every time she moved of the pleasures she'd be missing now that she'd left those perverted, wonderful men. "It's just…Gavin isn't interested in me."

Marnie's dark eyes turned shrewd. "I doubt that. I know him. I've been worried about him for the last ten years. When I heard he'd brought a woman here, I was so damn happy. Now that I've met you, I'm even happier. You're what he needs. I'm guessing you're already involved with Slade and Dex, while Gavin is being the stubborn holdout."

Hannah flushed. "You're perceptive."

"Well, sweetie, men don't usually give edicts about whether a woman can wear delicates unless they're involved, and I know Slade and Dex have been looking for a woman to share for a long time."

"That's a way of life around these parts, Miss," the large man with the thyroid issue said with a big smile. "We ain't got a lot of women here. We have to share. And if the James boys are only offering you three men, well, me and my brothers are willing to offer you five."

"Not really a selling point," Hannah said, unable to keep the horror from her voice. What on earth would she do with five men? Most likely, she would go crazy. The amount of cooking and laundry alone would make her suicidal.

"Don't mind them." Marnie reached out and covered Hannah's hand with her own. "So you say Gavin doesn't want you?"

Tears threatened. "Yes. He's made it clear that I'm not good enough for him."

"Horse pucky," Marnie replied. "He's been on a path to self-destruction for years. Ask yourself why he brought you here if he isn't interested."

"Well, I seem to have some sort of stalker…"

Marnie shrugged. "Dex's area of expertise. That don't require Gavin being here."

Good point. Hannah hadn't considered that. Everything lately had been such a whirlwind. The time to think between all those orgasms had been short.

Why would Gavin need to be here? The trouble at the site was either computer or mechanical. That was Slade's end of the business. Dex was security, and he'd taken the lead on working with the Lenox brothers, as well as looking into the malicious virus at the River Run office. Gavin didn't need to be here at all. Had he come simply because he wanted to?

"You might be right."

"'Course I am." A satisfied smile crossed Marnie's face. "I talked to him yesterday. He always calls me when he's coming in. I asked him what he was doing here, and he did that sputtering thing that men do when they can't really explain themselves. I'll bet Dex and Slade could have handled everything. Gavin should probably be in Dallas, but he chose to come here with you."

"What you're saying makes sense, but he pushed me away, Marnie. He said some really ugly things."

"Men don't always make the best decisions when it comes to admitting they're in love. Stop thinking about what he said. Start thinking about how he's treated you since you met him. That's what his heart is telling you, even if his mouth is lying."

How had Gavin treated her? She'd been so hurt by his slurs that she'd almost forgotten everything else between them.

He'd trusted her with a job she hadn't been entirely qualified for. He'd been patient and kind while she learned. When she'd been rear-ended on the freeway, she'd called Gavin to let him know she would be late to work. Minutes later, he'd appeared at the scene, just as the police were taking her statement. He'd lifted all the responsibility off her shoulders, including getting her car towed and driving her to work while it was in the shop.

Gavin didn't do that for all his employees.

She also bet he hadn't put his last secretary on his piano and made love to her like he was a dying man and she was the only one who could save him. She could be pregnant with his child right now…and a part of her didn't hate that idea. At the time, all she'd been able to think about was getting closer to him. Because she loved him. Maybe Gavin had been under the same spell.

And maybe she was making excuses for him because the alternative hurt too badly.

"It doesn't matter," Hannah said with a sad sigh. "He might have feelings for me, but he won't face them."

And she wouldn't come between him and his brothers. Her own family had been so fractured that she couldn't stand being the reason Slade, Dex, and Gavin fought.

Would Slade and Dex accept her goodbye? She doubted it. They would probably be on the next plane to Texas once they figured out she'd gone. They would hunt her down. Because they loved her.

Was it too late? Had she already come between them and Gavin? Was she giving up Dex and Slade for nothing?

"I'm not being very smart about this, am I?" Hannah asked Marnie.

"Walking away isn't the answer, girl."

"I don't know what to do." Hannah's misery washed over her. There was a big part of her that wished none of this had happened. Then she would just be at home, cuddled up with her cat, continuing to dream about her men.

But that was no longer an option. So now what? She'd always thought that love would be easy-breezy and bring her nothing but joy. Nope. It was hard, like everything in life. Maybe harder because it was so precious. Yet, she hadn't fought for it at all. She'd gotten almost everything she wanted, and now she was willing to throw it all away because it wasn't quite perfect enough?

Marnie leaned across the bar, propping her chin on her fist. "Do you think you gave Gavin any reason to push you away?"

She shook her head, fighting tears as she remembered that horrible scene. "No. He had no reason to talk down to me that way. Bastard."

He'd treated her like an annoying pest when all she'd done was offer him comfort. Well, and a blowjob. She'd given the man her very first blowjob. Shouldn't that count for something? Yes. But she hadn't fought, hadn't told Gavin how his words made her feel. She hadn't stood up for herself.

She pounded a fist on the bar.

"Now, you're getting mad." Marnie grinned. "That's the reaction you should have had."

The woman was right. Gavin had been a total jerk to her. Why had she cried over him and been willing to walk away from two men who did treat her right? She knew he was hurting, but that didn't give him the right to hurt others. Why should she give up her future with Dex and Slade because Gavin wanted to wallow in the past?

"Hey, Marnie, why'd you have to go and do that?" Six-foot-five-guy frowned. "She was real sad. Sad women are easier to comfort than mad ones. Now we ain't ever going to get her to come back to our place."

"You step one inch closer to her and your place is going to be a pine box six feet under," a low voice threatened.

Afternoon sunlight slanted in through open saloon doors. Slade, Dex, and Gavin stood in the doorway, looking like gunslingers about to start an Old West-style fight. Hannah's heart took a nosedive.

Individually, they were gorgeous. Together, they were positively heart-stopping.

Not one of them had on their usual, expensive suit. Instead, they all wore jeans and cotton shirts that proved they were far more rugged and male than the average executive. Slade was long and lean and bulged in all the right places. His face had such beautiful angles, it looked chiseled. Those blue eyes were sharp with intelligence. And under it all, a barely concealed power that pulled at her.

Dex was all dangerous cowboy. He was built more like a linebacker than his brothers. His biceps were huge and that cut torso of his tapered into a lean waist and the finest butt she'd ever had the joy to see on a man.

And Gavin looked like a fallen angel. His face was all kinds of stunning, which matched his body. Those lips of his, so skilled, so demanding, just unraveled Hannah completely. She couldn't help but think about how it had felt to have those lips on her skin, loving her.

None of them looked very loving now, though. As they stared down the crowd, they looked ready to kill.

All the other men froze.

"Now, Dex," Gavin said in that smooth-as-silk voice of his, "I don't think we need to spend the money on a pine box. We'll just toss his carcass off the mountain or let the bears take care of it."

Hannah slid off her barstool and faced them. It was time to start putting her dainty foot down. "You have no right to talk to them that way. You don't own me,

Gavin James."

Slade stepped forward and grabbed her arm. His grasp was gentle but unmistakably firm. "He might not own you. But we damn sure do."

"Damn straight." Dex crossed his arms over his massive chest and pinned her with a dark stare.

Hannah narrowed her eyes. "Do you have any idea how arrogant the two of you sound? I'm not a piece of property. No one *owns* me. Let's get that straight right now."

Dex shook his head. "You became ours when you gave yourself to us, darlin'. There's no going back."

"And you've earned some swats from all of us for leaving without explanation, except that little note on your computer," Slade said, his voice taking on that dark, deep tone that let her know she was in trouble.

Hannah turned to see if any of her admirers planned to back her up. Only Marnie stood behind her.

"They left the minute the James Gang walked in the door," Marnie murmured. "They ran out the back."

"Good to know they have survival instincts." Gavin snorted. "Get ready to feel my hand on your ass, sweetheart."

He stood in between his brothers, as though he had some sort of right to be there.

Hannah fumed. "I might be willing to hear this from Slade and Dex. Maybe. But why are you here, Gavin? You're no longer my boss. I quit, remember? You denied being my lover or having any feelings for me, so what I do is none of your business. You certainly can't threaten to spank me."

"Oh, I'll do more than threaten once we get all this settled." Gavin raised a brow, then his expression

193

gentled. "Hannah, I didn't mean a word of anything I said this afternoon. I'm willing to do whatever it takes to prove that."

His words made her pulse jump, but Hannah hesitated. She had to be careful that she didn't misunderstand him. "If you're just trying to hire me back, the answer is no."

Gavin smiled, looking supremely amused. "I loved having you as my assistant, and I'd hire you again in a heartbeat. But baby, my interest in you right now isn't at all professional. I'll be happy to prove it, starting with that spanking."

She managed to hold in a gasp—barely. "You don't touch me. I don't want you anymore."

"Yes, you do."

"Now you think you're reading my mind?" Hannah thrust her hands on her hips, her expression all but daring him to claim he was psychic.

"No, your nipples are telling me everything I need to know."

Hannah gasped. She glanced down. Sure enough, the little traitors were standing straight up, poking out from behind her shirt. Hastily, she crossed her arms. "It's an involuntary reaction. It doesn't mean I want you."

"I want you, baby. You said that you care about me. I admit, I care about you." He stepped closer. "Now tell me, do you want me?"

His voice had become a deep, male caress. Hannah actually felt more blood rushing to her nipples...and down between her legs, making it hard to think. Why was Gavin pushing this? Had he truly had a change of heart or was this some new game?

"I don't know." *A huge lie.* Hannah bit her lip. But darn it all, she wasn't ready to confess everything in her heart again only to have it thrown in her face.

"Boys, do you think she wants me?" Gavin slanted gazes to Dex and Slade, who flanked her in an instant. Dex grabbed her free arm and reached for the hem of her skirt.

"What are you doing?" she screeched as he lifted her skirt to her thighs. "This is a public place!"

"Everyone's gone, including Marnie. She just slipped out the back."

Of course the woman would choose her "boys" over someone she met less than an hour ago, but still, with Marnie went her last hope for an ally.

A second later, it didn't matter because Slade had popped the buttons of her blouse open, exposing her hard nipples, and Dex's fingers skimmed the embarrassingly wet folds of her pussy. She caught her breath then moaned when he grazed her clit.

Flashing her a wicked smile, Dex withdrew his fingers and held them up for Gavin. "Would you look at that. All pretty and very, very wet."

"I think I've made my point," Gavin drawled.

She smacked Slade's hands away and folded the edges of her blouse back together as she twisted away from Dex. Her skirt fell to her knees. "That was for your brothers," she told Gavin. "They were touching me. My arousal has nothing to do with you."

Gavin paused, shrugged. "Okay, then. I'll just sidle your way and see if I can make you come. That should prove something."

It absolutely would. She'd melt quickly into a puddle at his feet. Then he'd know he could play with her anytime he wanted, and her body would respond. Maybe she should stop fighting him and just ask what the hell he wanted.

"Fine. I want you. I admit it. What's the point?"

"The point is, things aren't right between us. We have to talk."

"Please, just listen." Slade turned to her and sighed. "Gavin has a few things he wants to say to you."

Gavin had already said enough. She'd been hauled bodily to Alaska, forced to miss her visit with her grandmother. She'd had her cell phone taken away. She'd lost her virginity and her ability to wear underwear. Gavin had ripped her heart out, forced her to admit that she wanted him, and *now* he had something to say? Marnie had told her to get mad. Well, she was mad.

Hannah picked up her shot glass and threw it straight at Gavin's head. "I'm not listening."

"Fuck," Gavin cursed as the shot glass whizzed past his head and smashed against the wall behind him, shattering.

Hannah reached for another on the bar nearby. Gavin strode toward her, the promise of punishment ripe in his eyes. She threw the glass in her grip. It pulled left again.

Slade and Dex seemed content to just watch the whole thing play out with barely repressed smiles.

"Hey, Gavin, before you spank her, you *did* promise to grovel." Dex leaned against the bar.

Gavin's eyes narrowed. "I can't grovel if she's throwing shit at my head."

"You, groveling? Ha!" Hannah reached for a

nearby glass tumbler and raised it over her head. If she was having trouble with the smaller missiles, she'd go bigger. "That'll never happen."

Hannah aimed carefully. She would only get so many chances before Slade or Dex put a stop to her retribution.

"If you're going to hit him, aim for the face, darlin'," Dex said. "He's going to be tender there."

"Absolutely," Slade agreed. "Dex and I both slugged him earlier today."

"Why did you hit Gavin?" And now that she thought about it, why had they allowed her to pitch fastballs at their brother's head. It wasn't like them. One of them should have had her over their knee before she could let the first one fly. Yet here they stood, watching as she took out her frustrations on the barware.

"For a couple of reasons," Slade explained. "First, he should never have said the things he said to you."

"He told you?" Why would he have told them? If he'd really been trying to push her away, he should have used the opportunity to shove a wedge between her and his brothers.

"I told them everything, sweetheart." Gavin stood up, the look on his face so regretful that Hannah put the glass down. She hadn't really looked at him before. She'd simply reacted to his presence. His handsome face was slightly swollen on his left jaw, and his right cheek, near his eye, had started to swell.

"Dex hit him for what he said to you. I hit him for not using a condom," Slade explained.

Dex's eyebrows climbed up his forehead. "He did *what*?"

Hannah set down the wine glass and held up a hand. "Stop. Back off on the barbarian act." She turned back to Gavin. "Why did you tell them?"

"I was confessing at the time. Everything." Gavin stared at her. She could feel his will pounding at her. "I told my brothers all the mistakes I've made. Pushing you away was one of the stupidest."

"Why do you think that?"

"Because I love you, Hannah."

She was suddenly just tired. "I'm sorry, Gavin, but I don't know if I can trust you. I believe that you *think* you mean what you're saying. I can even believe that you have feelings for me, but I'll always be a country girl with a community college education. I can't change that. I won't ever really care about the stuff those society women do, like fashion designers or what kind of car I drive. I can't be the kind of wife you need."

"You're exactly the kind of wife I need." Gavin closed the last few steps between them. "Loving. Kind. Smart. Loyal. Hannah, I can't imagine loving another woman the way I love you. I screwed this up. I just hope you'll give me a second chance."

She wanted to, but he'd battered her heart pretty badly.

Dex's phone trilled. He cursed under his breath as he pulled it out and answered it. "It's the site. I'll be right back."

Dex stepped away. Slade's hands came out to cup her shoulders. "Hannah, he's been scared. Please give him a chance. He really is crazy about you, just like I know you are about him."

Gavin was willing to admit he cared about her

right now, but what happened when people questioned him? And how was the relationship supposed to work? If Gavin was ashamed of her for her background, how was he going to react when people got wind of his ménage relationship?

Dex strode back into the room, his face pale. He clutched the phone tightly. "That was the one of the sheriff's deputies. They found Preston dead. He apparently hanged himself in one of the conference rooms."

Slade's hands dropped. "Dear God. What… I escorted him off the premises. How did he get back inside?"

Hannah hadn't much liked Preston Ward III, but she certainly hadn't wanted him dead.

"I don't know. Maybe he wanted to make a statement." Dex turned to Hannah. "We fired him earlier today. We think he might have been your stalker. Damn it. I need to go to the site."

Slade stepped close to Dex. "I'll go with you. I'm the one who fired him. He didn't take it well, but I never expected this."

"It wasn't your fault," Hannah said, wrapping her arms around him. "His wife had left him recently, too. There could be a lot of reasons he chose this."

She could feel the coiled tension in Slade's body, but he hugged her close. Dex came around her back and held her. She was surrounded by their warmth.

"We'll talk about it later," Slade replied. "I would feel safer if you went home with Gavin. You don't have to talk to him. Just don't beat him to death."

"Please, Hannah." Dex's hand tangled in her hair. He tilted her head up, twisting her slightly, brushing his lips against hers. "Give him a chance."

She nodded. She couldn't tell them no. She kissed Slade and they left.

Hannah was left alone with the man who'd broken her heart.

Chapter Twelve

Gavin turned the Jeep onto the road that led home. The gravel crunched beneath the wheels. His brothers were going to have a fun time coming home in the golf cart on these rustic roads. It was a testament to Hannah's desire to be away from him that she'd managed to drive to town in the miniature vehicle.

He glanced at the woman beside him. Her beautiful face was set in stubborn lines, her focus firmly on the road ahead. She hadn't looked at him once since they'd left the Angry Moose. Gavin sighed. Of all the people he'd hurt with his refusal to forgive himself, he regretted Hannah the most.

God, he hoped he hadn't lost his chance with her.

"Hannah, I would really like to talk to you."

"I'm not sure it would do any good," Hannah said. Her West Texas drawl always deepened when she got serious. That twang dripped now as she spoke. "I think we've said just about all we have to say."

"That's not true. I told you a bunch of lies meant to protect myself. Will you let me explain?"

She hesitated, and after a halting nod, Gavin went on. "In college, I met this girl named Nikki…"

He explained the entire story, every terrible detail,

including his failure to act on her suicide threat. When he finished, the car was dead silent. She was probably judging him, and he deserved it, but Gavin wasn't ready to give up. It had taken a lot of courage to tell someone with a heart as big as Hannah how small he'd been in the past.

Finally, she said, "It wasn't your fault. Nikki made a choice. I'm sorry you've been living with so much guilt."

He breathed a sigh of relief. She didn't hate him. "I have utterly regretted my part in Nikki's death. And I've been convinced since you walked in my office and shook my hand that, while I might love you, I'd be poison to you. When you said you loved me, my first instinct was to push you away. But you just wouldn't be deterred, my lovely, stubborn girl."

She smiled softly, and the crushing weight began to ease off his chest.

"I promise, I didn't mean a word I said to you." His hands tightened on the steering wheel as he tried to figure out how to convince her of his sincerity.

She turned those green eyes on him. They were so big and pure. God, nothing he or his brothers could do would ever wipe away the innocence that seemed an innate part of Hannah.

"But on some level, you did mean it, Gavin. There was a lot of truth in those words. Otherwise, they wouldn't have hurt so much. I don't fit into your world. I don't even know that I want to. It's easier with Slade and Dex. They don't really care what others think."

Gavin sat back in the driver's seat with a sigh. Just because she was innocent didn't mean she wasn't wise. Hannah wouldn't fit easily into his world. She would always run the risk of being ridiculed. It would happen behind her back because he had the money and clout to hurt whoever rejected her, but he was too worldly to believe it wouldn't happen.

But Hannah was wrong about one thing. "You're mistaking political savvy for caring, sweetheart. I don't give a damn what anyone outside my family thinks. I am very good at corporate politics, but they don't mean anything to me. Outside of work, none of that matters."

He would never go to another party, charity event, or social gathering if it meant making Hannah miserable.

"But all you do is work, Gavin. That's your whole life."

It had been, until he'd realized how important she was to him. Now he wanted something so different. He'd chosen his executive team carefully. Black Oak Oil could do with less micromanaging from him and still run like a well-oiled machine.

Gavin tentatively reached out and put his hand over hers. She didn't wrap her fingers around his hand, but she didn't move away, either.

"You've made me realize that I want something different. I've proven myself as a CEO. Now I want to prove to you and my brothers that I can be a good husband and someday, hopefully, a father."

She slanted her gaze his way and pulled her hand back. Gavin missed its warmth. "After this afternoon, someday might come around sooner than you think. I'm not sure I'm ready for that. I'm not sure you are, either."

He let his hand find the steering wheel again. He'd dug a very deep hole with Hannah. He needed to patiently fill it back in. "I *am* ready. If you're pregnant—and even if you're not—I want to prove to you that I'll be here every step of the way. We'll all be here for you."

Because he and his brothers were in this together, he wouldn't have to worry about Hannah or their children if anything ever happened to him. Dex and Slade would protect and shelter her and the kids. They would pick her up if she was down. No way would his tragic history repeat itself with her.

Something warm and infinitely secure settled in Gavin's heart. It felt so right. This was exactly the family he wanted, three planets rotating around one beautiful sun—with lots of little moons to follow.

"If I have a baby, and he's not biologically yours, I won't let you turn your back on him."

Hannah's words hit him straight in the gut. She really believed he'd abandon her or any of her children? Of course, what else would she think after hearing his part in Nikki's death? His satisfaction and rosy outlook for the future dissipated. A million gut-wrenching worries rushed to the surface. How could he convince her that he'd changed?

He raked his hand through his hair then pinned her with an earnest stare. "Never. I will never put myself before you again. I will never turn away if you or one of the children needs me. I know it must seem like I would after hearing about Nikki, but I really didn't think she was serious or pregnant. Please believe me."

The long silence nearly sliced him in two. He had way more fences to mend with her than he'd believed. What the hell was he going to do?

"Gavin?" Her voice trembled and went straight to

his heart.

God, he was afraid to look at her if her opinion of him was that low. But he'd promised just moments ago to be there for her. He couldn't renege now. He faced her.

Her eyes were wide, pooling with unshed tears. "I'm sorry you had to live with that. I'm sorry you've been hurting. The man I know would never abandon his own child—or anyone else's." Hannah shook her head, her blonde hair brushing her shoulders. She reached for his hand, and he gave it to her. "When you found out Dex existed, you moved heaven and earth to find him. You paid for his college, gave him a good job, and brought him into your family. Many people wouldn't have done half so much."

"I couldn't leave him there. He's my brother. I just wish I'd known sooner."

Gavin remembered walking into the dingy house where Dex had lived for the last year of his stay in foster care. More like confinement. The house had been filthy. His foster mother had cared far more about herself and her damned dogs than the kids in her care. Before Dex could even say hello, Gavin had tossed a wad of cash at the woman and packed his brother up in the Benz. Everything Dex had owned fit into a grocery sack.

"Of course." She squeezed his hand. "You mean the world to him."

"I haven't always done a good job of showing that I care for him, too."

"You'll be a great father, Gavin."

"I'll do my best every day. I can't promise everything will be perfect, Hannah. I can only promise that I'll try. You'll get everything I have to give, if you give me a chance."

She sniffled and released him, then folded her hands together in her lap. He wanted to hold her, but he hadn't earned the right yet. "Can I think about it for a while?"

At least she wasn't saying no. Or blaming him for the deaths of Nikki and their unborn child. Or throwing things at him.

He wouldn't admit it to her, but she'd been hot as hell when she was mad. Hannah in a fury had done all sorts of things to his cock. Even as he'd ducked, all he'd been able to think about was throwing her on the pool table and fighting his way inside her.

"Of course, sweetheart. Take all the time you need. I want you to be sure."

The house loomed ahead. He wished the drive was longer. Even with all the tension between them, he enjoyed just sitting with her.

He sincerely hoped that Preston had been Hannah's stalker. If so, with him dead, she would finally be safe, and he and his brothers could all concentrate on loving her. Gavin knew he should feel something for his former CIO, but after the way he'd treated Hannah, Gavin merely wished he'd gotten a piece of him before he'd taken the coward's way out.

If the threat to Hannah was gone, they had no reason to rush back to Dallas. He hadn't taken a vacation in years. Maybe they could keep Hannah captive just a bit longer.

With a grin, he thought about the items his brothers had brought. Whips and handcuffs and paddles, not to mention vibrators, nipple clamps, and that pretty pink anal plug—all the things a Dom would need to torture and pleasure a pretty little submissive. The idea of Hannah in nipple clamps, bound and trussed for his pleasure, really turned him on. Because it would be the woman he loved truly trusting him in every way.

"I don't like that mischievous look on your face." She frowned, lips pouting.

He'd like to shove his rock-hard cock past those plump lips. "Which look is that, sweetheart?"

"You remind me of a wolf about to eat a fuzzy little bunny."

His dick twitched. If she knew just how predatory he felt, she might jump out of the car. "Thanks to my brothers, the little bunny I'm thinking of tasting right now isn't fuzzy anymore."

Hannah gasped and turned the most perfect shade of red. "Gavin…"

"I barely got the time to look earlier. Am I right?"

As he parked the car, Hannah stayed utterly silent. Finally, she turned, wearing the naughtiest grin on her face. "This bunny might not be fuzzy anymore, but she is hopping away. For now."

She opened the door and slid out. Gavin followed, watching her ass sway.

Their talk had been more promising than he could have hoped. She hadn't condemned him, hadn't judged. Her understanding warmed his heart and made him more certain than ever that Hannah was the perfect woman for him. Gavin prayed like hell that he'd get his second chance.

* * * *

Slade's stomach turned as he looked down at Preston's body. On the surface, the man didn't look so terribly different from the one he'd fired just hours before. He wore the same suit. His eyes were closed, but he lay too still to be merely sleeping. There was nothing left of Preston Ward in the vessel that lay before him. He was a cold, dead being.

"That's him." Slade forced himself to acknowledge Preston's identity. He was relieved when the sheriff pulled the sheet back over the man's lifeless face.

The sheriff nodded shortly. Mike Akna was a quiet but professional man. As far as Slade knew, he'd never had to handle a case like this. River Run was hardly a hotbed of activity, but Mike radiated a competence that earned Slade's trust.

"Thanks, Mr. James. We knew who it was, but paperwork demands a formal identification of the body. We have witnesses who say you and Mr. Ward had an argument earlier today."

"I fired him and told him to fly back to Dallas, if that's what you mean."

"Did you or did you not threaten to kill him?"

Slade felt his eyebrows raise. He looked to his younger brother.

"I thought this was a suicide," Dex asked. "When your deputy called, he said Preston had hanged himself."

Mike held Dex's stare, gripping a notebook in his hand. "Someone wants me to believe that."

Slade's stomach plummeted to his knees. "I didn't kill anyone."

Dex thumped a hand across his chest to shut him up then slipped into professional mode. "What was the time of death?"

Slade thought if Gavin hadn't offered Dex a cushy job, he would have made a damn fine homicide detective.

"No TOD yet. Doc's not here to take a liver temp. I have a timeline, though. The last time anyone talked to the victim was 2:35 p.m. Preston called the two techs he'd brought with him from Dallas, Scott Kirkwood and Lyle Franklin, and advised them to make arrangements to return home."

"He'd been fired," Slade ground out. "That wasn't his call."

"And they stayed put here for that very reason, according to Ben Kunayak. Ben said that Preston was madder than a wet hen when you threw him out of the office, not depressed. In the parking lot, security heard him shouting that he was going to call Gavin and demand his job back or sue."

"Did you check Preston's cell?" Slade asked. "Had he called Gavin?"

"I found his cell, but it was demolished." The sheriff pointed to a table off to the side. Slade could see the decimated phone. It didn't just look broken, but like someone had tried to disintegrate it.

"Is the SIM card inside?" The SIM card would tell them who Preston had called. Slade stepped toward the table, but Dex put a hand out.

"Don't touch it. Chain of evidence is important. If this isn't a suicide, then we don't want to fuck up the evidence since you might be the prime suspect in a murder investigation."

Dex always knew how to put things as succinctly as possible. Slade looked to the sheriff, who solemnly nodded his head.

"You're involved, either way," Mike explained. "He was your employee, and you had an altercation with him shortly before his death. I am definitely going to need a statement. Now, rumor has it that you and both of your brothers were at Marnie's recently, and there was quite a scene. This man hasn't been dead for long. There's no rigor, and his body was still warm when we tried to revive him. I think the TOD will clear you, but we have to go through the motions first. And you're right, the SIM card is missing. There are also some signs of struggle."

"I punched him before his death," Slade admitted. "That should account for the bruising on his face."

Mike nodded, jotting a few notes. "Thanks, but there's more. Quite frankly, his skin isn't the right color for a hanging. I don't believe for a second this man died of asphyxiation. This room has an eight foot ceiling, not high enough for the long fall necessary to break someone's neck. Yet it appears that's what happened. It takes more force than you would guess to kill a man that way. None of this adds up."

Dex looked around the room. The belt that had been used in the hanging still swung from the ceiling. "How did he get up there? Did you move a chair? A table?"

Mike wiped a hand across his face and looked like he would really rather be fishing. "That would be question number three. Nothing has been moved except the body, and that was only moved in an attempt to revive him. Ben took him down and tried CPR, but he was gone."

Slade came to several conclusions, none of them pleasant. Preston hadn't been the tallest man, maybe five foot nine inches. The ceiling was at most eight feet. He would have needed something to lift him to the right height. "So unless he jumped, then someone helped him up there. That means someone killed Preston because he knew something or did something."

"Anything going on at Black Oak that I should know about?" Mike asked. "Any takeover attempts? Corporate espionage?"

Corporate politics could be nasty, but Black Oak Oil was solid. They weren't developing anything another company would want. They were in the business of finding oil and refining it. Slade had a bad feeling that this wasn't about Black Oak Oil at all. This was about Hannah. Everything had been about her, he suspected, like the virus being uploaded to the site. Someone had followed his obsession over three thousand miles. That was sick dedication.

Someone had watched Hannah much more closely than they'd imagined.

"Where are the techs, Scott and Lyle?" Slade asked, his voice hoarse.

He ran through the series of events and came to one conclusion: The murderer—and Hannah's stalker—had to be one of them. Lyle had been in the office when Dex had carried Hannah out. Scott had planned an "important" lunch with her that very day. Gossip being what it was, either could have easily found out where he and his brothers had taken her. Either could have uploaded the virus.

"As far as I know, they're at the lodge. I was going

to head over there and talk to them as soon as we wrapped everything up here. They can't go anywhere until tomorrow. The only way out is by plane, and Jimmy is passed out, according to Marnie," Mike explained.

Whichever tech was the guilty party, he wouldn't want to leave. He would still want Hannah—quickly—before anyone had time to figure out that Preston had been murdered and who'd been the culprit. Reaching Hannah meant traveling to the house. Anyone with access to a car could do that.

His blood running cold, Slade punched in Gavin's number. He would tell his older brother to take Hannah into the mountains. Gavin knew that terrain in a way Scott and Lyle wouldn't. Hunting cabins dotted the mountainside. Anyone who wasn't familiar with the area would need a map to find them. She would be safe. Gavin would shoot anyone who came her way.

But damn it, the call wasn't connecting. Poor signal all of a sudden. His phone was useless.

"I can't get a signal." Panic threatened to overtake him. He picked up the nearest landline and dialed the house.

After ten rings, he gave up. Dex stared at him as though willing Slade to give him good news.

Slade wished he could lie. "He isn't answering."

Dex swore. "I'm not wasting time. I'm going after her."

Slade agreed. "Sheriff, we're going to need to borrow a car."

* * * *

Hannah left the bathroom feeling a bit more relaxed. She'd showered and finally taken that darn plug out. She'd likely get in trouble for removing it, but she seriously doubted that Dex or Slade had intended that she wear it all day.

Besides, she wouldn't really mind the spanking she would get. In fact, she might actually like it.

Hannah Craig liked spankings. *Bye bye, good girl.*

But maybe enjoying a good spanking didn't make her a bad girl. Maybe it just made her honest with herself. She'd spent so much of her life trying to be what everyone around her expected that she'd forgotten to just be her.

As hard as she might try, Hannah couldn't see anything really wrong with loving three men. They weren't hurting anyone. Why did there have to be a boundary on love?

She didn't bother to close the curtains as she walked into the bedroom suite. Someone had left them wide open, and the big bay windows offered an amazing view of the mountains. Alaska was stunning. It was such a change from the big city and encroaching summer heat of Texas. Everything seemed lush and vibrant in air so fresh and crisp that it was a joy to breathe.

She felt truly alive for the first time in her life. Being in Alaska helped that feeling, but it was more about her men. Was she really going to let that feeling go because she was mad at Gavin? Yes, he'd said some ugly things. But the Lord above knew that she'd said some things in the past that she'd regretted. She didn't think Gavin would hurt her again. And if he did, Dex and Slade would kick him back in line.

The sun streamed through the windows, and Hannah opened the French doors that led to the patio with a smile. She was only dressed in her robe, but there wasn't anyone around to see her.

It was nice to be alone for a minute. If those boys had their way, it wouldn't last for long.

She breathed in the slightly chilly air and thought seriously about dropping the robe to feel the breeze on her skin. If she did, the brothers would find her that way, lounging naked on the patio, reveling in her newfound sensuality. Dex would be the first to attack her, and Slade would follow, their hands, lips, and tongues roaming her body feverishly.

She would look up, and Gavin would be watching, waiting to see if she would let him in.

Making love with him would be a nice way to let him know she was willing to talk. Well, maybe not to talk, but she was willing to try. She couldn't let her fear rule her. If Gavin walked out again, then she would deal with it. That was a risk every woman took.

Her hand grasped the tie of her robe. She was just about to let it drop when she heard a voice.

"Hannah?"

She looked up—and realized that she wasn't so safe here after all.

Chapter Thirteen

"Scott?" Hannah blinked, unable to believe he'd come here and found his way to the patio beside her bedroom. Why would he do that? He'd been desperately trying to see her the day the James Gang had dragged her off to Alaska. She could only think of one reason he'd come now.

He was her stalker.

Hannah took a step back, panic flooding her system. She was brutally aware that she was alone. The quiet of the afternoon, once so peaceful, now felt ominous. She glanced over her shoulder, past her bedroom, to the empty hallway. Where was Gavin?

"I'm so glad I found you." Scott sighed. "I feel like I walked miles to get to you. But I couldn't stop. I had to see you. Hannah, I need to talk to you." Scott's face was bunched up, some unnamed emotion animating him. He looked young and slightly vulnerable standing there with the early evening light lighting up his pale hair like a halo. But it was all an illusion.

"If you wanted to talk to me, you should have given me a call." Of course, it wasn't as if she and Scott were best friends. A phone call would have been suspicious. If he had, that likely would have tipped her off. Or if she hadn't grasped his guilt right away, one of her hovering men would have.

She wished those men were here now. Slade and Dex were back in River Run investigating Preston's suicide. Or had his death been suicide at all? Hannah nibbled nervously on her bottom lip as all kinds of possibilities rolled over her. Had Scott killed Preston? How far was he willing to go to take her?

Would Gavin be able to hear her if she screamed?

"I tried to call. I can't get cell service." Scott's gaze bounced all over, clearly skittish. "I think he's blocking it. There are several ways to block local signals. He's way smarter and more devious than I gave him credit for."

Hannah looked back to the French doors. Could she make it through them and into her bedroom before he caught her?

If she hadn't been so damn stubborn, she would have been with Gavin, talking through their problems.

"Where's Mr. Townsend? I tried the front door, but no one answered. I really need to talk to him, or Mr. James. Hannah there's something you need to know."

Hannah stopped and let his words sink in. "You tried the front door?"

Scott nodded. "Yeah. I knocked. I didn't, like, open it or anything. This is a rich folks' place. You never know, they might release the hounds or something. I thought maybe everyone had come out back, but...Hannah, someone's after you."

"I know." She couldn't keep the fear from her voice.

"Oh, crap. You think it's me." Scott shook his head and held his hands up, showing her he'd come unarmed.

"Well, you're here, not in Dallas where you're supposed to be. The whole reason Slade, Dex, and Gavin brought me up here was to escape this stalker."

"That makes sense. I was on my way to your office to pick you up for an early lunch so I could warn you when I saw your…exit. But he saw it, too. An hour later, a virus had crashed the River Run facility. So I volunteered for this assignment, hoping I'd get a chance to see you and—"

"Who saw my exit? Who are you trying to warn me about?"

"Lyle."

The truth washed over her. Lyle Franklin. She'd met him her first day on the job. He'd brought her laptop and helped her set it up. He was the head of the help desk, but he'd found time to help a new girl out. He'd been patient with her. She'd heard rumors that he was difficult to work with, but brilliant when it came to systems upkeep and repair. She'd never found him difficult. Anytime she'd had trouble and called the help desk, he'd come personally.

At the time, she'd thought he'd taken care of her because she was the boss's admin. There wasn't an employee at Black Oak who didn't want Gavin James to owe him or her a favor. She'd had lunch with Lyle on a couple of occasions in large groups, but turned him down for dinner because it had seemed too much like a date, and she hadn't wanted to lead him on. She'd never felt anything beyond vague friendship for the lanky, self-conscious man.

How much had he hidden from her?

"I think I should go and find Gavin." Hannah knew she needed to be cautious. She wasn't about to fully trust anyone except her men. She would go and get Gavin, and they could talk to Scott together.

Unless Scott was lying to gain her trust. Then he wouldn't let her move an inch off this patio.

She backed toward the French doors, easing closer to them. She would lock them behind her and find Gavin. They could get the sheriff, who could sort out everything in a nice, safe interrogation room where all the employees had guns and the right to shoot people.

That sounded like a plan.

"That's a good idea, Hannah." Scott's voice had taken on a soothing quality. He sat down at the patio table, carefully placing his hands on top. "Please tell Mr. James not to shoot me on sight. I get that you have to be cautious. I do. I'll wait here."

Hannah still didn't turn her back on him.

"And Hannah, if your computer's on, turn it off."

"Why?" She'd turned it on earlier in the day hoping to check her e-mail. It was still sitting open on the desk in her suite. She almost always left it up and ready to use.

"You have a webcam on that computer, Hannah. He's been watching you through it for months. It's how I figured out his scheme. Preston made us share a conference room back in Dallas for one of those installation task forces on Monday. Lyle left to go do something, and I was looking for a missing file. Instead, I saw videos of you."

"Me?"

Scott flushed a bit. "Yes. He has a ton of videos of

you. He's been watching you day and night. Some are just long videos of you lying around in your undies reading a book or talking on the phone. It looks like you're in the bedroom."

That bastard. He'd set up her computer. Lyle knew how computer illiterate she was. He'd told her she didn't need to know more, that he knew enough about computers for both of them. They had laughed about it at the time.

All along he'd been watching her, stalking her.

He'd been the one sending her threatening notes. He'd tried to kill her cat.

His expression earnest, Scott went on. "When that virus hit the site's computer, I knew someone with access and knowhow had uploaded it. Lyle fits the bill."

Everything Scott said made perfect sense.

"I'm going to go get Gavin. Don't go anywhere. I believe you, Scott. Thank you."

She was just about to turn when a bang cracked the air around her. Scott grunted, and his face became strangely blank. Red bloomed across his shirt.

Blood. He'd been shot.

"You're not going anywhere, Hannah." Lyle stepped from behind the house and pointed the gun at her.

Scott slumped forward, his head hitting the table with a nasty thud. Bile crawled up her throat.

Lyle Franklin stood roughly five feet seven inches tall. His hair was cut far too short for his round features. His eyes were too close together, giving him a slightly seedy look. His body was awkwardly thin, as though he'd never outgrown his teenage years and would never have the body of a man. But Hannah didn't doubt for a second that he could overpower her. His arms looked scrawny compared to her men's, but Lyle had already proven he had plenty of nerve and few qualms.

"Y-you killed him." Hannah couldn't believe he'd shot Scott right in front of her. How could he be lying there dead? She'd just been talking to him moments ago. Scott couldn't be much older than her. He should have had a whole lifetime to look forward to, but now, because he'd tried to help her, he'd taken his last breath.

"He was trying to keep us apart, dear. I can't allow that. How can I call myself your man if I let other men come between us?" Lyle lowered his arm, letting the gun rest at his side. But Hannah didn't doubt that he could have her in his sights in an instant.

She had to be careful. "Did you kill Preston, too?"

His small eyes softened, and he smiled as though inordinately proud. "I did it for you. I heard what he did to you, trying to force you to kiss him. I couldn't let him live after that. If I'd been there, I would have protected you, Hannah. That's what I do. I protect you."

By trying to kill her cat? By terrorizing her? She could try to reason with him, but she doubted negotiating with a lunatic would work. He was either here to rape or kill her—or both.

"In fact, I've been watching over you for a while now. I knew the moment I saw you that we were meant to be together. You felt it, too. Don't try to deny it. I saw the way you looked at me that day."

She barely remembered that day. Hannah wanted

to scream, but the trail of mayhem and murder was too long to risk making him angry. Heck, the proof of his evil was still warm and slumped over the patio table. She took a tentative step back.

Lyle's face hardened like he was about to explode in a tantrum. Unfortunately, his tantrum included a gun. "Don't run, dear. I'm done playing games with you. If you run, I'll chase you down. I want our first time together to be special."

Oh, God. She needed time. Her men would come for her. Sooner or later, Gavin would come looking for her. Slade and Dex would figure out her stalker's identity, and they would try to find her.

And Lyle would shoot them.

The thought of Gavin's big body slumped over, never to rise again, made her nauseous. Why hadn't she told him she loved him?

She loved all three of them, and she sure as hell wasn't going to let this deranged creep kill them.

Hannah looked around, seeking any sort of weapon she could use against him. Then she noticed Scott's body jerk slightly. His chest still moved up and down with shallow breaths. *Thank you, God!* He was still alive.

Lyle sighed and moved toward the man at the table. "Motherfucker. He's tougher than I gave him credit for."

Lyle lifted the gun.

"Don't," Hannah yelled. She couldn't stand there and watch him kill Scott.

Lyle's eyes narrowed. "You want to save him, Hannah? He wants to split us up."

"No, he just wanted to talk to me. You know, we

were supposed to have a meeting yesterday to talk about how the CEO can work better with his teams. It was just business." God, she hoped he hadn't heard much of their conversation.

His face turned vicious, and he gripped the gun more tightly. "You like your co-workers too much, Hannah. Didn't I tell you to stay away from those perverted brothers?"

Scott's previous words buzzed in her head. Lyle had watched her through the webcam. She'd had her computer open the night before. He might well have seen her give her virginity to Dex, then turn around and fully embrace Slade while Dex felt his way up her body and whispered hot encouragement.

"We should discuss this Lyle." If she could keep him talking, he'd be too busy to shoot people.

"The time to talk is over. I loved you, Hannah. I protected you. I was your angel." He heaved an angry sigh. "But you're just like the rest—a whore willing to spread her legs for rich men. Tell me something, Hannah. How could you let those perverts degrade you? Spank you and shove that…thing up your ass? I would have treated you like a princess. I wouldn't have let anyone else touch you. But they passed you around like a toy. How do you like being someone's live blow-up doll?"

"It wasn't like that." She tried to keep her voice calm. Scott's hand twitched. *Still alive.* How was she going to get him out of this before he bled to death?

He sneered. "I watched it. I heard it. It was disgusting. You let them turn you into a whore." Then his face fell, and he looked close to spilling furious tears. "I just…tried to love you."

222

Arguing with the crazy man holding a gun seemed very dangerous. "I know."

"I tried to save you. I knew what they were like."

She nodded. "You tried to tell me. I didn't understand. But I do now. I'm listening to every word."

He stared at her, his black eyes narrowing. "I didn't want to do it like this. I'd rather love you gently. But you don't like it that way, do you, Hannah? You're a little slut. I'm going to have to prove I'm more of a man than the three of them put together, aren't I?"

She didn't like the sound of that. "They won't let you take me."

"They're investigating Preston Ward's death. They won't be around for hours. I was surprised they left you here with the boss. I would have assumed they would protect their little slut, but maybe they're done with you."

He hadn't seen Gavin make love to her in the parlor. Lyle had no idea that Gavin would protect her. If she could just find a way to stall him and get help…

The cameras. During their brief tour of the estate yesterday, Slade had shown her the security cameras that dotted the estate. She let her eyes roam carefully as he continued on his diatribe. She was a whore, a slut, a bitch. That gun scared the hell out of her, and she couldn't stop trembling, but his words didn't touch her. She was loved. She was their woman, and anything she did with them was beautiful. Lyle was the perverse one.

There it was. A small, white camera pointed directly at her. It wasn't moving, but the red light was on. It was working. Of course, none of it mattered if Gavin wasn't watching. Even if he was, she feared that all he would see from that angle was her standing alone in the sunlight.

"Bitch, are you listening to me? Maybe I need to put another bullet in Scotty-boy to get your attention." Lyle put the gun to the back of Scott's head, and Hannah saw Scott tense. He wasn't as far gone as she'd feared. Scott had a chance to survive, but only if Hannah played her cards right.

And she really only had one card left.

"I heard you, Lyle. I just didn't understand everything. You didn't show yourself before. How was I supposed to know it was you? It could have been anyone."

The gun eased back, and he looked thoughtful. "I thought you would realize it was me. It was obvious."

She shook her head. "Not to me." *Not to anyone.*

"You're a lying, little whore. Why should I believe you?" A nasty grin came across his face. "I'll tell you what, Hannah. I'll let Scotty here live if you get in my car. We're going to go away, you and me. I'll show you a real man."

Oh, she couldn't get in that car. No way. No how. But if she got him away from Scott, she could run.

"A-all right." Her voice shook.

"It's not that easy, dear. First, I want a taste of what you've been giving the bigwigs. Take off the robe. Since you're a slut, you can ride without clothes. You didn't want to be my pure love? You can be my sex slave. I can beat you just like they did. I'll show you what kind of man I am."

Hiding her shudder, Hannah feared she already knew. He was a hateful misogynist who was so damaged, he would never heal. She wasn't sure what had warped Lyle's soul, and she didn't care. She only cared that he didn't kill anyone else.

Trembling, she let her hand find the tie on her robe. She'd wanted to be naked in the sunlight. She wanted to wait for her men to find her and love her.

Now she could only hope that they would save her.

* * * *

Gavin found just what he needed in the kitchen. Chamomile tea. Hannah'd had a rough day. He'd tried to back off, give her time and space. But leaving things unresolved between them was eating at him. He had to see her. So after a few minutes that had felt like months, he'd made her a nice cup of the steaming brew. It would give him an excuse to walk into her room. He'd listened in earlier and heard the shower running.

Trying to maim a man with shot glasses was dirty business. He wouldn't be surprised if Hannah was trying to unwind.

Maybe if he talked smoothly enough, he could coax her into resting her head on his shoulder. It would be an easy move to put an arm around her and hold her. That was all he wanted.

Bullshit.

His inner voice was back, but there was a marked change in it. Gavin found a saucer for the teacup as his new inner voice spoke to him.

You want to ease her back and kiss her. You want to show her you can be as tender as you were rough earlier. You want to prove you can be everything she needs. You can love her and protect her. You can change for her.

It isn't really change. It's getting back to who you are.

Gavin liked his new inner voice. He was surprised to find it sounded an awful lot like his Hannah.

He picked up the cup and started down the hall. He wasn't going to make love to Hannah right now, no matter how much he wanted to. He was going to hold her. The next time he made love to her, his brothers would be there. They would be a team, the way they were meant to be.

There was a distant ping, a sharp, familiar sound. Gavin had spent enough time in Alaska to know the sound of a gun firing. *Hunters?* They sounded awfully close to the house to be shooting big game.

There was a small room just off the kitchen that served as the housekeeper's office. It housed a computer and all the keys to the various buildings. Everything electrical in the house could be monitored from the office, including the security cameras.

Gavin let the teacup clatter to the desk as he flicked through the cameras. They had various views of the grounds. *Nothing, nothing...* His heart nearly stopped when he came to the feed for camera number four. Hannah stood on the patio outside the master bedroom. She wore a robe and faced the camera. Her hand was on the belt, and she slowly unknotted it.

A memory of Nikki assaulted his brain. She would fight him like a mad cat. Then she would tease him.

Just like Hannah was teasing him now.

Her hands fumbled as she released the tie. Slowly, very slowly, she brought her hands up to the lapels of the robe. He couldn't see her face clearly, but she seemed to be playing for the camera.

She took off her robe slowly, almost stiffly. To tease him even more? Her breasts came into view, nipples hard and pointed in the cool air. She looked beautiful...but then he noticed her tense expression, the terror in her eyes.

Gavin understood instantly. Hannah was nothing like Nikki. She hadn't invented a reason to fight merely for the drama. If she wanted to make up, she would tell him so straight to his face.

Hannah wasn't teasing him on camera; she was being forced.

The CB radio squawked, the sound jarring in the quiet room.

"Gavin. Gavin, this is Dex. Can you hear me? Please, God, hear me."

He picked up the radio, but he didn't take his eyes off the monitor. Who was just outside the camera's view? He prayed it was one of his brothers playing around with their soon-to-be wife.

"Dex, are you and Slade here on the grounds?" *Please say yes. Make this all a fun, little joke. I'll run out there and play with Hannah, too.*

"No, we're in one of the sheriff's cruisers," Dex shouted. "We're almost home, but you need to keep an eye on Hannah. Preston was murdered, and one of the techs is Hannah's stalker. I think it's Lyle. Slade noticed that he had scratches all over his arms. I have similar scratches from rescuing Mr. Snuggles. Is Hannah with you now?"

Gavin's heart felt like it was going to pound out of his chest. "No, but I think someone else might be. Hurry."

He tossed the radio down. He didn't have time to explain. He needed to get to Hannah.

After pulling out the key that opened the small gun cabinet, he yanked out a shotgun and quickly loaded it. He wasn't going to fail her.

Gavin ran down the hall and out of the house.

Chapter Fourteen

Gavin took a deep breath. The gun in his hand felt like an old friend. He silently thanked Marnie for teaching him how to use it years ago. She'd taken him and Slade hunting every summer when they were supposed to be learning accounting and how to work a rig. They'd learned those things, all right—but so much more. Most importantly, they had learned that they were brothers and could depend on one another, no matter what. Every time their father had tried to turn them into rivals, Gavin would remember bonding with Slade during those summers, teaching him the true importance of family for the first time. When Dex had come along, he'd become another brother to depend on, even if Gavin hadn't always shown it.

Now, he wanted his family to be one close-knit unit, sharing Hannah and her love.

As soon as he took out whoever threatened her.

He flattened his body against the brick and listened, trying to figure out the bastard's identity.

"You have a beautiful body, Hannah. Let the robe drop so I can see more than just your breasts. I want to know if that blonde hair of yours is real. I know how whores change their appearance to entice men."

Oh, he was going to kill that fucker. Gavin didn't care how or why this man had gotten so screwed up. No one was going to talk to Hannah that way.

Gavin peeked around the corner. Even from the back, he recognized Lyle from his severely short hair and his clothes. Goddamn the bastard.

Hannah stood with sunlight bathing her, clutching her robe around her waist, her green eyes flared with fear. She looked so young and vulnerable. So alone. She was his to protect. He couldn't let her down. He would rather die with her than live knowing he'd failed her.

"You're going to have some trouble figuring that out, but I'll tell you that I don't bleach my hair."

Hannah's sweet twang flowed over him. No panic in his girl. Her steady voice was music to his ears.

Gavin was a possessive man. He could share with his brothers, but anyone else was out of the question. Yet, he found himself willing Hannah to do whatever necessary to stay alive. No matter what, he would love her. And, in time, his unwavering love—and that of his brothers—would heal her.

Gavin edged around the corner and checked everyone's position. Hannah stood in the background. Lyle, the fucker, was roughly ten feet in front of her, with his back to Gavin. Another person sat at the table, head down on the wrought iron.

The other tech, Scott? He wasn't moving. Blood dripped slowly onto the stone patio. Maybe Lyle shooting Scott had been the noise Gavin had heard. If Lyle had already killed someone, then Gavin could fire at will—if he could just get Hannah out of his direct line of fire. As it was, if Gavin shot at Lyle and missed,

Hannah would suffer.

With a brief nod, he caught Hannah's gaze. Her bright green eyes widened. He willed her to do whatever she had to.

I love you, Hannah. He mouthed the words.

With a gaze that told him she understood his reassurance, Hannah dropped the robe, fully displaying her beautiful body. Then she jumped out of his line of fire.

It had the intended effect. Lyle cursed savagely and charged her, intent on attack. That left Gavin free to act.

Sucking in a calming breath, he stepped out from behind the house, aimed, and fired.

After a quick pull of the trigger, Lyle's body jerked. Then blood began soaking his shirt at the right shoulder. Hannah screamed and ran toward Gavin. But Lyle wouldn't let her go that easily. He lunged for her, catching her ankle in a death grip.

"You're staying with me, whore," he snarled.

Gavin's heart lodged in his throat.

"Let her go and you might live," he growled at Lyle, circling in front of the asshole and closing in.

"She's mine. If I go down, I'll take her with me." Lyle raised his gun with his free hand. A ghastly smile contorted on his face. "She's mine."

"No, she's not, motherfucker." Gavin didn't hesitate. He raised the shotgun and fired again. And again.

Finally, Lyle's grip loosened. Hannah broke free and ran for him. Gavin caught her in his arms just as he heard his brothers shouting from the driveway.

Hannah's arms twisted around him. "I'm so sorry.

I should have told you sooner, Gavin. I love you."

His heart swelled as he kept the gun trained on Lyle, just in case. "Baby, I love you, too. So much."

His brothers raced onto the patio. Dex kicked Lyle's gun away, then bent down, fingers on the tech's carotid. "Dead."

Gavin thought that perhaps he should feel bad that he'd taken a life, but all he felt now was profound relief. Peace and rightness followed when his brothers surrounded them. Their arms encircled Hannah.

Their woman was safe, and his family was finally complete.

* * * *

Hours later, Hannah walked into the house, her hands still trembling. She could still see Lyle's desperate face, feel the bite of his grip as he clutched her ankle, trying to drag her down with him. So much pain and anger had flared in his eyes just before Gavin had delivered the fatal blow. She'd never forget the rage bubbling in his expression just before he'd fallen back, dead. Hours later, she was still shaking.

"Hannah?" Slade inquired softly as he entered the room. "I thought you'd like to know, Scott made it to Anchorage. He's in surgery now, but the doctors said he's going to be fine. The bullet missed his lungs. If Lyle had shot him again..."

Lyle would have killed him, like he would have killed her in the end. Like he could have killed them all.

Slade's arms wrapped around her, pulling her into the comfort of his chest. "Baby, you can cry. Let it all out."

She allowed Slade to wrap her in his protective embrace. "I was so scared."

"I know. We all were. But you were magnificent, Hannah. You didn't panic. You held your ground and bought Gavin time to bring Lyle down ."

"I swear my life flashed before me when I saw you on that security monitor." Gavin stood in the doorway.

She sobbed, and it felt good to cry. She'd forced herself to be strong while they'd taken care of Scott and waited for an ambulance. She'd held it together at the sheriff's office as she had given her statement. Now, she wanted the comfort of their arms around her, but only Slade seemed willing to come near her. She didn't understand.

"Did you think I was doing something I shouldn't?" Hannah asked. When she'd stood in front of the camera, she'd known that Gavin would only be able to see her. What had he thought she was doing?

His flush told her all she needed to know. "For a moment, I thought you were teasing me, like Nikki used to."

Dex turned on his brother, his face going mulish and stubborn. "Asshole, she's nothing like Nikki."

"I know. And I figured out quickly that something was wrong."

But Gavin still hadn't held her since that moment when she'd run into his arms. After that, he'd picked up her robe and covered her, his touch almost impersonal. He'd found her skirt and blouse, but he hadn't offered to dress her. Nor had Dex. They were both so polite and distant.

She needed to feel alive—and loved. But Dex

merely leaned back against the wall, watching her, his eyes hooded with anxiety. Gavin held back, his face concerned, but he made no move toward her.

Slade smoothed back her hair and tilted her chin up to him. "I see that you need something, baby. Tell me what."

Hannah didn't hesitate. "All of you. Together with me."

She needed to lose herself in the pleasure they gave. She needed them surrounding her.

"Hannah, you've been through a lot." Gavin said one thing, but his eyes said another. They were eating her up, and her sex clenched at his hungry expression. So why wasn't he moving toward her?

"You should rest," Dex insisted softly, but he refused to look at her. "I can sleep in one of the other bedrooms. You need your rest tonight."

"I'll do the same," Gavin offered, the desire on his face dissipating. "And there's another room for Slade. I'll have it made up, too."

Slade's arms tightened around her. "I'm staying with Hannah."

He was the only one? The others didn't want her anymore? Her first instinct was to cry, but anger rose faster.

Before she could confront them, Slade stepped in. "You'd better explain yourselves, brothers. Or she might start throwing things again."

"Never mind." Hannah couldn't believe they were done with her. But if Dex and Gavin didn't want her, then she would take Slade and pour all her love into him. "We'll be fine on our own. They can sleep wherever they want. But they should go now because

I'm going to kiss you, Slade James. I want you."

A long, slow smile crossed his ridiculously handsome face. "I want you, too, baby. You wanna play?"

That sounded wonderful and mind-consuming. "Please."

"You want to play *now*?" Dex stared at her in disbelief.

"You heard the lady. Find your position, Hannah," Slade murmured. "And stop topping from the bottom."

Hannah fell to her knees. "I don't know what that means."

A low chuckle rumbled from Slade's chest as he touched her head. "It means you're trying to manipulate me to get what you want."

Hannah shrugged. She wasn't going to stop doing that. Slade would have to get used to that bottom topping thing.

"It makes you a bratty little sub," Dex said, his voice taking on the low growl that made Hannah's heart race. When he finally looked her way, his stare was hot and dark with the threat of sin.

"We agreed to give her time," Gavin said. But he was pushing away from the wall, closer, stalking her.

"Time to what?" Hannah shivered as they closed in.

They all could have died today. She didn't want to waste time. She just wanted to feel them.

Slade's hand tangled in her hair. The little bite of pain made her moan. "Are we playing?"

Hannah knew where he was going with this. "Yes, Sir."

"Then obey me. Your Masters need to talk. No

interrupting." He smiled. "Listen for a bit. You might learn something."

Maybe...but she'd probably have trouble keeping quiet. Even so, Hannah was done questioning whether she was capable of this relationship or good enough for them. She was exactly what these three men needed.

And she needed them. She needed the deep understanding and soul connection she'd found with Slade. She craved Dex's crazy alpha male dominance. And she wanted Gavin's duality. He was all smooth operator on the surface, but underneath he needed her more than the other two.

"She's been through a terrible ordeal. She's got to be traumatized. Do you really think she needs us to spank her and tie her up now?" Gavin asked.

That was exactly what she needed, especially if they brought out that spreader thingee. Hannah opened her mouth to tell them, but Slade's expression made her stop.

"I think Hannah has stated what she needs. I believe playing rough with her would reassure her that we're here for her in whatever way she needs." Slade sounded very reasonable. He always understood her.

"Lyle made her undress. We don't really know what else he did to her. How will we know if something we do will bring it all back?" Dex sounded tortured.

Hannah looked up at Slade, trying without words to make her needs plain.

Slade sighed. "Tell them. They won't believe me."

"He didn't do anything awful to me. Gavin got to him before he'd really laid a hand on me. I took off my robe because it bought me some time. I didn't like him looking at me, but even if he'd raped me, I would still be yours. I'd still need this. But you're hesitating. Should I be worried that you don't want me anymore? Maybe now that the danger is over and your protective instincts are down, you don't find me as appealing. If that's the case, then you should run along to your own beds."

She was very satisfied when Gavin's mouth dropped open and Dex's eyes narrowed.

"That's over-the-line bratty." Dex's body language changed. He popped his shoulders back and firmed his jaw. His demeanor went from hesitant to commanding in a heartbeat. "I don't like that, Hannah. What do you call me when we're playing?"

"Sir." She repressed a smile. Yes, she was probably going to top from the bottom a lot.

"I prefer Master, baby," he drawled. "And I have a few questions for you. Care to explain why you were alone outside the house when you had a stalker after you?"

Hannah bit her bottom lip. Put that way, it sounded a bit careless. "I was getting some fresh air and enjoying the sunlight."

"What were Master Gavin's instructions?" Dex barked.

Boy, when he decided to go into Dom mode, he went all the way.

"He told me to stay in the house. But I didn't really think about the patio not being a part of the house." She hadn't been thinking at all.

"I like the way Master Gavin sounds, Hannah." Gavin looked down at her, hovering close. "You'll call me that in the bedroom from now on. Let me hear it."

Hannah knew he was still worried about being on the outside. "Yes, Master Gavin."

"Did you disobey a direct order given for your safety?" Gavin growled.

She nodded, wincing. She might be in more trouble than she'd imagined. She suspected that her backside was about to get very sore.

"Hannah, pick a safe word." Dex touched her head, his hand stroking her. She couldn't miss the way his cock strained against his jeans.

They were all so worried about her. Only Slade understood that she needed them full throttle and hard to handle. And she needed them now. She wanted everything the James Gang could dish out.

"How about elephant? I promise to use it if things get to too tough to take, but I want something from you, too, Dex."

His eyes warmed. "I might be willing to grant you a favor, baby."

"Change your name."

He stepped back, scowled. "What?"

Dex might be shocked, but his brothers were smiling.

"We tried to convince him to do it, sweetheart." Slade's hands were on the buttons of his shirt.

"He refused because he said he didn't want the last name of the man who'd abandoned him," Gavin explained.

Hannah looked up at Dex. "But it's going to be my name, too. Unless you think I should keep mine. We could have a very modern marriage, keep everything separate."

"Hell, no. There isn't going to be any of that,

Hannah. You will take your husbands' name and that's that," Dex said with finality. "I'll talk to the lawyer tomorrow. We need to tell him to stop the mess Gavin started, too."

Slade knelt behind her and slid his hands under her shirt, slipping it off and exposing her to the chilly air and his brothers' heated gazes. He cupped her breasts, and she sighed in his arms. This was what she'd needed. She felt safer now that they surrounded her.

Gavin watched the hands on her breasts. "I don't believe I'll stop the distribution of stock, merely alter it. I'm going to split the company four ways. I think our wife should have a say, too."

Tears filled Hannah's eyes. "You can't do that. Gavin, I was ready to sign whatever prenuptial agreement you wanted."

His eyes hardened. "No, Hannah. This is going to work, and this is going to be your company, too. Do you understand?"

She nodded. They were giving her a great gift, but it went far past the monetary value. They were giving her a family she could count on. "I love you, all of you."

Gavin got to one knee and kissed her soundly. "I will never make you regret that."

"But I might," Dex said. "You've had all the concessions you're getting for the night. Now present that ass to your Masters for punishment."

"First, pass me the clamps. I want to see these nipples decorated." Slade pinched at them, rolling Hannah's nipples between his thumbs and forefingers.

Hannah tried not to squirm. She watched Dex walk to the small closet and pull out a box. Slade thumbed and twisted her nipples while Gavin tossed his shirt aside, exposing his wide, hard-muscled chest.

"I don't think they're hard enough yet." Gavin tweaked one of her nipples.

"Perhaps a little tongue play would get them where we need," Slade suggested.

"I was thinking the same thing." Gavin bent his head and sucked a hard tip into his mouth.

As he drew her nipple into his hot mouth, the sensation shot straight from her breast to her pussy. Hannah gasped. Gavin sucked hard, his teeth just grazing the edge of her flesh, lighting her up. He bit down gently as his hand found her thigh.

Dex knelt beside Gavin, a small piece of jewelry in his hand. He held it up for her perusal. "This is a clamp, Hannah. I'll clamp your nipples when you've been a bad girl, or simply because I want to decorate my gorgeous girl's body."

Hannah hissed a little as he pinched her free nipple, then clamped it. Gavin worked on her other nipple, sucking and laving it with affection. Then Dex clamped that one, too, before gently hauling Hannah to her feet. The clamps jangled, the weight of them making Hannah incredibly aware of her breasts.

"See, that's just pretty," Gavin said with a sweetly lecherous smile.

Dex tugged carefully at one, grinning when Hannah shivered. "So sensitive. It's time to light up that lovely backside of yours. Bend over and put your hands on the table. I want that ass in the air. Do you need a gag?"

"I don't know. Will I?" The question came out as a breathless little squeak.

"I love hearing your cries, baby. It makes my cock weep, but Gavin is new to all this."

"Why don't you let me decide what I can handle?" Gavin shot back.

Slade's lips quirked in a sarcastic grin. "We could give him a safe word, too."

"Fuck you, Slade. Hannah, your Master gave you an order. Why aren't you obeying?" Gavin demanded, his voice all deep and dark.

Slade chuckled, and Hannah breathed a sigh of relief. She had her men exactly how she wanted them—working together.

She walked to the table and placed her palms flat on the walnut table. She arched, raising her ass to them.

"This won't do," Slade said as he yanked on her skirt, tugging it down, then kicking it away. "That's better. Do you have any idea how much I love you? Sometimes I think my life really began the day you walked into it."

Hannah twisted to gaze up at him. The warmth in his blue eyes made her heart well with emotion.

Slade's hand caressed down the line of her spine, then he dropped a kiss between her shoulders.

"I thought I was going to die when I realized how close that asshole had gotten to you." Dex chimed in, his big, rough hands caressing her hips. "I don't know what I would have done if he'd hurt you."

"It would have been bad, brother," Gavin said, his hand tangled in her hair. He moved closer, then whispered in her ear. "You did what I couldn't. You made us a family, sweetheart. I promise to love you for the rest of my life. I won't let you down again."

He kissed her cheek—and dropped a blindfold

over her eyes.

Hannah barely had time to wallow in the sweetness of their devotion before it began. *Smack.*

"This isn't going to go easy, darlin'," Dex intoned, his Texas accent more pronounced as he became aroused. "You owe us twenty-five for disobeying."

Smack. This one on her right cheek had to have come from Slade. Tears formed, hot and desperate, in her eyes. "And another five for trying to top from the bottom."

She didn't point out that she hadn't tried; she'd done it. She had everything she wanted, including this spanking.

Smack. The hardest one yet, and it had landed right between her cheeks, heating up the crack of her ass.

"That's for throwing glassware at my head." Gavin hummed. "Fuck, that's pretty. It's so pink."

She felt someone pull her cheeks apart.

"Where is the plug, Hannah?" Displeasure resonated in Dex's voice.

She'd forgotten about that. "I took it out."

Hannah didn't mention that she'd thrown it away.

All three men growled.

The smacks rained down, one after another. She heard them counting, but somewhere at ten they seemed to recede until all she felt was her body and its sensations. Tears squeezed from her eyes. Even that felt good. The pain released not only the fears and worries she'd buried deep inside her, but it freed up some reserve and uncertainty that she'd kept chained up. She was safe here. She could trust her men and discover herself.

Heat lit up the flesh of her ass. It only started out

as sharp, stinging pain. Then...it morphed into a deep warmth, seeping beneath her skin. Every nerve in her body leapt to life, kindling need in her veins. Her breasts, weighed down by the clamps, brushed the cool wood of the table, setting off another wave of awareness. Everything inside her seemed awake and alive.

"Add another twenty for taking out the plug." Slade's demand brought Hannah out of her pleasant haze.

A hand smacked her already sore ass once more. God, how was she going to take another twenty? They were going to make her, and that fact sent pleasure hammering straight between her legs.

She gasped as big, male hands, Slade's she thought, pulled her cheeks apart and cold lube dribbled onto her rosette.

"Is she ready?" Gavin asked.

Hannah tensed, her stomach knotting. She knew what they were talking about. She was nervous but ready. Her first brush with real anal sex might be rough, but she wasn't about to shy away. She wanted to be filled with her men.

"God, she's going to be so tight." Dex's voice spoke as she felt a new plug begin to breach her ass. A familiar ache started. Jittery, jangled sensations sparked to life deep inside. "This is the medium plug, baby. You should know that I'll regularly plug you as a part of our play. If you take one out without permission, I'll just use a bigger one next time. We'll never run out of ways to fill you up."

She knew they would keep her full in more ways than sexually. They would fill her life, her heart, and one day, her womb. What had seemed so empty just days before now burst at the seams, giving her hope, anticipation for the future, and perfect contentment.

She breathed out and arched her back further. The plug slid home. She would never deny them what they needed.

"Very good, baby." Dex walked around and lifted the blindfold. A warm smile creased his face, and his voice had softened. "Are you trying to get out of the last count?"

She shook her head. "No. I want it. I want everything my Masters want to give me."

He chuckled and kissed her forehead. "Masters. We all know who's really in charge. Give it to her. I'm dying to get to the part where we make her come."

The slaps started again, Slade and Gavin seeming content to take turns. When the heat sank into her skin, they caressed her with a gentle but firm hand. One of them pressed and played with the plug while the other found her pussy. She whimpered at the feel of deft fingers teasing her folds and brushing her clit for a moment before retreating. Then the spanking began once more.

Over and over they repeated the process until Hannah was so aroused she thought she would scream.

Finally, after what seemed like a lifetime, Gavin finished counting, then teased between her legs again. "She's very wet. I think our little sub liked her spanking."

So much. Hannah was taut with hunger, her body nearly screaming in need. "Please."

Dex bent to her. "What did you say, darlin'?"

"Please, Dex. I need you."

His lips split into a wide smile. "I'm right here. I'm not going anywhere."

"That isn't what she's saying, and you know it." Slade was the soft touch. Hannah felt fingers press against her clitoris. "She's desperate to come. Are we going to give our bratty little sub permission?"

"Hell, no," Dex insisted.

"Please, Slade."

A thunderous frown rolled across his face. "Not until we get inside you. What are you supposed to call me?"

Perhaps he wasn't all that soft on her, after all.

"Master," Hannah sighed as Slade hauled her into his arms. She wrapped her arms around his neck as he carried her to the bedroom.

She looked over his shoulder. Dex and Gavin walked side by side. Both had shucked their clothes, and their gorgeous bodies were on full display, complete with impressive full-staff erections.

Slade set her on her feet and turned her face up to his. "Are you sure you're ready for this, sweetheart? We're going to be demanding."

Hannah's tender backside could attest to that. "I can handle the three of you."

He leaned over and brushed his mouth against hers, licking across her lips until Hannah allowed his tongue to slide against hers in a silky dance. As she kissed Slade, she felt another body at her back.

"Give me a little of that, darlin'." A rough hand turned her face to the right.

Dex kissed her long and slow while Slade toyed with her nipples and the jewels that dangled from them.

"Hey, don't forget me." Gavin pulled her his

direction. He kissed her hard, his mouth dominating hers with commanding, seductive power.

"It's time, baby." Gavin released her. "Ride Slade."

Hannah looked to the huge bed. Slade laid across the soft comforter, holding his big cock up, waiting for her to sheathe him.

"Go on, darlin'." Dex urged her forward, his hand smoothing across her tortured backside.

Hannah crawled up on the bed, careful to keep the plug in. She kissed her way up Slade's body from his feet to his strong thighs to his lean waist, all the way up to his lips. Slade. Her soul mate.

"Kiss me, too, darlin'." Dex took his place at the head of the bed. His cock thrust toward her. Hannah let him plunder her mouth once more. Dex. Her champion.

Gavin's strong hands cupped her hips. "I'm here, too. And I'll never leave you alone again."

He planted soft kisses along the sensitive skin of her neck, making her shiver. Making her feel so adored. Gavin. Her savior.

Her men. It was past time to be with them all.

Slade had a condom in his hand. He rolled it on that big cock, stroking himself as he prepared to fill her. "Come here, baby. Let me get inside you."

Dex held her hands, and Gavin moved her hips into place. She sighed as Slade's huge cock eased inside her pussy.

"God, I love the way you feel." Slade pushed up, deeper into her. "She's so tight with the plug."

He was right. Her pussy felt stretched and deliciously invaded.

Gavin groaned behind her as he gently pushed her

forward. "She's going to get a lot tighter. I think Dex needs a little attention, too."

Dex was at the head of the bed on his knees, cock in hand, waiting for her. The bulbous head wept with a creamy drop of semen. Hannah sighed as she licked at it, then pulled the head into her mouth. Dex tasted masculine and salty and she reveled in it as Slade thrust up and impaled her on his cock.

"I'm going to take the plug out, Hannah." Gavin's voice was a deep groan. "Don't you lose Dex."

Hannah whimpered around Dex's cock as it filled her mouth, while Gavin slowly removed the plug from her ass. She felt its loss, but there was no time to bemoan it. Dex fed her his length inch by inch. Slade pumped softly up, finding a place deep inside her pussy that had her pleasure building to a crescendo.

More lube coated her anus. Fingers massaged here there. She'd never imagined it could feel so good. Gavin rimmed her, preparing her to take something she knew was far bigger than the plugs they'd used.

She tensed when she felt Gavin's cock at her tight entrance. It burned as he pressed against her tight, untried muscles, but she wasn't about to back down.

"Steady, sweetheart. You're very, very tight." Gavin's hands felt like brands on her hips. He held her tightly as though he was afraid to let go.

"God, that feels good." Slade's breath came in deep pants, his control obviously slipping. "Arch a little, baby. Let Gavin slip deeper inside."

"Hurry. Her mouth is killing me." Dex pushed his way back in, filling her up.

Hannah felt like she might splinter into a thousand pieces as she followed Slade's order. When she raised her ass, Gavin's cock tunneled deeper. More burning and stretching. She wasn't sure how much more she could take, but the delicious bite of pain tore at her composure. She moaned and clawed at Dex's thighs.

"Relax, baby," Dex's voice soothed. His hands petted her hair, and he gentled his strokes. "You're so fucking gorgeous. You're more than enough woman for all of us."

"You're our everything, Hannah," Slade added. "Relax and let us take care of you. Take a deep breath and push out. Allow Gavin in so we can all love you."

"Yes. Christ, let me in, Hannah. I'm dying to be deep inside you. I've never wanted anything as much as I want this sweet ass." Gavin pressed in, inexorably forcing her to take a bit more of his wide cock with every little stroke.

Slade pulled on the clamps, twisting her nipples. As she moaned, he reached around and spread her cheeks wider for Gavin. "Come on, baby. Don't resist. Take all of him."

Hannah whimpered in little cries of pleasure around Dex's cock as Gavin slid completely into her ass. The burn was there, but so was a crazy jangle of sensation, a fullness that stimulated a host of new nerve endings.

As he eased back, Slade pumped deep into her pussy. "God, that's tight."

"Yes," Gavin hissed. "She's taking every inch of my cock and it's so pretty. I'm never going to leave you, baby. I'm always going to want to be inside you like this."

His words made the warmth inside her flash hot. As he shoved inside her again and praised her once more, Gavin pushed her closer to climax. As he slid back, Slade thrust up, nudging her cervix. She cried out in bliss. Inflamed, aroused, desperate, she pulled on Dex's cock, bringing him almost to the back of her throat.

"Fuck, guys, I'm dying here." Dex's voice sounded strangled.

"Damn straight," Slade said. He shoved his cock up again

"She's like a vise on my dick. This is too good. I won't last. Hannah, you come for you Masters." Gavin fucked her in long, luxurious strokes.

The others joined in. They were like a well-oiled machine. When Gavin pressed deep in her ass, Slade pulled out. When Slade fucked into her pussy, Gavin dragged his cock out, almost withdrawing. Every pleasure sensor in her body lit up. They exchanged panting breaths and devotion. Slade plied his tongue around her sensitive, clamped nipples. Gavin nibbled at her neck, his hot affection making her shiver all over.

"Finish off," Slade told the others. "I don't know how long I can hold out. She feels so good."

"I'm close." Dex's hands tangled in her hair. "Relax, baby. Just breathe deep and take me."

He fucked into her mouth in deep strokes, his cock swelling against her tongue as the other two grew larger and more insistent inside her. Pleasure built fast and hard, tearing at her composure. With every stroke, they sent her farther into an abyss of need so deep, Hannah wasn't sure she'd ever leave. She didn't want to. Her body rode the wave of sensation they heaped on her. All she had to do was let go and feel.

She softened her throat. Dex surged into her

mouth, and his body stiffened. He shouted, sounding desperate, dying. Then warm seed coated her tongue. Tangy, an unexpected salty shock. Then instinct took over, and she drank him down. All the while, Slade and Gavin plundered her mercilessly, their hands tightening on her like they never wanted to let her go.

When Dex withdrew from her mouth, she fell against Slade, reveling at the feel of his heart pounding against her. Almost immediately, he propped her up until her stare met his. Dex eased his hand onto her belly, forcing it between them.

"This is just what you need, baby." Dex's finger found her clit. "Ride it. Come for us."

"Now, Hannah," Gavin commanded. "I'm going to come."

"Me, too. I can't hold off any longer." Slade surged up, keeping his head up long enough to remove the clamps.

Blood rushed back to them in a hot surge of delicate pain as Dex circled her clit. The pleasure overload, coupled with the friction, catapulted Hannah into a blinding ecstasy she'd never experienced. She gasped as the orgasm raced through her body. It started in her core, building, building, and then spread like a wild fire until it culminated in one huge explosion that engulfed her, ripping a scream from her throat.

As she took off flying, Slade and Gavin gave in to the need. Slade's cock pulsed inside her. His gorgeous face contorted, his blue eyes fused to her like his world began and ended with her. Gavin came in strong bursts, coating her ass with his essence, his hands clutching her like he'd never let her go.

They fell together in a heap of warm, satisfied

flesh. Her head rested on Slade's chest. She could hear the strong beat of his heart as he wound down. Gavin's body pressed her into Slade's, the weight a welcome warmth. Dex stretched out beside her, his face in line with her own. He looked satisfied and happy, as though a huge weight had been lifted.

"I love you, Hannah," he said solemnly and kissed her forehead.

"The best thing we ever did was kidnap you and take you to our lair." Slade smiled.

She could feel their connection all the way down to her bones. Even when they were apart, she would be able to feel them.

"I like the way you boys treat a captive," she said, snuggling down. She suspected she was in for a long night.

Gavin pressed her hot cheek to his. "Get used to it. I don't think we're ever letting our captive go."

That was fine with Hannah.

Chapter Fifteen

One year later

With a fully-healed Mr. Snuggles purring around his ankles, Gavin took off his tie and tossed it aside. It felt so good to leave work today. His new Vice President of Operations had given him hell. She'd been in place for almost nine months and had big plans for changing the way Black Oak Oil did business. She was very employee oriented. Already the woman had opened a day care on site, talked him into a better health insurance plan, and forced him to build better facilities at the Alaska site. She had a head for business and could argue all day long when she believed in something.

Of course, he always took it from her because she looked awfully good in a bikini.

"Hey, you took off early!" Slade walked in from the pool. "Dex was just about to start up the grill. You want a beer?"

"Absolutely. I'm on vacation, after all. Does she know?" Gavin stared outside where Hannah splashed in the pool, her blonde hair in a messy pile on the top of her head. Her baby bump wasn't showing yet, but in a few weeks, it would. Knowing he'd soon see the evidence of their passion, of the life they'd created, growing inside her turned him on.

Slade smiled. "She has no idea. She thinks she has a meeting with the head of technology tomorrow."

"Excellent." Gavin shrugged out of his suit coat. Scott had proven not only a great manager, but a successful conspirator. "Everything is in place. The plane is ready. Marnie knows we're coming. Have the contractors finished out the playroom?"

"Yes, just today. I sent you the pictures. I assure you we now have the perfect space to play with our wife for the next month. And Dex decided he's going to tie her up this time. He's going to march into the conference room and lasso her before we pick her up and take her out. You know she likes the cowboy thing."

Gavin threw back his head and laughed. His sweet Hannah had a vivid imagination. She had taken to play like a duck to water.

He looked forward to spending the month focused on nothing but her.

Hannah looked up, and he knew the moment she saw him. Her green eyes lit up. She rushed to the edge of the pool and raced up the steps. Dex turned from the grill and nodded his way.

Dex James. His brother. It was all legal now. He smiled.

Hannah walked toward him, her breasts barely encased in a yellow bikini top. She never wore that suit in public, but damn he liked to see it on her in private.

"Watch out," Slade said, pressing a cold beer into his hand. "She's going to throw herself in your arms. If you don't want to get those clothes wet, I would run."

She would just chase him down. His wife never let him get too far. Anytime the pressure got to him, she drew him back in with the sunshine of her smile. His world finally had a center, and he was content to orbit around her.

Hannah did just what Slade had promised. She threw herself into his arms, plastering her body to his.

"Welcome home, Mr. James." She pressed a little kiss on his lips. "I missed you."

He missed her every minute he wasn't in her presence. "Me too, love. Are you ready for your meeting tomorrow, Ms. VP?"

"Absolutely, boss." Hannah loved her new responsibilities, and the employees adored her.

"Make sure you're not late."

She frowned at him and wrinkled her nose. "I'm never late, Mr. James. Are you going to come swimming with me? The water's great."

"As I'm already wet, I think I will." He slapped her ass playfully as she walked back to the pool.

Gavin stripped off his shirt.

"Has our little pool party taken a distinctly adult tone?" Dex asked, a wide smile on his face.

"Hannah likes to play cowboys and captive, doesn't she?" Gavin asked. "I think the James Gang is going to ride tonight."

"Dinner can wait," Dex said. He dove into the pool.

"Hallelujah. She kills me when she wears that bikini. I always just want to strip it off her." Slade followed his brother.

Gavin shucked the rest of his clothes. He didn't

need them.

The James Gang had a captive, and they weren't ever going to let her go.

Their Virgin's Secret
Masters of Ménage, Book 2
By Shayla Black and Lexi Blake
Now Available!

Two Men on a Mission

Security Professionals Burke and Cole Lennox
have shared women before but never meant to fall in
love with one. Their lives are precarious, always on the
edge of trouble. But Jessa Wade is too tempting, too
perfect, to let go. They're on a dangerous mission, but
they can't help but get close to the beautiful, innocent
artist. When their mission takes them to a foreign land,
they reluctantly leave their love behind, promising to
return for her one day.

A Woman with a Secret

After her lovers disappear, Jessa Wade bravely
moves on with her life, protecting her secret. But when
she becomes the target of one of Burke and Cole's
enemies, the men leap into action, vowing to save their
woman and to never leave again. As danger stalks all
three, they must come together and face the mistakes of
their past. On the run and out of time, Burke and Cole
will fight for their future with Jessa. But will Jessa's
secret bring them together....or tear them apart?

Cole stood, buttoning the jacket of his suit coat. "It's time for me to leave. She's too innocent for what I need. I can't put that on a virgin. Besides, she's more interested in you. I'll go back to the hotel. We do have work to do, remember?"

Burke's face fell. "Can't we talk about this?"

"What the fuck is there to say?"

She sat there watching them, wishing she hadn't ever spoken up. They could still be sitting here having a nice dinner and planning to go to a movie or a show together. But no, she'd needed to forge her own path. She always did. She could hear her mother complaining in her head about what an ungrateful daughter she was for turning aside all their plans for her and making her own. Painting, not international business. Two men, not one.

Jessa listened to them argue. She was on the outside now, but then she'd felt that way all of her life. Even at the lavish parties her parents had thrown, she'd been on the outside. When she'd tried to fit in, going to a school she didn't want to go to, studying what she didn't love, it had been terrible. Always on the outside.

The best thing she'd ever done had been defying her parents. She'd stood up and gotten kicked out, but it had been for the best. She would have suffocated if she'd stayed. She'd been happier since leaving all that behind and didn't regret her choice for a minute. So why was she retreating now instead of fighting for what she wanted? Wasn't she simply proving Cole's point that she was too inexperienced to handle him?

She wasn't a child. She might not have slept

around, but that didn't mean she couldn't deal. She looked at him, really looked at him. She tried to look past her insecurity and see him as he truly was. Jessa gnawed at her lip. How would she draw Cole in this moment? His face was all broad lines and bleak angles, but under the pain she saw gentleness lurking. Yearning even. She would love to draw him, then transfer that image to canvas, the colors of her palate bringing everything to life. Time slowed for Jessa. She studied him as she would a subject she painted, looking deep. Bold colors. He required them. He wasn't as black and white as he tried to portray. He was a million shades, just like his brother.

He turned to her, and she realized his carefully blank stare wasn't about her. He was scared of something.

Maybe she was fooling herself or seeing what she wanted to see, but his sudden refusal didn't make a lick of sense. For four days, Cole had been right beside her, eating her up with his stare again and again, silently seducing her with the desire in his remote eyes. Burke was more blatant, but she hadn't imagined Cole's attraction to her. What was he afraid of?

"Goodbye, Jessa." His voice sounded ragged. "You have a good time with Burke. He'll take care of you, baby."

"No." The word slipped out. Now that she'd truly seen him, she knew deep down that if he let his fear win, it would haunt them all.

Burke smiled, but Cole scowled, suddenly on the offense.

"No?" Cole challenged, leaning in. "What is that supposed to mean?"

Stopping him in his tracks emboldened her. Jessa stood, certainty running through her veins, settling her face inches from his. She was still nervous, but no one got what they wanted by giving up. And she just knew she was doing the right thing.

"It means that you two are a packaged deal. I won't settle for half, and that's what I would get if I only gave myself to Burke. I would get the good and the gentle, but there'd be no balance."

"Fuck balance. Stick to Prince Charming. I'm a ruthless bastard." Cole's eyes narrowed. His fists clenched.

She was getting to him.

"I don't need gentle all the time," Jessa assured him softly. "I need what you can give me."

Cole sunk his hand into her hair and pulled slightly. "I don't have gentle in me. I'm brutal. I'll demand everything from you, then want more. I'll want to give you a little bite of pain, then I'll get hard at all your little cries. I'll want to tie you up, spank your ass, and share you with Burke. You're right; we aren't exactly whole. And we won't do this for fun. We'll consume you."

They needed to share her. They balanced each other in every facet of their lives, even sexually. As an artist, she understood symmetry completely.

She smiled at Burke who sat patiently, awaiting the outcome of their little skirmish with a faint smile. She drank in strength from his encouragement before rising up on her tiptoes and brushing her mouth against Cole's. The kiss was a soft, sweet caress of lips that had her longing for more.

"I'm game to try every dirty, dark thing you can

think of," she whispered. "But can you ease me into it? Let me have a lover…" She grinned. "Or two. Then I'll be ready."

"Fuck." Cole fisted her hair in his hand and pulled, pinning her with a wracked blue stare for a long moment. She could sense the war inside him, the need clashing with the caution. Then he took her mouth.

Jessa held on for dear life. She'd been kissed before, but not like this. She'd been pecked and bussed, and a couple of boys had thrust their tongues at her, but Cole dominated. His kiss made her really understand the word. He was in total control. Using his tongue, he surged in, not asking but demanding entry. She gave it because she wanted him inside. She ceded control to him, riding the wave. Her body flooded with a hot swell of desire as his tongue rubbed against hers in a silky slide. She could feel her pussy tightening, her folds warming and softening. Moistening. It was unlike anything she'd ever imagined before. With those hard, sinewy arms, Cole dragged her in, his chest impossibly solid and wide against her breasts. His hips slammed against hers, and she could feel the long, thick line of his erection.

He wanted her. She trembled. God, she wanted him.

He lifted his head, his lips almost a snarl, his voice a harsh rasp. "Kiss Burke. Let me watch you."

Burke stood, smiling and open, as though something had blissfully fallen into place. "You should do what he says, sweetheart. He's incredibly bossy."

For all the dark passion she'd felt with Cole, a light-hearted joy stole over her as Burke took her in his arms. He kissed her every bit as passionately, but playfully. He nipped, flirted, toyed with her lips, his fingers sliding down her back to rest playfully on her ass.

Everything. She could have everything. It was right here in her grasp.

Burke's tongue found hers and they danced, a teasing waltz of desire. When he released her, his deep blue eyes found hers, and he kissed her forehead with such tenderness it brought tears to her eyes.

"Thank you," he whispered.

"Take me to your room. I want you both so much."

Theirs To Cherish
Wicked Lovers, Book 8
By Shayla Black
Now Available!

The perfect place for a woman on the run to disappear…

Accused of a horrific murder she didn't commit, former heiress Callie Ward has been a fugitive since she was sixteen—until she found the perfect hideout, Club Dominion. The only problem is she's fallen for the club's Master, Mitchell Thorpe, who keeps her at arm's length. Little does she know that his reasons for not getting involved have everything to do with his wounded heart…and his consuming desire for her.

To live out her wildest fantasies…

Enter Sean Kirkpatrick, a Dom who's recently come to Dominion and taken a pointed interest in Callie. Hoping to make Thorpe jealous, she submits to Sean one shuddering sigh at a time. It isn't long before she realizes she's falling for him too. But the tender lover who's slowly seducing her body and earning her trust isn't who he claims…

And to fall in love.

When emotions collide and truths are exposed, Sean is willing to risk all to keep Callie from slipping through his fingers. But he's not the only man looking to stake a claim. Now Callie is torn between Sean and Thorpe, and though she's unsure whom she can trust, she'll have to surrender her body and soul to both—if she wants to elude a killer…

* * * *

Callie trembled as she lay back on the padded table and Sean Kirkpatrick's strong fingers wrapped around her cuffed wrist, guiding it back to the bindings above her head.

"I don't know if I can do this," she murmured.

He paused, then drew in a breath as if he sought patience. "Breathe, lovely."

That gentle, deep brogue of his native Scotland brought her peace. His voice both aroused and soothed her, and she tried to let those feelings wash through her. "Can you do that for me?" he asked.

His fingers uncurled from her wrist, and he grazed the inside of her outstretched arm with his knuckles. As always, his touch was full of quiet strength. He made her ache. She shivered again, this time for an entirely different reason.

"I'll try."

Sean shook his head, his deep blue eyes seeming to see everything she tried to hide inside. That penetrating stare scared the hell out of her. What did he see when he looked at her? How much about the real her had he pieced together?

The thought made her panic. No one could know

her secret. No one. She'd kept it from everyone, even Thorpe, during her four years at Dominion. She'd finally found a place where she felt safe, comfortable. Of course she'd have to give it up someday, probably soon. She always did. But please, not yet.

Deep breath. Don't panic. Sean wants your submission, not your secrets.

"You'll need to do better than try. You've been 'trying' for over six months," he reminded her gently. "Do you think I'd truly hurt you?"

No. Sean didn't seem to have a violent bone in his body. He wasn't a sadist. He never gripped her harshly. He never even raised his voice. She'd jokingly thought of him as the sub whisperer because he pushed her boundaries with a gentleness she found both irresistible and insidious. Certainly, he'd dragged far more out of her than any other man had. Tirelessly, he'd worked to earn her trust. Callie felt terrible that she could never give it, not when doing so could be fatal.

Guilt battered her. She should stop wasting his time.

"I know you wouldn't," she assured, blinking up at him, willing him to understand.

"Of course not." He pressed his chest over hers, leaning closer to delve into her eyes.

Callie couldn't resist lowering her lids, shutting out the rest of the world. Even knowing she shouldn't, she sank into the soft reassurance of his kiss. Each brush of his lips over hers soothed and aroused. Every time he touched her, her heart raced. Her skin grew tight. Her nipples hardened. Her pussy moistened and swelled. Her heart ached. Sean Kirkpatrick would be so easy to love.

As his fingers filtered into her hair, cradling her scalp, she exhaled and melted into his kiss—just for a sweet moment. It was the only one she could afford.

A fierce yearning filled her. She longed for him to peel off his clothes, kiss her with that determination she oft en saw stamped into his eyes, and take her with the single-minded fervor she knew he was capable of. But in the months since he'd collared her, he'd done nothing more than stroke her body, tease her, and grant her orgasms when he thought she'd earned them. She hadn't let him fully restrain her. And he hadn't yet taken her to bed.

Not knowing the feel of him deep inside her, of waiting and wanting until her body throbbed relentlessly, was making her buckets full of crazy.

After another skillful brush of his lips, Sean ended the kiss and lifted his head, breathing hard. She clung, not ready to let him go. How had he gotten under her skin so quickly? His tenderness filled her veins like a drug. The way he had addicted Callie terrified her.

"I want you. Sean, please . . ." She damn near wept.

With a broad hand, he swept the stray hair from her face. Regret softened his blue eyes before he ever said a word. "If you're not ready to trust me as your Dom, do you think you're ready for me as a lover? I want you completely open to me before we take that step. All you have to do is trust me, lovely."

Callie slammed her eyes shut. This was so fucking pointless. She wanted to trust Sean, yearned to give him everything—devotion, honesty, faith. Her past ensured that she'd never give any of those to anyone. But he had feelings for her. About that, she had no doubt. They'd grown just as hers had, unexpectedly, over time, a fledgling limb morphing into a sturdy vine that eventually created a bud just waiting to blossom . . . or die.

She knew which. They could never have more than this faltering Dom/sub relationship, destined to perish in a premature winter.

She should never have accepted his collar, not when she should be trying to keep her distance from everyone. The responsible choice now would be to call her safe word, walk out, quit him. Release them both from this hell. Never look back.

For the first time in nearly a decade, Callie worried that she might not have the strength to say good-bye.

What was wrong with her tonight? She was too emotional. She needed to pull up her big-girl panties and snap on her bratty attitude, pretend that nothing mattered. It was how she'd coped for years. But she couldn't seem to manage that with Sean.

"You're up in your head, instead of here with me," he gently rebuked her.

Another dose of guilt blistered her. "Sorry, Sir."

Sean sighed heavily, stood straight, then held out his hand to her. "Come with me."

Callie winced. If he intended to stop the scene, that could only mean he wanted to talk. These sessions where he tried to dig through her psyche became more painful than the sexless nights she spent in unfulfilled longing under his sensual torture.

Swallowing down her frustration, she dredged up her courage, then put her hand in his.

Holding her in a steady grip, Sean led her to the far side of Dominion's dungeon, to a bench in a shadowed corner. As soon as she could see the rest of the room, Callie felt eyes on her, searing her skin. With a nonchalant glance, she looked at the others scening around them, but they seemed lost in their own world of pleasure, pain, groans, sweat, and need. A lingering sweep of the room revealed another sight that had the power to drop her to her knees. Thorpe in the shadows. Staring. At her with Sean. His expression wasn't one of disapproval exactly . . . but he wasn't pleased.

Dungeon Royale
Masters and Mercenaries, Book 6
By Lexi Blake
Now Available!

An agent broken

MI6 agent Damon Knight prided himself on
always being in control. His missions were executed
with cold, calculating precision. His club, The Garden,
was run with an equally ordered and detached
decadence. But his perfect world was shattered by one
bullet, fired from the gun of his former partner. That
betrayal almost cost him his life and ruined his career.
His handlers want him to retire, threatening to revoke
his license to kill if he doesn't drop his obsession with
a shadowy organization called The Collective. To earn
their trust, he has to prove himself on a unique
assignment with an equally unusual partner.

A woman tempted

Penelope Cash has spent her whole life wanting
more. More passion. More adventure. But duty has
forced her to live a quiet life. Her only excitement is
watching the agents of MI6 as they save England and
the world. Despite her training, she's only an analyst.
The closest she is allowed to danger and intrigue is in
her dreams, which are often filled with one Damon

Knight. But everything changes when the woman assigned to pose as Damon's submissive on his latest mission is incapacitated. Penny is suddenly faced with a decision. Stay in her safe little world or risk her life, and her heart, for Queen and country.

An enemy revealed

With the McKay-Taggart team at their side, Damon and Penny hunt an international terrorist across the great cities of Northern Europe. Playing the part of her Master, Damon begins to learn that under Penny's mousy exterior is a passionate submissive, one who just might lay claim to his cold heart. But when Damon's true enemy is brought out of the shadows, it might be Penny who pays the ultimate price.

* * * *

"I'm going to kiss you now, Penelope."
"What?"
"You seem to have an enormously hard time understanding me today. We're going to have to work on our communication skills." Damon moved right between her legs, spreading her knees and making a place for himself there. One minute she was utterly gobsmacked by the chaos he'd brought into her life in a couple of hours' time, and the next, she couldn't manage to breathe. He invaded her space, looming over her. Despite the fact that she was sitting on the counter, he still looked down at her. "You said yes. That means you're mine, Penelope. You're my partner and my submissive. I take care of what's mine."

She swallowed, forcing herself to look into those stormy eyes of his. He was so close, she could smell the scent of his aftershave, feel the heat his big body gave off. "For the mission."

"I don't know about that," he returned, his voice deepening. "If this goes well, I get to go back out in the field. It's always good to have a cover. Men are less threatening when they have a woman with them. If you like fieldwork, there's no reason you can't come with me. Especially if you're properly trained. Tell me how much your siblings know."

She shook her head before finally realizing what he was asking. His fingers worked their way into her hair, smoothing it back, forcing her to keep eye contact with him. "Oh, about work, you mean. Everyone in my family thinks I work for Reeding Corporation in their publishing arm. They think I translate books."

The Reeding Corporation was one of several companies that fronted for SIS. When she'd hired on, she'd signed documentation that stated she would never expose who she truly worked for.

"Excellent. If they research me, they'll discover I'm an executive at Reeding. We've been having an affair for the last three months. You were worried about your position at the company and the fact that I'm your superior, but I transferred to another department and now we're free to be open about our relationship."

"I don't know that they'll believe we're lovers."

"Of course, they will. I'm very persuasive, love. Now, I'm going to kiss you and I'm going to put my hand in your knickers. You are wearing knickers, aren't you?"

"Of course."

He shuddered. "Not anymore. Knickers are strictly forbidden. I told you I would likely get into your knickers, but what I really meant was I can't tolerate them and you're not to wear them at all anymore. I've done you the enormous service of making it easy on you and tossing out the ones you had in the house."

His right hand brushed against her breast. The nipple responded by peaking immediately, as if it were a magnet drawn to Damon's skin.

"You can't toss my knickers out, Damon. And you can't put your hand there. We're in the ladies' room for heaven's sake."

"Here's the first rule, love. Don't tell me what I can't do." His mouth closed over hers, heat flashing through her system.

His mouth was sweet on hers, not an outright assault at first. This was persuasion. Seduction. His lips teased at hers, playing and coaxing.

And his hand made its way down, skimming across her waist to her thigh.

"Let me in, Penelope." He whispered the words against her mouth.

Drugged. This was what it felt like to be drugged. She'd been tipsy before, but no wine had ever made her feel as out of control as Damon's kiss.

Out of control and yet oddly safe. Safe enough to take a chance.

On his next pass, she opened for him, allowing him in, and the kiss morphed in a heartbeat from sweet to overpowering.

She could practically feel the change in him. He surged in, a marauder gaining territory. His tongue commanded hers, sliding over and around, his left hand tangling in her hair and getting her at the angle he wanted. Captured. She felt the moment he turned from seduction to Dominance, and now she understood completely why they capitalized the word. Damon didn't merely kiss her. She'd been kissed before, little brushes of lips to hers, fumblings that ended in embarrassment, long attempts at bringing up desire. This wasn't a kiss. This was possession.

He'd said she belonged to him for the course of the mission, and now she understood what he meant. He meant to invade every inch of her life, putting his stamp on her. If she proceeded, he would take over. He would run her life and she would be forced to fight him for every inch of freedom she might have.

"That's right, love. You touch me. I want you to touch me. If you belong to me, then my body is yours, too."

She hadn't realized her hands were moving. She'd cupped his bum even as his fingers slid along the band of her knickers, under and over, sliding along her female flesh.

He'd said exactly the right thing. He hadn't made her self-conscious. He'd told her he would give as good as he got. It wasn't some declaration of love, but she'd had that before and it proved false. Damon Knight was offering her something different. He was offering her the chance to explore without shame.

About Shayla Black

Shayla Black (aka Shelley Bradley) is the New York Times and USA Today bestselling author of over 40 sizzling contemporary, erotic, paranormal, and historical romances produced via traditional, small press, independent, and audio publishing. She lives in Texas with her husband, munchkin, and one very spoiled cat. In her "free" time, she enjoys reality TV, reading and listening to an eclectic blend of music.

Shayla's books have been translated in about a dozen languages. RT Bookclub has nominated her for a Career Achievement award in erotic romance, twice nominated her for Best Erotic Romance of the year, as well as awarded her several Top Picks, and a KISS Hero Award. She has also received or been nominated for The Passionate Plume, The Holt Medallion, Colorado Romance Writers Award of Excellence, and the National Reader's Choice Awards.

A writing risk-taker, Shayla enjoys tackling writing challenges with every new book.

Connect with Shayla online:

Facebook:
www.facebook.com/ShaylaBlackAuthor
Twitter: www.twitter.com/@shayla_black
Website: www.shaylablack.com

About Lexi Blake

Lexi Blake lives in North Texas with her husband, three kids, and the laziest rescue dog in the world. She began writing at a young age, concentrating on plays and journalism. It wasn't until she started writing romance that she found success. She likes to find humor in the strangest places. Lexi believes in happy endings no matter how odd the couple, threesome or foursome may seem. She also writes contemporary Western ménage as Sophie Oak.

Connect with Lexi online:

Facebook: Lexi Blake
Twitter: twitter.com/authorlexiblake
Website: www.LexiBlake.net

Sign up for Lexi's free newsletter at www.LexiBlake.net!

Also from Shayla Black and Lexi Blake

Masters Of Ménage
Their Virgin Captive
Their Virgin's Secret
Their Virgin Concubine
Their Virgin Princess
Their Virgin Hostage
Their Virgin Secretary, Coming April 15, 2014

Also from Shayla Black/Shelley Bradley

EROTIC ROMANCE
THE WICKED LOVERS
Wicked Ties
Decadent
Delicious
Surrender To Me
Belong To Me
"Wicked to Love" (e-novella)
Mine To Hold
"Wicked All The Way" (e-novella)
Ours To Love
Wicked and Dangerous
Forever Wicked
Theirs To Cherish

SEXY CAPERS
Bound And Determined
Strip Search
"Arresting Desire" – Hot In Handcuffs Anthology

DOMS OF HER LIFE
One Dom To Love
The Young And The Submissive

STAND ALONE
Naughty Little Secret (as Shelley Bradley)
"Watch Me" – Sneak Peek Anthology (as Shelley Bradley)
Dangerous Boys And Their Toy
"Her Fantasy Men" – Four Play Anthology

PARANORMAL ROMANCE
THE DOOMSDAY BRETHREN
Tempt Me With Darkness
"Fated" (e-novella)
Seduce Me In Shadow
Possess Me At Midnight
"Mated" – Haunted By Your Touch Anthology
Entice Me At Twilight
Embrace Me At Dawn

HISTORICAL ROMANCE (as Shelley Bradley)
The Lady And The Dragon
One Wicked Night
Strictly Seduction
Strictly Forbidden

CONTEMPORARY ROMANCE (as Shelley Bradley)
A Perfect Match

Also from Lexi Blake

CPSIA information can be obtained at www.ICGtesting.com
Printed in the USA
BVOW02s0630030815

411420BV00001B/40/P

9 781936 596065